Bedtime, Playtime

Bedtime, Playtime

JAID BLACK

RUTH D. KERCE

SHERRI L. KING

POCKET BOOKS
New York • London • Toronto • Sydney

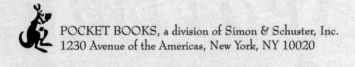 POCKET BOOKS, a division of Simon & Schuster, Inc.
1230 Avenue of the Americas, New York, NY 10020

ISBN-13: 978-1-4165-3614-7
ISBN-10:   1-4165-3614-0

This Pocket Books trade paperback edition May 2007

10 9 8 7 6 5 4 3 2 1

POCKET and colophon are registered trademarks of
Simon & Schuster, Inc.

Manufactured in the United States of America

For information regarding special discounts for bulk purchases, please
contact Simon & Schuster Special Sales at 1-800-456-6798 or
business@simonandschuster.com

Contents

Bedtime, Playtime

Warlord

JAID BLACK

Prologue

The Isle of Skye in the Scottish Highlands, 1052 AD

EUAN DONALD WATCHED DISPASSIONATELY as the decapi-tated body of the Hay fell lifelessly at his feet. Blood oozed out from where the laird's severed head had been but moments prior, pooling around him in a river of dark red.

Sheathing his sword, the Donald's dark head came up, his black eyes boring holes into the anxious faces of those Highlanders surrounding him. None would rebel. None would second-guess his decision to execute the Hay chief-tain. None would dare.

'Twas not bravado on his part, not even ego. Not really.

'Twas simply the way of things, the territory that came with being the Lord of the Isles, the king of the High-landers, a god unto himself. Euan's word was law, as it had always been, as had the word of his father, as had the word of his father's father, and so on.

At the age of five and thirty, Euan had been chieftain to the Donalds and Lord of the Isles for over fifteen years. The price of being the master of all he surveyed had been paid in full.

His six-foot-six-inch body was heavy with muscle and riddled with battle scars. The harsh angles of his face were chiseled into a stone-like façade and hinted at no compassion, no mercy for any who would come up against him. His eyes were as black as his hair, calculating pools of obsidian that broached no argument and conveyed no emotion at all.

To come up against the Donald was to die. This fact was one that kinsmen and Outlanders alike understood well.

Today, as he did on most days, Euan wore his plaid of muted blue and green, a large emerald brooch holding the material together at his shoulder. 'Twas a fitting banner for the man who ruled the Highlands with an iron fist and who dwelled on an island many said was close to the heavens themselves, for it was surrounded on all sides and in all views by a formation of impenetrable clouds.

"'Tis done then." Graeme Donald, youngest brother to Euan, nodded toward a bevy of soldiers, indicating 'twas time to remove the Hay's bloodied carcass from the great hall. Turning to scan the nervous faces of the clan chieftains behind him, he waved a hand toward them and bellowed, "Will another amongst ye dare tae steal from the Donald?"

Murmured nays floated throughout the great hall, all eyes shifting from the Hay's remains to Euan's stoic form.

Graeme's upper lip curled wryly. "Weel then, 'tis time tae make merry, aye? Ye came fer a feast and a feast ye shall have."

Oppressive silence filled the chamber for a suspended moment. None were certain what to make of such an odd declaration. They had come for a wedding feast, every last one of them. They had journeyed from the protection of their respective keeps to witness marriage rites betwixt the Lord of the Isles and the first-born daughter of the Hay.

Not a one amongst them had ever fathomed the possibility that Tavish Hay would refuse to deliver the Donald's betrothed to her own wedding. Not a one amongst them would have credited the notion that the Hay would have been daft enough to allow Moira to break her sacred agreement and run off to the northlands with the brother of a Viking jarl.

For that matter, not a one amongst them would have been lackwitted enough to deliver such news to the Donald himself. Nay. They would have run hightail in the opposite direction. But then the Hay had never been renowned for his thinking abilities.

At last the laird of the lesser MacPherson clan broke the uncomfortable spell with a forced chuckle. "I will drink tae that." He lifted his goblet toward Euan. "Tae the Donald," he toasted, "and tae, err . . ." He shifted uncomfortably on his feet, the color in his face heightening. "Tae . . ."

Swallowing roughly, the MacPherson met Euan's black gaze. "Weel . . ." He lifted his goblet higher. "Tae the Donald."

"Tae the Donald."

The others were quick to chime in, all of them lifting their ales and meads in toast to the Lord of the Isles. Graeme's brow shot up, forming a bemused slash over his eyes as he cocked his head to regard his brother.

Euan smiled humorlessly as his dark gaze flicked from Graeme to the men standing behind him. Saying nothing, he stalked toward the dais that had been prepared for him in a slow, methodical stride. The great hall was so silent that each of his footfalls could be heard effortlessly, rushes on the ground or no.

When at last he reached the raised dais, he lifted the goblet that had been prepared for him and turned on his heel to face his rapt audience. Nodding once, he prepared to down the honeyed mead. "Aye," he rumbled, "I will drink tae that."

"WHAT WILL YE DO now, brother?"

Euan lifted a curious brow but said nothing. Standing atop the battlements, he scanned the outside perimeter below their position and absently awaited Graeme's meddling. His youngest sibling was the only one in god's creation who could get away with such. 'Twas mayhap because he had raised him and felt him more a son than a brother.

Graeme waved a hand absently through the air. "Aboot getting wed, aboot siring an heir, aboot—"

"Graeme," Euan said quietly. "I'm no' lackwitted, mon. I ken your meaning."

Graeme nodded. "Then what will ye do?"

Euan shrugged. He had known three wives and had lost

all of them to laboring his bairn. Out of all three pregnancies and subsequent fatal deliveries there had been but one survivor, and that was his six-year-old daughter Glynna. After losing so many wives and babes, 'twas nothing really to lose a betrothed.

He turned his head to look at his brother, his facial features reflecting the fact that he had not a care one way or the other. A woman was a woman. Any woman of breeding years would do. "Get another wench tae take Moira's place in the bedsheets."

Graeme chuckled at that. "Mayhap had ye tumbled the Hay's daughter before the wedding she would have shown up."

One dark brow shot up. Euan shook his head slightly and looked away, his gaze flickering back down below the battlements. His hands fisted at his hips, the thick muscles in his arms bulged further in response. "I'm glad she dinna," he said honestly. "Truth be told I think a troll would be better bedsport than Moira."

Graeme grinned. "Ye have seen her before then?"

Euan shook his head. "Nay. But on Michaelmas three years past 'twas said by her own clansmen that she is possessed of an awkward appearance."

"I was no' there. That must have been whilst I still fostered under the MacPherson."

"Aye."

The brothers stood in silence for a long moment, breathing in the crisp night air. 'Twas May so the days were longer now, darkness still not having descended though it was well past the time of the evening meal.

Graeme's chuckle at last broke the silence. "I was thinking . . ."

"Hm?"

"Aboot the Hay."

Euan craned his neck to glance toward his brother. "Aye?"

"He owes ye a bride."

Euan waved that away. "I did no' kill the mon over Moira, though I know 'tis what the other lairds think. I killed him for betraying me. 'Tis a difference." He shrugged his broad shoulders. "Besides, the mon is dead," he rumbled. "His debt has been paid."

"No' really."

Euan sighed. It had been a long day and he was in no mood for conversing let alone for solving riddles. His youngest brother was mayhap lucky that he was able to rein in his temper where he was concerned. "Explain yourself."

Graeme thought to tease him a bit, but relented when he saw his brother's lethal scowl. He sighed. Why couldn't the man learn how to make jest? "As to that, 'tis true the Hay paid the price for helping Moira in her deceit, yet did he no' deliver another bride tae take her place in the bedsheets."

Euan grunted. "'Tis true."

Graeme stood up straighter, his back rigid with determination. "Then mayhap a wee bit o' reivin' might be in order."

"Reivin'? Ye want tae go steal some *cattle*?" Euan said the last incredulously. "'Twill no' even the score."

Graeme's face flushed at the criticism for which the

Donald felt an uncharacteristic pang of sympathy. He knew that the boy had only been trying to help lighten his black mood. What his sibling seemed unable to understand on his own was that his mood was always like this. After ten and eight years the boy should know that. But he didn't.

Sighing, Euan forced a grin onto his face and ruffled Graeme's hair affectionately. "Ye are just wanting tae prove that ye learned things from the MacPherson more useful than merely how tae bed a wench. Aye, that's what it is I'm thinking."

Graeme chuckled, no longer embarrassed. "Mayhap."

Euan considered the idea more thoroughly before responding. Mayhap his brother was on to something. Not something quite like Graeme had envisioned—he hardly needed more cattle on Skye for the love of the saints—but something vastly more important. He did, after all, need a wench to take to his bed and get her with heir. Besides, as black as his mood had been as of late a bit of thrusting between a wench's legs was an enticement unto itself.

The Donald's black gaze flicked over the castle walls and toward the rock-strewn beach below. 'Twas not so long a boat ride to the mainland. And from there mayhap a sennight's journey to Hay lands at best. "I think," he murmured, "that ye might be right, brother."

Graeme's eyes widened in surprise. "I, uh, I . . . am?"

Euan couldn't help but to grin at the boy's astonishment. 'Twas true he wasn't a man known for changing his mind. Set in his ways he was. "Aye." He nodded, his demeanor growing serious. "We shall depart on the morrow when the sun falls."

Graeme smiled broadly, unable to contain his excitement. 'Twas the first reiving the Lord of the Isles had made him a part of, brother to him or no. 'Twas past the time to prove he was now a man and no longer a boy. "'Twill be a good time, thievin' the Hay's cattle."

Euan shook his head slowly as he met his brother's eager gaze. "'Twill no' be cattle we steal, boy."

Graeme's eyebrows shot up forming an inquisitive dark slash. "The Hay's sheep are sorry I've heard it be told. No' verra wooly at all. Nay, brother. I dinna think their sheep are worth the time."

Euan shrugged. "'Twill no' be sheep we reive either."

"Then what? What will we be reivin'?"

The Donald arched one arrogant black brow. His upper lip curled into a mirthless smile. "Wenches."

Chapter One

Nairn, Scotland, Present Day

EYES NARROWING, JANET DUVAL'S lips pinched together as she studied her outfitted form in the inn room's unflattering and depressingly accurate mirror. Nobody had ever accused her of being too skinny, she thought grimly, but lordy did she look pudgy in this number.

Twirling around to get a better look at her backside, she qualified that mental statement a bit. She didn't just look pudgy, she looked downright fat.

She wanted to go on a diet—really she did . . . !— but she knew at the same time that she never would. Janet morosely considered the fact that her body seemed to be at its happiest when she was about twenty pounds heavier than what was considered cosmopolitan back home in the States.

Ah well. C'est la vie.

Unzipping the fashion monstrosity that she was supposed to wear to her business meeting tomorrow, she threw it into a pile on the nearest chair and fished around her suitcases for a comfortable sundress. Janet told herself as she climbed into the cotton, clingy number that nobody at the whiskey distillery cared one way or another how she dressed up for meetings anyway. So long as she showed up tomorrow with a hefty check and purchased a ton of Highlander whiskey for the American-based firm she worked for, they'd all be happy.

After she'd donned the thigh-length, spaghetti strap green sundress, Janet took a speculative look at herself in the mirror and as usual found her attributes lacking. She wasn't gorgeous, she knew, but she oftentimes doubted that she was even remotely passable.

But then, Janet was the sort of female who would need a miracle before she'd realize her worth as a person and as a woman. Where Janet would have called her long, tawny-colored hair unremarkable, others would have noted the sleek beauty of it, not to mention the unruly curls that gave her a sensual, freshly bedded look.

Where Janet would have said her lips were too big and her smile too wide for her face, others would have thought her mouth lushly formed, her smile able to brighten even the blackest of black moods.

Where Janet believed her body to be too fat for a man to get turned on by it, men conversely tended to think of her curves as fleshy and voluptuous, the kind of body a man could cuddle up with on a cold night and love until all hours of the morning.

But Janet Duval never saw that possibility. Never even considered it. Not even once.

Turning away from the mirror, Janet glanced about her private quarters in the local inn until she located her favorite pair of sandals. Stepping into them, she grabbed her cloak from a wooden peg jutting out from the bedroom wall just in case it got a bit chilly out.

It was May, that much was true, but even in May the Highlander climate never surpassed the seventies. At night it could get downright cold.

Throwing her cloak absently over one shoulder, Janet picked up her purse and headed for the door. Tonight was, after all, fish and chips night at the local pub.

As she threw open the heavy door and closed it quietly behind her, she grinned to herself that no pudgy girl worth her salt would ever let a Scottish fish and chips night go by unattended.

Being pudgy might not be in vogue, but it beat the hell out of eating salad.

"ACH EUAN, I DINNA KEN why we are no' wearing our own plaids. Why must we sport these . . ." Graeme swept his hand to indicate the nondescript, black garments they'd all donned and frowned. ". . .things."

Euan and Graeme's middle brother Stuart chuckled and answered the question instead. "Graeme boy, half the fun o' reivin' is leaving the mon ye reived tae guess who it was that did it. Ye dinna wear your plaid like an emblem dunderhead."

Defensively, Graeme's chin tilted upwards. "I knew that."

Euan shook his head at Stuart. He didn't think it wise to undermine the boy's pride before a dangerous activity. 'Twas mayhap only another few minutes' ride into the heart of Nairn, the village where his riders had followed the Hay entourage to.

'Twas luck, that. The Donalds wouldn't have to ride all the way into the eastern Highlands to abscond with Hay wenches after all. In another hour or two they'd have their pick of the lot.

For whatever that was worth.

Euan nodded toward Stuart, indicating 'twas time to fall behind him in the line. Stuart acquiesced, nodding toward Graeme to do the same.

The predatory thrill of the hunt flowed into the Donald's veins, fixing his features into their usual harsh relief and causing his muscles to cord and tense.

'Twas time for the Lord of the Isles to find a wife.

Chapter Two

OH MORAG YOU'RE TERRIBLE!" Janet shook her head and grinned at her best friend's story. She had met the rascally redheaded Morag three years past when she'd first started working as the liaison between her firm and the whiskey distillery in Nairn. The duo had hit it off famously and had been inseparable ever since. "Did he really call it . . ." She waggled her eyebrows and chuckled. ". . . a love hammer?"

Morag snorted at that. "Yea he did. Can you imagine? That wee bitty thing . . . having the nerve to call it a hammer!"

Janet stretched her arms above her head as she yawned, absently thrusting her breasts outward. Many a man in the pub noticed and appreciated the view, but as usual, she was oblivious to their perusal.

Her green eyes sparkled playfully. "I've never seen it," she grinned, "but you've told me enough about it that I'd have to agree with you."

One red eyebrow shot up mockingly. "More like a love *pencil,* I'd say."

The women laughed together, then moved on to another topic. Morag waved her fork through the air, punctuating her words as she spoke. "So are you going to take that promotion or no'?"

"I don't know." Janet sighed, her demeanor growing serious. "It would mean a great deal more money, but it would also mean that I wouldn't be traveling to Nairn every few weeks anymore. I'd be at corporate headquarters instead."

Morag's chewing ceased abruptly. Her blue eyes widened. "You wouldn't be coming to Scotland?"

Janet looked away. "No. Not very often."

"How often?"

She shrugged, though the gesture was far from casual. "Once or twice a year," she murmured.

"Once or twice a year?" Morag screeched. "Oh Janet, that's no' verra good news."

She could only sigh at that. "I know."

The women sat in silence for a few minutes, both of them lost in the implications of what it would mean to their friendship if Janet took the promotion her company was preparing to offer her. They'd hardly see each other. And they both knew it.

"Well," Morag said quietly after a few more heartbeats had ticked by, "selfish or no', I'm hoping you don't take the offer."

Janet's tawny head shot up. She searched her best friend's gaze for answers. "What will I do if they fire me?"

Morag thought that over for a minute. "We've talked about going into business together more than once," she said hopefully.

"True."

Morag grinned. "Sounds like the perfect time to do it then."

Janet's lips curled into a wry smile. "I hadn't considered that option."

"Then consider it." Morag glanced down at her watch. "But consider it as we walk back towards the inn. I'm on duty for the late shift tonight."

"Oh of course." Janet stood immediately, having momentarily forgotten that it was her best friend's job to run the small cozy inn her family owned and operated in the middle of Nairn. But then Morag didn't typically work nights. She only was this week because her brothers were off visiting friends in Inverness.

Janet didn't particularly care for either of Morag's brothers. In her opinion, they treated their twenty-five-year-old sister more like a worker bee than as a sibling and an equal partner in their deceased parents' heirloom of an inn. But Janet had never said as much to Morag. She figured if her friend wanted to talk about it, well, then she knew she was always willing and happy to listen.

The women paid their tabs and said their goodbyes to the other pub patrons, then made their way towards the door. Janet pulled on her cloak and buttoned it up after the brisk Highland winds hit her square in the face, underscoring the fact that the temperature had plummeted in the little time they'd been squirreled away inside of the tavern.

"It's foggy out there tonight," Morag commented as she donned her own cloak. "More so than what's normal."

Janet studied the tendrils of mist with a curious eye as an inexplicable chill of uneasiness coursed down her spine. Shrugging off the bizarre feeling, she closed the pub's door and followed Morag outside into the dense cloudy formation.

"Yes," she agreed as they walked down the street. "It's strange out tonight."

"MORAG," JANET SAID as her eyes struggled to penetrate the surrounding mist, "I can't tell which way is up let alone which way heads east toward the inn."

"Neither can I." She sighed. "Good god Janet, this fog is like nothing I've ever seen before."

Janet nodded, though Morag couldn't see the affirming gesture through the swirling mist. The fog was so dense that the friends were holding hands lest they lose each other in it.

Janet looked left then right, but had no more luck seeing one way than she had seeing another. She used her free hand to burrow further into the cloak. Her heartbeat was accelerating, her skin prickling, and she wasn't altogether certain as to why. The fog was thick, yes, but that hardly accounted for the feeling of near panic that was swamping her senses. "We better be careful," she whispered. "We could run smack dab into a wall and not know it until it's too— *oomph*."

"Janet!" Morag said worriedly, unable to see exactly

what had happened. She only knew for certain that she'd come to an abrupt stop. "Are you alright, lovie?" When she didn't answer right away, Morag squeezed her hand tighter, urging her to speak. "Janet!"

"I'm fine." Janet giggled. "Remember how I said we could walk smack dab into a wall and not know it?"

"Yeah."

"I did." She giggled again, her wide smile beaming. "Be careful, but come here and feel."

Morag pivoted slowly in a circle, allowing her best friend to lead her slightly to the right and place her hand on a cold stone wall. She chuckled when she realized that, indeed, Janet truly had walked into a wall. "This will make for a good story." She grinned, her eyes at last finding Janet's through the layers of mist. "I can't wait to tell everybody about—"

A shrill scream pierced their ears, abruptly bringing a halt to whatever Morag had been about to say. Their eyes widened nervously.

Janet's tongue darted out to wet her suddenly parched upper lip. "D-Did you hear that scream too?" she said in an urgent tone beneath her breath.

"Y-Yeah." Morag swallowed a bit roughly as she glanced about.

Squeezing her best friend's hand, Janet attempted to steady her breathing, but found that she couldn't. "We must leave here," she said, her heart feeling as though it might beat out of her chest. "But I can't see which way to go."

"Neither can I," Morag murmured. "Oh god Janet there's another scream!" she whispered in a panic.

"It wasn't the same as the first." Eyes rounded in fright, Janet used her free hand to clutch the wall that was now beside her rather than in front of her. She sucked in her breath when her hand didn't come in contact with a stone wall like it should have, but with a wall that felt as though it were made of . . . earth and twigs?

"What the hell?" she asked herself almost rhetorically. "Morag this wall isn't right!"

Morag didn't know what to make of such an odd declaration, so she ignored it. "Come. Behind the wall," she whispered. "The fog does no' look so thick back there."

Janet glanced toward where her friend was pointing and nodded. She said nothing as she retreated a few steps backward, stepping behind the wall she had just clutched onto, a wall that looked to belong to a home of some sort. Only that couldn't be right. Homes in the Highlands were no longer made of thatch, and they hadn't been for years and years.

Shaking her head, she thrust the odd feelings at bay and followed quietly. Only when they'd gained their position did she speak. "The fog seems to be lessening a bit," she whispered.

Wide-eyed, Morag nodded. "That could be good or bad, I'm thinking."

"I know." Janet squeezed her hand and breathed in deeply to regain her composure. She could be of no help to either Morag or herself if she wasn't thinking clearly. "If the fog lifts we'll be able to see who's causing the screams, but . . ."

Morag closed her eyes and said a quick prayer to Mother Mary. "They will also be able to see us."

"Yes."

Morag closed her eyes to finish her prayer, leaving Janet to keep vigil.

Not even a moment later, Janet watched in horror as the fog lifted a bit and the surreal scene before her revealed a large barbaric-looking man clamping his palm over a young girl's mouth and lifting her up into his overly muscled arms. He passed the girl up to another man mounted atop a horse, only then glancing over in their direction.

Janet shuddered as her large green eyes made contact with piercing black ones. She tried to clutch Morag's hand tighter, only then remembering her friend had released hers to say a prayer. "Shit," she whispered frantically, "he sees us."

"Oh my god," Morag cried out, "we've got to—"

Morag's scream caused Janet to whirl around on her heel. She watched in helpless horror as a mounted rider flew by on horseback and snatched Morag off of the ground with one sweep of a heavily muscled arm. Tears of overwhelming fright gathered up in Janet's eyes. In shock, she drew her arms around her middle and hugged herself as she listened to Morag wail for her to go get help.

Help. Yes, help.

The reality of the fact that there was aid to be found within running distance helped to snap Janet from her state of frozen shock long enough to get her to move.

She would get help for Morag. Oh god . . . Morag!

Pivoting on her sandal, she turned toward the enveloping mist, preparing to dash into it, uncaring of the fact that she would be nearly blinded, unable to see through the thick fog. Braving one last glance over her shoulder, she clamped her hand over her mouth when she heard Morag's scream and watched as her best friend's captor held her securely while riding off to only god knows where with her.

Janet's gaze was drawn toward where the lone dismounted man stood, the largest and most frightening looking of all these marauders. He was watching her, seemingly undisturbed by the fact that he knew she was about to run.

She sucked in her breath as his black gaze found hers and his lips slowly curled into a terrifyingly icy smile.

Saying a quick prayer of her own, she broke his stare and fled into the mist.

Chapter Three

JANET RAN AS FAST AS her feet would carry her. She sprinted at top speed toward . . . anywhere. She had no clue as to where she was going. She could see nothing, hear nothing, feel nothing that wasn't associated with acute fear.

The cold didn't matter. The fact that she'd tripped at least twice already and had skinned up both of her knees didn't matter. The only sight she could conjure up was the mental image of Morag screaming. The only sounds she could hear were the beating of her own heart and the gasps of air her lungs sucked in as she heaved for each breath.

She'd been running for what felt like hours but had only been minutes. She dashed through the fog, refusing to slow down no matter how weary and pummeled her body felt. She might never make it to help before she was murdered on the streets of Nairn, but she'd be damned if she wouldn't go down trying.

Pumping her arms back and forth as her body treaded through the boggy mist, she let out a small whimper of relief when she noticed a break in the fog just ahead. Dashing toward it with everything she had left in her, she came to an abrupt halt once she reached her destination.

"Oh my god," she muttered in between pants. Her eyes darted back and forth, taking in the bizarre scene around her as she doubled over to catch her breath. "Where in the hell am I?" she rasped out.

Janet's mouth dropped open in morbid fascination as her eyes flicked about the row of crude mud and thatch huts that she'd wandered into the midst of. She'd never seen anything like them. Well, she'd never seen anything like them outside of lands that had been preserved for their historic value, she mentally amended.

Snapping out of the reverie that had swamped her, she took a deep breath and reminded herself that she needed to find some sort of help. Morag was in danger. God in heaven, she thought hysterically, her best friend had literally been kidnapped off the streets! She could only hope Morag's captor didn't force himself on her before she could be rescued.

Steeling her nerves and forcing herself to behave with a calm she was far from feeling, Janet took a tentative step out of the mist and toward the row of thatched huts just ahead. She *would* get help. For Morag she would find a way.

Janet tried with every fiber of her being to make that mental vow a reality, but before she could take another step from the fog a heavily muscled arm whipped out and snatched her back into the eerie cloud formation. She opened her mouth to scream, but was forestalled from carrying it out by a large, callused hand clamping roughly over her lips and grinding into her mouth.

Frightened and quite certain he meant to kill her, she bit down as hard as she could on whatever skin she could find, bearing down until the metallic taste of blood trickled onto her tongue. It wasn't enough. The small nick she'd given him hadn't even caused him to flinch.

Flailing madly about, she gave him her full weight then, hoping it would induce him to drop her long enough to allow her precious moments to make good on another escape. Anything—even a single moment's hesitation on his part—and she'd try to flee into the mist again.

But that wasn't to be. When Janet's feet purposely shot out from beneath her and she tried to fall buttocks-first toward the ground, the same heavily muscled arms that had caught her in the first place merely swept her back up as though she were a rag doll. He whirled her around to face him, his large hand still clamped over her mouth.

"Seall dè fhuair mi," he said in a chillingly controlled tone. "Nach e tha mear."

Janet's green eyes rounded uncomprehendingly as her head shot up. She'd never heard such a language. It sounded vaguely similar to the Gaelic she'd heard some of the Highlanders in these parts speak and yet so different at the same time.

Breathing rapidly, Janet determined to look up—way up in fact—and meet her captor's eyes. He might kill her, and was no doubt preparing to do so, but she'd be damned if she'd act the coward while taking her last breath.

She was afraid to look at him, terrified in fact. She'd never encountered a man so huge, so powerfully built. The arm he had wrapped about her felt as heavy as a tree trunk, so roped with muscle it was. He was shirtless, making it easy to ascertain the fact that his equally massive torso was riddled with . . . battle scars?

Janet sucked in a deep breath from behind the giant's hand and, casting her fears behind her, shot her gaze up to meet her captor's dead-on. And then she wished she hadn't.

His black eyes drilled into her, piercing her with a possessiveness she'd never before witnessed, never experienced. The look he was bestowing upon her was so primal that it terrified her.

He didn't mean to simply kill her, she now knew. No. Escaping him would never be that easy. He meant to have her, to rape her.

Janet's last coherent thought before falling into the first faint of her life revolved around whether the barbarian would choose to kill her before, after, or . . . *during?*

And then the blackness overtook her and she thankfully knew no more.

EUAN HELD ONTO THE wench's middle as her limp body sagged against him atop the destrier. 'Twas just a wee bit further they'd go before making camp for the night, getting their party as far from the scene of the reivin' they'd just done as was possible in a night's journey. The Hay would definitely retaliate. He planned to be on his own lands when they did so.

Graeme had been right after all, the Donald thought in a rare flash of humor. The reivin' had been a spot of good fun.

As he ran his hand over his future bride's plump breast and felt a nipple pop up through the fabric of her finely made outer tunic, he conceded that he'd especially enjoy reaping the benefits of tonight's coup. He could scarcely wait to rut between his wench's legs. His manhood was painfully erect just thinking about it.

Euan absently toyed with the nipple, plumping it up between his forefinger and thumb as he considered where the closest village with a priest might be located.

He wouldn't fuck her wee body until he owned it by law, so he'd have to make certain she was his in posthaste.

The Lord of the Isles would be made to wait but so long.

Chapter four

"JANET, WAKE UP. PLEASE LOVIE please . . . *wake up*."

Janet could hear Morag calling to her from somewhere in the back of her mind. But everything was so hazy, so obscured. Her best friend's voice seemed miles away. Her eyelids felt heavy, the muscles of her body were on fire, her knees felt as though someone had raked them across a serrated blade.

"Janet *please* . . . please wake up."

Black eyes. A man. Morag's screams.

The night's activities slowly began to unravel in the fogginess clouding her brain . . .

But she'd gotten away! She'd fled into the mist for help. For—Morag. Oh god . . . Morag!

But no. The man had stopped her. The battle-scarred . . . warrior? A warrior?

"Janet, for the love of Mary would you open your eyes." This in urgent tones from Morag.

Morag? Morag was here? She'd gotten away? Oh . . . Morag!

Ice-cold water pelted Janet in the face, waking her up instantly. She bolted upright, sucking in huge gasps of air, the frigid liquid shocking her into alert mode.

She blinked a few times in rapid succession as her eyes took in the strange surroundings. Animal rawhides enclosed her on three sides, the bark of a large tree on another. The tiny space she was sitting in consisted of earth and animal furs.

A tent. She was sitting in some sort of primitive tent. Her gaze clashed with Morag's. "Where are we?" she whispered.

"Oh lovie," Morag said as she ran a hand through Janet's mane of unruly tawny curls. "I didn't think you'd ever wake up."

"I'm fine." Janet sat up straighter and forcibly shook the remaining cobwebs from her brain. "I'm awake. Morag, what's going on? Who are those men? Where have they taken us?"

"I don't know." Morag worried her bottom lip as she threw a long red tress over her shoulder. "I can no' understand a bloody word of what they are saying to me, Janet. These men . . ." She lowered her voice and leaned in closer to her best friend. "These men are dangerous. We must run away!" she said urgently. "Preferably *before* they come back to interrogate us again!"

"Interrogate?" Janet's eyes widened. "They've interrogated you?"

"They've tried." Morag sighed. "Janet, they can no' understand what I am saying to them any more than I can comprehend what they are saying to me."

"How can that be?" Janet shook her head slightly, more confused than frightened, which was saying a lot. Her eyes darted back toward Morag's. "That makes no sense."

"I know." Morag was quiet for a pregnant moment as she studied her friend's features.

"What Morag? What is it?"

"It's just . . . it's . . ."

"Yes?"

She sighed. "Janet, something verra strange is happening here. Something . . . something isn't right."

Janet was surprised she was able to find a chuckle amidst the chaos, but she did. "No kidding," she said wryly.

Morag didn't return her mirth. "I'm serious Janet. I do no' just mean the fact that we were kidnapped in the heart of Nairn by a bunch of over-large, non-English speaking men. It's . . . it's . . . more than that." She took a deep breath and glanced away.

Janet clasped her hand and squeezed it. She had felt those same odd premonitions since she'd first laid eyes on the fog when they'd trekked out of the pub. "Tell me," she said under her breath. "Tell me what you think is going on."

Morag nodded, deciding to waste no more time. "Bear in mind before you dismiss my musings as nonsense that I have been awake since this entire sordid mess began. I have seen things you have no' seen, or things you have no' seen yet anyway."

Janet's heartbeat picked up. Her skin began to tingle as it had back in the mist. She didn't have any idea what Morag was about to say, but whatever it was she knew she wasn't going to like it. "Go on."

"These men . . ." Morag's eyes widened as her voice dropped. "These men are no' like any men of our acquaintance, Janet. Their bodies are covered in battle scars, they ride upon horses instead of in cars." She waved a hand through the air. "They carry swords and wear almost no clothing save scratchy blackish plaids for the love of Mary!"

Janet drew her knees up against her belly and wrapped her arms around them.

"We traveled on horseback for hour upon hour last evening and no' once, *no' even once*, did I see a home of normal appearance." Morag began to shiver. She rubbed her arms briskly, warding off the chill. "Every last home I saw with my verra own eyes—every last one, Janet!—was made of thatched twigs and clay."

"Like something out of a history book?" Janet murmured. She closed her eyes briefly, remembering only too well the row of thatched huts she'd run into before the gigantic dark-eyed man had captured her.

"Yes," Morag sobbed quietly, "just like something you'd see in a history text, or on a tour of preserved relics. Only people *live* in these relics."

Janet sucked in a deep tug of air. Her lungs burned, felt heavy. "So what you are saying," she rasped out, "is that . . ."

No! Things like that don't happen!

"What I'm saying," Morag continued for her, "is that . . ." She looked away, couldn't go on.

Janet closed her eyes. ". . . That we've traveled through time."

The words hung there between them, feeling more than a bit strange on the tongue and yet, perversely, feeling more than a bit right as well. Morag was the first to speak. "Well," she murmured, "as fantastical as it sounds, I for one do no' think we are in our own time any longer."

Janet's eyes flew open. She blew out a breath. "You sound quite calm about such a terrifying possibility."

Morag shrugged helplessly. "I've had more hours awake to deal with all of this than you."

"True," Janet murmured. She searched Morag's eyes as she considered for the first time since she'd awakened just what else her best friend might have seen, might have been made to endure. "Morag . . ." Her throat felt dry, parched.

"Yes?"

"The man who took you. Did he . . . I mean . . ." She stumbled over her words, unable to find the right ones. "Did he . . ."

"No." She shook her head. "He fondled me a wee bit, but he did no' rape me thank the lord."

Janet released a shaky breath. "Thank god for that at least."

"But he will," Morag said quietly. "They mean to do with us what they will, Janet. Make no mistake." She shivered. "The way the fairer-headed man looks at me, the way I saw that brutal-looking black-haired man staring at you . . ." She let her words trail off portentously, not finishing her sentence.

"Shit." Janet drew her knees in closer to her body. "What do we do?"

"We escape."

"But how?"

Morag found her first chuckle. "I have no' got that far in my plans."

Janet snorted at that. "And if our time travel theory is correct and we are indeed existing in some prehistoric, barbaric era . . ." She shook her head slightly as her gaze found Morag's. "Then what good is escaping? Where will we go?"

Morag nodded definitively. "Back toward Nairn."

Janet raised a brow as she considered that. "Good idea. Maybe that weird fog will still be there and we can get back home."

"Exactly."

"Or maybe this is just a dream."

"Maybe."

Janet sighed. "But you don't think so."

"No." Morag shook her head. "I do no' think so."

The women stared at each other until Janet broke the silence. "Well then, the only thing left to figure out is how we get out of this . . ." She flung a hand towards one animal pelt wall. "Thing."

Morag chuckled softly. "Unfortunately, that will be the most difficult part to figure out." She patted Janet reassuringly on the knee, causing her to wince. "But we—oh dear, what's wrong? Is it your knee, lovie?"

"Yesss," she hissed as she sucked in air between her teeth.

"Let me see." Morag undid the buttons on Janet's cloak, carefully tugged it open, and quickly ascertained how

bad the situation looked. Since Janet was wearing a sundress that only came to mid-thigh while standing, it rode up
even further while sitting, making it easy to see that her
knees were badly skinned up. "Ouch." Morag winced sym-
pathetically. "I take it you got scraped up whilst running?"

"Yes. I—"

One of the animal pelt walls flapped open and the figure of a brooding, dark-haired man emerged. Janet's heart
rate picked up, pounding inside of her chest. The women
huddled closer together, a natural reflex given the situation.

The giant's gaze sought out Janet's, but was snagged a
moment later by the sight of her naked leg. She swallowed
roughly in reaction as she watched the barbarian study the
thigh most adjacent to him. His eyes trailed from the knee
upward, slow and lingering, his possessive gaze burning into
her so harshly that she hysterically wondered if a cattle
brand would magically appear on her leg. Why not? Everything else about this situation was insane.

He wanted her. She'd be a fool not to see it. His burning eyes said so. His meandering gaze said so. The thick
erection poking against the kilt-like blackish covering he
wore said so. She averted her gaze and quickly looked away.

The heavily muscled giant stood there for another moment before making his way further into the tent. His
movement caused Janet's head to snap up and her body to
huddle impossibly closer to Morag's. The warrior noticed
her reaction and, oddly enough, slowed his movements
down, approaching her in a manner that was surprisingly
non-threatening for one so large and obviously lacking in
grace and finesse.

Everything about the battle-scarred man spoke of command and authority. He was a warrior accustomed to taking what he would when he would. And yet he approached Janet cautiously, the way an adult would when trying to lessen the fright of a skittish child.

His large, callused hands placed softly on her knees caused their gazes to clash. Janet's eyes widened nervously. She glanced toward Morag who was shaking like a leaf, then back to the warrior squatting before her.

One hand slid slowly down her right thigh, the leg opposite the side Morag was sitting near, so her friend didn't know what the stern-looking giant was about. His grim black eyes were glazed over with desire as he trailed his hand gently over the expanse of her warm, soft flesh. He touched her as though he couldn't seem to help himself, as though there was nothing in the world he wanted or needed more.

Such a response from a man might have been an aphrodisiac under normal circumstances, but under the current ones it was gut-wrenchingly frightening. Janet began to swallow convulsively.

Her reaction didn't go by undetected. Again, at odds with the warrior's harsh exterior, he showed her the kindness of dropping his hand from her thigh and settling it back upon her skinned knee. His eyes sharpened almost instantly, as if he had momentarily forgotten himself but was now back in control.

And then he was preparing to leave. Just like that. He dropped his hands from her knees and stood up from his squatting position.

Janet couldn't help but to notice how heavily muscled

his legs were when they flexed into standing mode. Indeed, the warrior's entire body looked almost godlike it was so formidably carved.

Janet watched him exit the tent, watched as the animal skin flapped shut behind him, then cocked her head to gawk at Morag whose own jaw had dropped open. "What was that about?" she whispered.

"I don't know." Morag swallowed a bit roughly. She squeezed Janet's hand. "I-I thought he meant t-to . . ."

Janet breathed in deeply. "So did I. I—"

The tent flapped open again and her gaze clashed with the warrior's. His mask was back on, that stony impenetrable façade that she would have thought he always wore had she not witnessed that blazing look in his eyes a minute prior herself.

Her green eyes widened noticeably as he lowered his powerful thighs before her and squatted between her legs once again. Her breathing became shallow and choppy as she prepared for the worst.

Would he rape her right here in front of her best friend? Would Morag be made to watch so she'd know what was in store for her as well? The mere thought of such humiliation caused tears to form in her eyes.

Large, callused hands thrust her legs open a bit wider. Janet looked away and bit down hard on her lip. She could feel Morag's breathing growing labored as they both prepared for Janet's assault. Morag cried out softly as the warlord settled himself intimately between Janet's thighs.

No! Janet thought hysterically. This couldn't be happening! Please god . . .

Janet closed her eyes and bit down harder on her lip. The metallic taste of blood trickled onto her tongue. Her heart was beating so rapidly she could hear nothing but the pulse of it. She squeezed Morag's hand as she felt the warrior's breath come closer.

And then she felt *it*—the hardness of his erection brushing up against her leg from beneath his coarse wool covering. Panting almost hysterically, Janet clamped down on Morag's hand as the warrior placed . . . a wet rag on her knee.

A wet rag on her knee?

Confused, Janet's eyes flew open and darted toward the giant. Her breathing slowed so rapidly it halted completely for a lingering moment. The warrior was . . . good lord he was tending to her wounded knees.

Eyes rounded, she looked quizzically at the giant who didn't seem to notice her. He was busy patting icy cold rags on her knees, tenderly wiping away the dirt that had mingled with the blood on her exposed, raw flesh.

Flicking her eyes toward Morag, Janet couldn't help but to notice the bemused expression on her best friend's face. It was that of a deer caught in headlights. Clearly, she had assumed the battle-honed giant had meant to harm her as well. Playing nursemaid was the last thing either had expected of this formidable man.

Janet's gaze slowly raked over the giant's austere features. He wasn't a bad looking man, she admitted to herself. In fact, if she'd met him under any circumstances other than the one she currently found herself in she would have found him superior in appearance.

His features were grim, but handsome. Black as midnight hair flowed a bit past the shoulders and was swept out of his eyes by a Celtic braid plaited at either temple. His eyes were dark, so brown they almost looked black. She noticed for the first time that the iciness of his gaze was lessened somewhat by sweeping, inky black eyelashes that formed an impressive crescent when his eyes were shuttered as they were now while he studied her knees.

She shouldn't be noticing these things, she told herself stiffly. The warrior might be showing her a kindness by tending to her wounds, but they were wounds his pursuit of her had caused in the first place. She was, Janet reminded herself, no more than a prisoner to him. She asked herself not for the first time, however, just why she and Morag had been captured to begin with.

Her inward musings were brought to a halt when the warrior finished his task and began to speak. His voice was a deep bass, the richest rumble she'd ever heard. She definitely didn't understand a word of what he was saying though.

"Madainn mhath. Ciamar a tha thu?" His black gaze swept over her breasts, settled on her face.

Janet pretended not to notice his perusal of her anatomy. She shrugged and answered his question with a perplexed look.

He tried again. "Dè 'n t-ainm a th'ort, te bheag?"

Her green eyes merely grew larger. She glanced toward Morag, then back to the grim-faced warrior. She shook her head slightly, again shrugging her shoulders in a helpless gesture. "I don't understand your words," she said quietly.

Comprehension dawned in the giant's eyes. They widened almost imperceptibly before he recommanded them and the façade was neatly back in place. He seemed to turn things over in his mind for a moment or two, then pointed to himself and rumbled out a word. "Yu-an."

Janet shook her head, not understanding.

He pointed toward himself again, thumping a callused hand in the vicinity of his chest. "Yu-an."

She was about to shake her head again when the significance of the giant's actions at last dawned on her. Euan. He was telling her that his name was Euan. Glancing first toward Morag whose rounded eyes indicated she still hadn't caught on, she looked back at the warrior and pointed toward herself. "Ja-net."

"Joo-nat." His deep voice repeated her pronunciation— sort of.

She didn't know why, but she felt the need to correct him. "Jaa-net," she said louder, more distinctly. She pointed at him. "Yu-an." She pointed back toward herself. "Ja-net."

He smiled, giving him a softer appearance. A dimple popped out on his left cheek, which Janet found oddly fascinating. "Jah-net."

She nodded, then smiled in spite of herself, weirdly elated by the fact that they'd managed that small communication, no matter how insignificant, and no matter that she was still his prisoner.

EUAN WALKED FROM THE tent feeling more than a wee bit daft. The purpose of yestereve's reivin' had been to steal

Hay women. The comely wench was clearly not Hay, may-hap not even Scottish. So why did he think to keep her regardless? He shook his head and sighed as he strutted toward the campfire where his brothers and men awaited him. Wenches did strange things to men. Especially wenches who sported creamy thighs and fleshy bosoms.

He came to a halt in front of his siblings, then nodded toward Stuart. 'Twas Stuart who had caught the red-headed wench and had a wish to keep her. "'Tis as ye suspected, brother. The wenches do no' speak our tongue."

Graeme chuckled, earning him a punch in the side of his jaw from Stuart. That didn't hold back his mirth, though. "At least my fair Elizabeth kens what I say tae her."

Stuart rolled his eyes and looked back to Euan. "Ye are certain?"

The Donald nodded briskly. He thought back to the conversation that had just taken place in the makeshift tent.

"Madainn mhath. Ciamar a tha thu?" Good morning. How are you?

Nothing.

"Dè 'n t-ainm a th'ort, te bheag?" What is your name, little one?

Again, nothing.

"Aye," he confirmed, grinning a bit at the memory of he and Janet pointing towards themselves and pronouncing their names as slowly as lackwits. He quelled the small smile, his features quickly shifting back in place. "I dinna ken from where they come, but 'tis sorely apparent they do no' comprehend a word of what I'm speaking tae them."

Stuart grunted. "I dinna care, brother. I want tae keep the fiery-haired wench." He waggled his eyebrows and grinned. "I'll teach mah wee bride Gaelic betwixt thrusts in the bedsheets."

Now it was young Graeme rolling his eyes. He decided to ignore Stuart. "What of ye, brother? Will ye keep the other one?" He nodded toward Euan as he considered her appearance. "She is comely for a certainty."

Euan grunted as he shook his head wryly. "Aye. And one hell of a good runner."

A few of the soldiers surrounding them laughed at that.

Stuart grinned. "'Twill no' be easy tae chase your wench down long enough tae thrust, brother. 'Twill mayhap be a while before that bride learns Gaelic."

The laughter evolved into guffaws. Euan acceded to it good-naturedly, uncharacteristic though it might be.

The Lord of the Isles needed an heir and therefore a wife. Janet was the comeliest lass he'd ever laid eyes upon. Big, sparkling green eyes. A lush bosom. The sort of fleshy body he could lose himself in, pumping away into oblivion. His mind was made up. Why bother looking elsewhere when perfection was already awaiting him in yon tent?

"Aye," Euan rumbled. "I will keep her."

"Then ye best get busy." This from Graeme.

Euan lifted one dark brow.

Graeme grinned, then bowed mockingly toward his elder siblings. "Your comely wenches?"

"Aye?" they asked in unison.

Graeme jerked his head toward the tent where even as

he spoke two women were emerging, making efficient bee-lines toward the thick of the forest, dashing off into it at top speed. "I dinna think they ken the honor ye give tae them, making them Donald brides." He chuckled. "In fact, looks tae me as though they are getting away."

Chapter Five

JANET GLOWERED AT THE giant brute standing beside her, his bulging and vein-roped arm plastered about her waist. So much for her ill-fated escape attempt, she thought glumly. The only thing it had garnered her was *his* undivided attention, not to mention being forcibly separated from Morag as though they were two naughty girls being grounded from playing with each other by their fathers.

So now she stood beside her captor who, much to her disgruntlement, looked extremely handsome now that he'd cleaned himself up a bit. Frightening, but handsome nevertheless.

He was wearing a clean plaid of muted blue and green with a white tunic beneath it. His plaid was draped over one arm and held together by a large emerald jewel at one shoulder. The garment fell just above his knees, showing off legs too well muscled to belong to a human.

Janet's lips pinched together. It wasn't fair that a man so dastardly should look so good.

Men who had the look of soldiers began to gather in on all sides. At first Janet thought it was to make certain she didn't try to flee—as if she could with Euan's tree of an arm clamped around her!—but now she wasn't so sure. They didn't seem to be paying her much attention in fact. Their interest seemed to lie with the short little man standing in front of her and Euan wearing a scratchy looking robe with a hooded cowl and speaking in some other foreign tongue she couldn't make heads or tails of.

Janet sighed. It had been a long day. It felt like days ago that she and Morag had attempted to fly the coop so to speak, but in reality it had only been what was probably ten to twelve hours.

After they had been recaptured, Euan and the fair-haired man that had stolen Morag had separated the women from each other's company. They'd been within seeing distance of the other at all times, but not within a range that allowed for conversation.

Janet had managed to scrape up her knees even worse while on the run, tripping over the fallen branch that had eventually permitted the big oaf at her side to catch up with her. Damn branch.

Following her rather ignominious capture, Euan had recleaned her knees in private then shut her cloak. He had pointed and growled at her clothing, making it apparent that she wasn't allowed to remove her outerwear for any reason whatsoever.

Not that she would have. She hardly wanted to show off skin to any of the men surrounding her.

Following his grunts and stern finger pointing lecture,

Euan had placed her atop a horse and jumped up to sit behind her on the mount. They had ridden that way hour after hour, stopping only briefly to eat and care for the animals.

If there had been any lingering doubts in her mind as to whether or not she and Morag had managed to do the inexplicable and travel through time, they had quickly been vanquished. There was no evidence of the modern age anywhere to be found. Nothing but horses, non-English speaking peoples, shabbily dressed villagers, the occasional man or woman hawking crudely made foods and wares, and wild animals galore.

Then they had come to this place. This hole in the wall village that boasted a few thatched huts and little else. Morag had been the first to be swept from her horse and squirreled away into the very forest clearing Janet stood in right now.

When Morag had emerged from the clearing a bit later, her face had been white as a ghost's. She had been trying to tell Janet something with her eyes . . . something, but what she hadn't any notion.

Janet's gaze had fallen to Morag's clothing. The cloak she wore hadn't looked torn or borne any evidence of a man trying to rip through it to force himself on her. That had been Janet's primary concern. When that fear had been wiped away, she'd been left in a quandary, knowing full well that her best friend had been trying to warn her of what would transpire in the forest clearing, but still unable to figure out what that something was.

So now here she stood, soldiers surrounding her on all

sides, Euan stoically planted to her left, a tiny Latin-speaking man just in front of her. Latin? Yes, come to think of it, his words sounded remarkably like Latin.

The smallish man produced a bolt of cloth, placed Janet's hand atop Euan's, and wrapped them together like that. Curious, Janet's gaze shot up to meet Euan's. He didn't return it. His solemn face was intent on whatever it was the Latin speaker was saying.

What was going on! she wailed to herself. If she even knew what time she was in she might be able to sort out all of these strange happenings . . .

"Tha." Euan nudged her gently, breaking her out of her reverie. "*Tha*," he repeated commandingly, nodding down to her so she'd know she was expected to repeat what he'd just said.

Janet nibbled on her lower lip as a sense of awareness slowly stole over her. *Tha*. She'd heard that word before in the Highlands. It meant *yes*. If she repeated it, what exactly would she be agreeing to?

She moistened her lip nervously with her tongue, in the end deciding that there was no point in arguing with the man. If he wanted a yes she'd give him a yes. Begrudgingly, she narrowed her eyes at Euan and phonetically repeated the word she'd been prompted to say. "Ha."

Almost immediately the Latin speaker followed up with a few more words of his own. He said . . . something. Something that made Euan smile for a fraction of a second before he lowered his face to hers and kissed her chastely on the cheek.

Congratulatory shouts rose up from the surrounding

soldiers, many of them thumping the giant beside her on the shoulder, almost as if they were saying to him "job well done."

Janet chewed that over for a moment. She stilled. Her back stiffened.

Her eyes shot up to meet Euan's as she gaped open-mouthed at him. His answering arrogant smirk was all the confirmation she needed.

Good lord in heaven, the man had just married her. And worse yet, she'd agreed to it.

Chapter Six

J ANET STOOD INSIDE OF the crude hut Euan had cloistered
her inside of an hour past, wondering morosely if this
pathetic place was to be her new and permanent home. The
hut boasted but one room . . . one single, solitary room. A
hay-strewn bed lay at one side of it, a kitchen-like area with
a few clay bowls on the other, and a solitary chair in the
middle. That was it. No tables. No more chairs. No anything. She hated it immensely.

Naked, Janet covered her breasts with her hands as
best she could while she watched two village women remove the crudely made tub she'd just bathed in from the
one-room hut. She nibbled on her bottom lip, hoping
that the women would hurry up and come back with her
clothes. She didn't want to be caught unawares when her
husband returned.

Her husband. Janet groaned. Good lord! How would
she ever get out of this mess, find Morag, return to Nairn,

and get back to the future? The task set before her was simply overwhelming.

The wooden door opened a moment later causing Janet's head to shoot up. Her breath caught in the back of her throat and her eyes widened skittishly when she realized that the new occupant was not one of the village women that had helped to bathe her, but instead the very man she least wanted to see while naked.

Dusk was just beginning to settle over the Highlands, so there was still enough light to see the heat in Euan's eyes as his black gaze raked insolently over her body. He was erect, very erect she could easily surmise, his penis bulging against the plaid he still wore.

He closed the door quietly behind him and made his way slowly towards her. Janet sucked in her breath and took a reflexive step backwards.

Euan stopped in his tracks, approaching her cautiously again, just as he had in the tent before tending to her knees. It was then that she noticed he carried a platter of some sort. Food. Against her will, her stomach growled hungrily in reaction to it.

"Hai." He dipped his head. His blazing eyes raked over her flesh once more, lingering over long at the clipped tawny curls between her thighs, but he made no movement to touch her.

"Hi," she whispered back. She gnawed on her lower lip and looked away.

It occurred to her that it was stupid to stand there shielding her breasts from his view when her mons was completely bared to him. But nonsensical or not, she continued to cup them.

Part of it was born of fear, knowing what he meant to do to her and knowing equally well she wouldn't have enough physical power to stop him when he did. But she had spent all day long with him, first while he tended to her knees and then again for the long trek on horseback to the rugged area of the Highlands they were now in. She was afraid of him yes, but not as acutely as she'd once been. He treated her too tenderly to fear him too much.

No, it was definitely more than fear that kept her hands cupping her breasts. It was also reflex, Janet's naturally shy reaction to standing totally divested of clothing in front of a male.

Back home in the States she had endured all manner of teasing as a child and then again as an adolescent. Pudgy. Plump. Fat. Fluffy. Big-boned. Piggy. She'd heard every derogatory term imaginable coupled with her name, every euphemism there was to express the fact that she wasn't a rail and would therefore never be as desirable as every woman wanted to be to the opposite sex.

But this man, she told herself staunchly, this man had captured her, made her his prisoner, taken her against her will, even married her for the love of god! If he wasn't happy with the end result that was his own doing. Perhaps he'd even let her go once he realized his mistake.

Firmly resolved to get it over with while she was still angry enough to do it, she dropped her hands from her breasts and thrust her chin defiantly up. Her nostrils flaring, she stood there and waited for him to reject her.

His reaction wasn't quite what she had been expecting.

Euan groaned, the fire in his eyes raging brightly, licking over every lushly rounded curve, every nuance of her fertile figure. He didn't seem at all put off by her body. In fact, he gazed at her with such obvious desire that Janet's nipples involuntarily puckered up for him and her breath caught for the briefest of moments.

Biting her lip, she glanced away, shaken by both of their reactions. Now what did she do? She'd feel like an idiot recovering her breasts at this point.

And then the decision was taken away from her as she heard him put down the platter of food and come to her. Two large, callused hands cupped her breasts and gently kneaded them like soft dough. He plumped them up with his hands, taking the nipples in between his thumbs and forefingers, and massaged them from roots to tips.

Janet closed her eyes and gasped. "No. Please. No."

From somewhere in the back of her mind it occurred to her that her voice sounded smoky with passion, not defiant with anger and fear. Euan didn't speak her language, she reminded herself, as he began to massage her breasts and nipples into a deeper state of arousal. If she wanted him to understand that his touch wasn't welcome, she'd better sound more forceful.

Janet's green eyes flew open and locked with Euan's black ones. He continued to stroke her, tug just the right amount on her nipples, just enough to where it didn't hurt but sent tremors of desire coursing through her blood instead. She opened her mouth to say no, but found herself sighing and her eyes glazing over instead.

He was handsome. Incredibly, impossibly, muscular and virile. The sort of man that would never look twice at her in her own time, but for some reason or another was fascinated by her in this one.

This was—madness. She couldn't even speak with him, couldn't converse with him, knew nothing about him beyond the fact that his name was Euan and he was well-versed in tending to wounded knees . . . among other things.

And then one of his hands dropped a heavy breast and a callused finger found the sensitive piece of flesh between her thighs and stroked it. "Oh god," she breathed out. Janet's head dipped back, her neck bared to him, all rational thought out the proverbial window. "Oh god."

Where a minute ago she would have tried to say no, she found in this moment that her feet were moving apart to give his hand better access to her clit. She closed her eyes against her worries and fears, accepting the pleasure, and moaned softly.

It was all the impetus Euan needed to further his ministrations. "Mmm, tha," he rumbled as his eyes watched her face, as his hand cupped her wet flesh and felt her liquid dewing up for him.

And then he was lifting her into his arms and carrying her to the bed. He sat her down on the edge of it and splayed her legs wide.

Janet offered him no resistance, opening them impossibly wider for him instead so that her labia was on prominent display. The entire scene felt surreal, like it had to be happening to any woman but her. A more brazen woman. A more wicked woman. Not the reserved and mousy Janet Duval.

He traced the slick folds of her flesh with one callused finger, the look on his face reminding her of someone who'd found the most glorious treasure on earth and wanted to explore every facet of it. His reaction to her body was heady enough to induce her nipples to pop out further as desire shot through her at lightning speed.

"Oh lord." He was rubbing her flesh again, stroking her clit, exploring every wet nook and cranny. Her head dangled backwards like a puppet. She leaned back on her elbows and splayed her legs as wide as they would go. He began to rub her more briskly, faster and faster. *"Euan."*

"Mmm, te brèagha," he rasped out.

Beautiful one. He'd called her *beautiful one.* She'd understood that, knew that expression from her friends in Nairn. Her breathing grew more labored with each touch.

Faster. Faster.

Oh god the stroking was faster, brisker . . . faster still. *"Oh god."*

She was soaking his hand, saturating his fingers. And still impossibly faster. *"I'm coming Euan."*

"Tha, te brèagha," he urged her on. *Yes, beautiful one.*

He didn't need to understand her language to comprehend what words she was groaning out. Her body was telling him.

"Euan," she moaned. *"Faster. Yes . . . god—faster."* On a final groan, her head snapped back, her nipples shot out, and her labia turned a juicy red as her orgasm blew. Blood coursed into her vagina and nipples, heating her body, burning even her face.

And then he was coming down on top of her . . . already naked? She didn't know when or how he'd discarded his plaid but didn't care either. She made him do a little groaning of his own when she pulled him roughly down on top of her and wantonly wrapped her legs around his waist. She wanted him to fill her—needed him to fill her.

Euan clenched his jaw as he poised his thick cock at her entrance. If she didn't slow down a wee bit he was liable to do her a damage. "Gabh do thìde," he gritted out. *Take your time.*

But she was wild for him, his beautiful wee wife. Hot and wild. He'd never experienced such a primal reaction from a wench, had never seen a woman filled with such passion as his Janet. He was more glad than ever that he'd snatched the wrong wench for a wife.

Instead of slowing down, she gyrated her hips, thrusting them upward towards his jutting cock. It was his undoing. There was only so much a man could take, the Donald or no.

Grabbing her by the hips, he thrust deeply inside of her tight, wet flesh, groaning like a man possessed as he did so. Christ but he'd never felt anything so tight and welcoming.

"Oh Euan."

She was breathing out his name in her passion already, he thought with more than a little arrogance. Grabbing his wife's large, elongated nipples, he settled his body atop hers and began thrusting into her in long, deep strokes. He rolled the nipples around with his fingers, tugging at them in the way he'd discovered she liked.

"Faster."

She groaned out that foreign word over and over again.

As much as he wished it otherwise, Euan knew not her meaning. He continued burrowing into her in long, agonizingly languid strokes.

"*Faster*," she all but shouted, this time arching her hips to pummel at his cock in quick strokes.

Ahh. Now *that* he understood.

Euan released his hold on Janet's breasts and came down fully on top of her. Twining a handful of her long, sweetly scented hair around his fist, he locked gazes with her just before he rammed himself home.

She groaned, her head falling back upon the bed as he rode her body hard, fucking her sweet cunt in fast thrusts. "Tha domh phuiseag fearachdainn math," he said hoarsely. *Your pussy feels good.*

Sweat-soaked skin slapped against sweat-soaked skin. The sound of Janet's sweet cunt sucking up his manhood reverberated throughout the shepherd's hut. Euan growled as he went primal on her, fucking her harder and faster, riding the body he now owned by law into ecstasy and oblivion.

"Euan."

His name on Janet's lips as her back arched and her body climaxed for him was powerfully arousing. She shivered and convulsed, moaning wantonly as she burst all around him.

In one fluid movement, he grabbed her hips and rammed himself inside of her body, over and over, again and again. Quick strokes. Deep thrusts. Flesh slapping flesh.

His muscles corded and bunched. His jaw clenched. He rode her fast, hard, like an animal. "*Leamsa.*" Mine.

And then he burst.

Nostrils flaring, Euan's black gaze collided with Janet's as he thrust home once more, then on a groan of completion, spurted himself deep inside of her.

They held each other like that, both of them spent and breathing deeply, both of them too exhausted and replete to speak.

Euan bent his neck to sip gently from her lips. Janet accepted him without hesitation, sweeping her tongue out to meet with his. They kissed slowly for a minute or two, sweet and languid brush strokes until their mingling stopped completely.

Entwined with each other in every way possible, they fell fast asleep.

Chapter Seven

SHE WOKE UP TO the feel of a tongue sliding along the folds of her swollen flesh. The tongue was tantalizingly rough and slick, rimming her labial folds with precision, flicking across her clit, rimming, flicking, rimming, flicking . . . *god*.

She moaned in reaction, her eyes not yet opened, her brain still drunk on pleasure and sleep.

The tongue was joined by firm lips, lips that closed over her swollen clit and helped the tongue to suckle her. Flick, suck, flick, suck, flick, suck . . . *oh yes*.

She ground her hips to meet the tongue and lips as her nipples stabbed up high into the air.

Flick, suck, flick, suck.

Suck, suck, suck, suck . . . *Euan*.

Janet's eyes flew open and her hips flared upward on a groan as she climaxed into his mouth. *"Oh god."* Instinctually she wrapped her legs around his neck and buried his face further into her flesh, wanting him deeper, needing him to suck her dry, wanting the pleasure-pain to never relent.

"Mmmm." He lapped at her like a dog, slurping up the juices that trickled out of her engorged flesh, then sucking again—harder, torturously harder until—

"*Oh my god.*" Janet reared up off the bed, screaming because the pleasure was so acute. "*Yes Euan.*"

Reflexively her body tried to disjoin from his mouth, uncertain it could handle falling over such an all-consuming precipice of pleasure. Euan grabbed her hips in reaction, simultaneously shoving his mouth deeper into her cunt and suckling from her clit harder.

"Oh Jesus god. Oh my . . . god!"

Janet's hips tried to thrash about, but he held her steady, not letting go, never relenting. "Mmmm," he growled, vibrating her clit all the more. His sucking became merciless, faster—harder.

Her head flew back, her nipples hardened and elongated impossibly further, blood rushed to her face. "*Yes . . . oh yes!*"

And then she was there, falling over the precipice, screaming from the ecstasy, wanting more, needing to be filled and fucked.

Euan flipped her over with a growl as he came to his knees, wanting to take her from behind on all fours. "Dinn," he gritted out, nudging the back of her head gently.

Lying on her elbows, Janet looked over her shoulder and made a face, not understanding. She arched an inquisitive brow at him.

"Dinn," he stated with more force, again nudging her head. His eyes were blazing, his muscles corded, his thick cock jutting and swollen. "Dinn."

Janet's lips formed an O. He wanted her upper body pressed down further. She complied readily, spreading her legs far apart, sliding off of her elbows and pressing her head and torso further towards the bed, her buttocks and labia dipping upward for his use.

He grunted arrogantly then cupped her labia from behind and pressed his palm and fingers upwards. "Suas."

That must mean "up," she told herself wryly. Her face heating up despite the night they'd already shared together, Janet submitted, keeping her head and torso down while simultaneously thrusting her labia and buttocks up into the air as high as they would go.

It was a wicked feeling, she thought, being on display like a man's personal whore. But when Euan expelled his breath on a groan while running his hand over her exposed flesh, she decided that wicked could be a good thing.

"Leamsa."

He growled out that word again, the word he had used the last time he'd fucked her, the word he was even now repeating over and over again as he rubbed her wet flesh.

Mine. Janet somehow understood that *leamsa* meant *mine.* Her body reacted to his possessiveness, her nipples hardening and her breath quickening.

"Leamsa."

She gasped as he impaled her, her flesh slurping up the impressive length of his cock, her labia reflexively arching skyward for more. He gave it to her.

Euan gritted his teeth as he slid in and out of her, thrusting into her depths in long, penetrating thrusts. "Leamsa."

"Oh god."

He pummeled faster, pounded harder, thrust into her to the hilt. Over and over. Again and again. "Leamsa."

The slapping sound of her soaked flesh sucking up his cock reverberated, grew louder and lustier as she grew wetter and wetter. "Leamsa."

Janet thrust her buttocks back towards him, meeting each of his thrusts as he gave them to her. The harsh jiggling of her breasts caused her already sensitized nipples to grow that much harder. "*Euan*," she moaned out. "*Oh god . . . Euan.*"

She buried her face in the bed furs as her body began to convulse, her labia contracting around his steely flesh. She half screamed and half sobbed from the pleasure, so powerful was her orgasm.

"*Leamsa,*" he roared possessively, his jaw clenching. His callused fingers dug into the flesh of her hips as he thrust faster and faster, harder and harder. His muscles were tensed, the veins in his neck and arms bulging, his balls impossibly tight from the need to burst.

Janet moaned, continuing to meet his thrusts with thrusts of her own. "*Yes Euan,*" she groaned, "*god yes.*"

And then she was coming again, pulsing around him again, contracting again, moaning like a mortally wounded animal because the pleasure was so acute as to border on the painful.

"Tha, te bheag," he gritted out, "taom a-mach e." *Yes, little one. Pour it out.*

"Oh god." Waves and waves and waves of pleasure shot through her, jutting out her nipples like hard gems, heating her face like a furnace, sending her over a cliff of sensation.

"Leamsa," he growled definitively, slapping into her deeply for a final thrust. Gritting his teeth and closing his eyes, he groaned as he erupted, spurting his orgasm deep inside of her.

A suspended moment later, when the intensity had died down a bit and some sense of rational normalcy settled in, Janet began to wonder why Euan was still holding onto her hips, thereby forcing her buttocks and labia to remain skyward. Confused, she drew herself up as far on her elbows as he would allow, then glanced over her shoulder to study his face.

The mask was back, that stone cold façade that broached no argument and allowed no leniency. And yet, conversely, his black eyes blazed more possessively than she'd ever seen them before.

A chill of foreboding swept through her, causing her eyes to widen and her throat to parch. He was about to do something—or say something—and she had no idea what. All she could do was wait. Sit there on all fours, her labia on display for him, and wait for whatever it was that he was about to command.

And then his large, callused hands were reaching under her and grabbing her breasts. He found the nipples, pinched them between his thumbs and forefingers, and locked gazes with her. *"Leamsa,"* he said softly. Too softly. He tugged at them a bit so there would be no mistaking his meaning. "Tha?" *Yes?*

Janet's eyes widened further.

"*Tha?*" he asked more sharply, pinching her nipples again.

He wanted her to say it. He wanted her to acknowledge an ownership of sorts over her. She hesitated for a moment, uncertain as to what she should do. She didn't want to stay in the past, no matter how enjoyable these past few hours had been.

Eventually, however, the look in his eyes scared her into nodding. She would not say the word, but she would nod.

When she submitted Euan released one nipple, then used his free hand to trail down to the soaked and swollen flesh between her thighs. He slid two large fingers in her to the hilt, then met her gaze once more. "Leamsa," he murmured, his deep voice a rumble of authority and power. "Tha?"

She nodded briskly.

"Tha?" he asked again, louder, angry now.

She nodded again, assuming he hadn't seen the small gesture.

"*Tha?*" he bellowed, thrusting his fingers in again and pinching one of her nipples.

Janet's eyes widened nervously. He wanted her to say it—aloud. He wouldn't settle for anything less.

She swallowed harshly as her gaze clashed with his for a final time. Clearing her throat nervously, she nodded once more. "Tha," she agreed quietly.

With an arrogant grunt, he began to massage her clit with one hand and the nipple he was still latched onto with the other. She groaned, her head falling limp as he rewarded her for her compliant answer.

And then he was impaling her all over again and Janet thankfully had to concern herself with rational thought and worries of ownership no more.

Chapter Eight

JANET HAD BEEN SURPRISED when Euan had awoken her a few hours later indicating that they were going to depart this place where they had shared so much passion together. He had taken her again, thrust himself into her with a groan as though he couldn't seem to help himself, as though her body was the most soothing place in the world for him to be. He had brought her to orgasm at least twice, maybe three times. She had been so groggy with pleasure and peaking she could no longer remember.

Euan had given her a new dress then, a floor length green number that was not only quite beautiful, but also more appropriate for his world. She could only assume that he'd somehow acquired it during the bath she'd taken after he'd married her.

And then he had taught her several new words by leading her outside and pointing to various things. He had been patient in his instruction, which had surprised her.

She didn't know why she was surprised really, for he'd been extremely gentle with her ever since he'd captured her.

Perhaps she'd been taken aback because of the way Euan bellowed orders at his men. She'd quickly surmised that he was the leader amongst the group for everyone catered to him efficiently and unquestioningly. If he barked out a command, it was obeyed and answered instantly. It was through these exchanges that by the second day of their journey from the village Janet found herself picking up more and more words from Euan's tongue.

Janet was pleased that she seemed to be learning key words and phrases from his language rather rapidly. Not enough to where she could yet carry on meaningful conversation—they'd been together but three days after all—but enough to where she was slowly beginning to comprehend what he meant without his having to point at whatever thing or action he was trying to describe.

The past three days had felt much like a dream to Janet. Riding through the Highlands on horseback, the brisk winds hitting her in the face, stopping to look at the wares of the occasional nomadic craftsman, making camp—and making love—with her husband at night.

Her husband.

The knowledge that she even had a husband, let alone one that had died hundreds of years before she'd been born, was what felt more surreal than anything else. And weirder still, she wasn't altogether certain how she felt about it.

Three days ago Janet would have escaped Euan at first opportunity. Today, if given the choice, she wasn't certain what she'd do. Such an admission was not only startling to her, but terrifying as well.

And Morag—oh how she missed Morag. Janet had no idea at all as to how her best friend was faring. Morag and her captor, a man Janet could safely assume was now Morag's husband, had ridden out ahead of she and Euan the morning following the weddings.

Where Morag had been taken Janet couldn't even begin to speculate. Worse yet, she wasn't well-versed enough in Euan's tongue to put such a higher level question to him. It was one thing to be able to ask for food and drink, quite another altogether to express feelings and concerns. She felt as though she were floating along like a piece of driftwood, unable to control her own destiny and uncertain as to where the waters would lead.

On the fourth day of their journey their entourage had been attacked by a group of bandits that outnumbered their party three to one. One minute Janet had been eating an apple as she rode in front of her husband on his mount and the next she was startled into dropping the piece of fruit by the sound of ear-piercing war cries followed by the thunder of hooves as a group of sword-wielding men assaulted them from the south.

Wide-eyed, her gaze had shot up to Euan's. He had paid her no attention, dashing off toward a tree with thick, high branches instead, and placed her into it for safe-keeping while he'd galloped back to charge directly into the fray.

Janet had been frightened. Not only for herself, but for Euan as well. Tears of frustration and terror had welled up in her eyes as she'd watched him ride off, watched him en-gage in a fight in which the numbers greatly out stacked any hope of a Donald victory.

A Donald. Janet now understood that her last name was Donald, or MacDonald. Apparently the two names were in-terchangeable, but since she knew from her own time that "Mac" meant "son of," she could assume that in these times the "Mac" was dropped as redundant, leaving what-ever name was behind it to stand solo.

Not that she'd thought about something as inane as name trivia as she'd watched the skirmish unfold. She had considered the naming business later on, after the Donalds had surprised her by quickly vanquishing the threat to them.

It had been chilling, watching her husband kill men be-fore her very eyes, watching as his heavily muscled and vein-roped arm had bore down on men with such force that his sword had neatly sliced through their now dead carcasses like butter.

He had worn that mask again, that stony façade that was so much a part of him . . . a part of him that was al-ways in place save for the moments of passion they claimed together at night. But she supposed such a mask was neces-sary in this world, a needed way of severing all emotion from whatever job had to be done in order to keep your wits—and life—intact.

And so now here she stood on the fifth day of her jour-ney, gazing out into the frigid Highland waters from shore as she watched a large boat being made ready for them to take to . . . well she didn't know where precisely, could only conjecture from the bits and pieces of Scottish history she'd gleaned while working in Nairn.

Janet knew that the clan MacDonald heralded from the Isle of Skye, that tiny dot of an island in the Hebrides where a man known as the Lord of the Isles had ruled as a king of sorts over the Highland clans in medieval times. She could only surmise, therefore, that since her husband's last name was Donald, or MacDonald, Euan must be of this lord's direct clan.

Janet felt weary, tired and bone-weary from their long journey. And she was confused, still overwhelmed by everything that had taken place this past week. And what's worse, at least to her way of thinking, was that she deeply suspected that she was beginning to grow feelings toward her husband that she wasn't particularly interested in having. Attached feelings. Caring feelings. Feelings of . . . love.

It was just that he was so . . . good to her. Euan made her feel special and loved and desired—three things she had never felt for a man back in her own world, most likely because no man had ever felt them for her either. The way he looked at her, the way he held her as though he'd never let her go or let anyone take her from him . . . it was heady stuff. Heady stuff that had little by little evolved into a deeper affection for him.

But how did he feel for her? she wondered. It was hard to speculate when she wasn't versed enough in his language to speak with him! But, Janet thought somewhat nostalgically, it was only when looking at her—just her—that his mask slipped from place, and bits and pieces of what in any other man would have been termed vulnerability could be seen.

Leaning against the bark of a tree, Janet had closed her eyes for barely a moment when the feel of soft lips placing kisses on her mouth startled her into opening her eyes. She kissed him back without qualm, then smiled up at the gentle giant towering over her. Well, gentle might not be the best term used to describe him, but he was gentle towards her at any rate.

Euan didn't smile at her, but then he never did. She could see the affection for her in his eyes though, the way they seemed to sparkle whenever he looked at her—and only when he looked at her. "Ciamar a tha sibh?" he asked somewhat briskly.

Janet cleared her throat a bit, answering him in broken Old Gaelic. "I am well. How are you?"

"Good. We will travel tae my lands today."

She looked at him quizzically.

"Land," he repeated quite patiently. He stomped his foot on the earth below him and repeated the word. "Land." When her eyes lit up with comprehension, he grunted, his usual response when pleased with her ability to learn quickly.

"We will go on the boat?" she asked him, pointing toward the large wooden vessel in case she was using the wrong word.

Apparently she hadn't. Euan nodded, speaking slowly so she'd understand him. "Aye, we will. 'Twill take most of the day."

Janet noticed that he didn't seem terribly put off by such a notion. And then she understood why when he backed her up against the tree bark and pressed his erection into her belly. The glazed over look in his eyes coupled with his thick erection let her know in no uncertain terms just what he planned to do with her to while the hours away on the boat.

"Mmm Janet," he murmured against her ear, "I need tae love ye."

Janet's body responded immediately, her nipples hardening and her breath catching. She knew her own eyes were glazed over, could feel them narrowing. "Yes," she whispered.

And then Janet did something she never would have been bold enough to do to a man in her own time. Reaching up under his plaid, she wrapped her palm and fingers around his thick cock and began to masturbate him.

Startled, though not unpleasantly so, Euan sucked in his breath. "Ah Janet." He closed his eyes, clearly trying to steady himself, and pushed at her hand. "Stop," he said gruffly. "Later, wife."

But Janet wasn't listening. She felt empowered by the response he always gave her, brazen and daring.

Euan was given only a moment to wonder at the mischievous look suddenly in his wee wife's eyes, his own nearly bulging from their sockets when she dropped to her knees and her head disappeared beneath his plaid. Right here under a tree. Where anyone could walk upon them. She was massaging his balls underneath his plaid.

"*Chan eil*," he hissed under his breath. *No.*

But again, Janet wasn't listening. She'd never done this for him before and suddenly she wanted to do it more than anything on earth. She took him into her mouth, sucking from tip to base, deep-throating him in one suck. She was elated when he gasped in astonishment, then acquiesced to her on a low moan.

Obviously this wasn't an activity women of his time knew much about. Good, she thought wantonly. The realization that for once he was more of a virgin in this arena than her made her all the more determined to bring him to orgasm.

"*Janet*," he said harshly, a disembodied voice from where she couldn't see him on the other side of the plaid.

And then she was pumping him in and out of her mouth in quick sucking strokes, letting his cock go almost the entire way out of her mouth before suctioning him back in with her lips and tongue. She knew the smacking sounds of her suckling were as much a turn-on to him as they were to her.

Janet realized the exact moment when Euan mentally capitulated. His breathing ragged and choppy, he thrust the plaid from around her so he could watch his cock disappear into the depths of her mouth and throat. He groaned at the wicked sight, his muscles cording and tensing. "Aye, Janet," he said hoarsely. "Dinna stop kissing me."

Grabbing her by the back of the head with both large hands, he helped to ease himself in and out of her mouth, riding her faster and faster, much as he did to her pussy while mating.

Janet gave him everything, holding back nothing. She sucked him hard, faster and harder, in and almost out, over and over, faster and faster. Kneading his tightly drawn scrotum with both hands, she suckled on him relentlessly, knowing from his now incessant moaning that he was about to burst.

"Tha, Janet," he gritted out between pants, his jaw clenching as he continued to ride her mouth, "doit mo bhod." *Suck on my cock.*

And then he was coming, riding her hard as he spurt into her mouth, moaning louder than she'd ever heard him moan before, uncaring if anyone heard what they were about.

Janet drank of him, sucked every drop of him dry, until his cock once again lay flaccid and sated in the nest of dark curls at his groin.

Euan drew her up to her feet, hugging her tightly against him, as if thanking her.

FIVE HOURS AND THREE blow jobs later, Janet decided that she had created a monster. Her jaw was sore, she was slightly seasick from the rough movement of the waters in a postage-stamp-sized cabin that boasted one tiny bed of animal furs and a few small slits for breathing in oxygen, yet she couldn't seem to stop herself from obliging his carnal longings.

Clearly, Euan was enthralled with the new form of pleasure she'd introduced to him. He hadn't left her side once. Not even to go check on the voyage's progress.

Three times now Janet had fallen asleep with a sated cock in her mouth and three times she had been woken up to a stiff, thick erection poking at her lips, wanting entry. She always gave it to him, of course, then secreted away a smile when she'd hear her husband moan as he closed his eyes and laid back to enjoy a special treat.

Janet honestly didn't know how her jaw was withstanding so much sucking, but it was. Every time she got sore to the point where she didn't think she could carry on, it took but one glance toward Euan's face to change her mind.

His expression while she sucked on his cock reminded her of what she assumed a little boy who'd discovered masturbating for the first time would look like—gloriously enraptured. A man who had found and captured Nirvana.

EUAN SIMPLY COULD NOT get enough of his wife's suckling. He knew he was being hard on her poor mouth, but he kept awakening from his slumber with a rock-hard erection and a new load of juice that needed to be relieved. And by the saints, 'twas bliss the way Janet relieved him. He'd never before experienced such a sinful delight.

"Ah Janet," he murmured, as he watched her beautiful mouth slurp up his cock, "keep kissing him," he groaned. "Dinna stop, love."

Love. Not a word he'd expected to feel for his wife. Not a word he'd felt for any female save his daughter Glynna.

Nay. With Janet he had felt lust upon seeing her, more lust than he'd ever entertained in his life. Lust that had driven him to capture her twice, lust that had speeded him towards the first village with a priest just so he could rut inside of her, lust that had kept his cock hard and pumping his cream into her more often than he'd believed to be possible.

But somehow over the course of the journey back home, over the course of fucking her mindless and spewing inside of her several times a night, the Lord of the Isles had fallen in love with his captured bride.

He would never let her leave him. Never.

Euan sucked in his breath and groaned as Janet released his cock from her mouth and bent lower to suckle of his man's sac. Running his fingers through her long curly hair, he closed his eyes and enjoyed the bliss.

Nay. He would never let her go.

Chapter Nine

THE CASTLE WAS BEAUTIFUL. Janet simply couldn't get over how gorgeous it was, a mythical looking place that was probably no more than a shell of a relic in her time if indeed it still stood at all. Honestly, she didn't know. Although she'd heard a great deal about the Isle of Skye, she'd never actually visited it. But she was here now. And wow was it awesome.

The entire island was the most lush, picturesque place she'd ever laid eyes on. Emerald green grass, true blue skies, fragrant bluebells that stood at attention in the wind. It was breathtaking.

And the castle—simply indescribable in its wonder. She gawked at the fireplace in the great hall where she was currently standing, taken aback by how large it was. She would easily be able to stand upright in it and still have a bit of head room. It was that tall. And the width—twenty replicas of her could stand side by side in it. She imagined it took a great deal of kindling to light so massive a structure every day.

And then there was the little girl. Glynna if she'd understood Euan correctly. She was roughly six years in age and about the prettiest little thing Janet had ever laid eyes on. There was no doubt as to who had fathered this child. If the jet black curls and stubborn jaw hadn't given away her parentage upon first glance, then the way she'd flung herself into Euan's arms upon seeing him certainly would have.

What's more, it was obvious that the father was deeply in love with the daughter. Euan had actually broken into a full smile upon seeing Glynna, bending down, scooping her up off the floor, and affectionately rumpling her fine coif of a hair-do.

Janet had smiled while watching, mesmerized by the sight of it. She'd always wanted children, but she had never thought she'd have one. She didn't know how she felt about having one now. Latching on to Glynna, a motherless little girl who even now was holding her hand as she stood next to Janet and watched her father order this man and that man about, was paramount to all but giving up any hope of returning to the life she'd known but a week ago.

But did she want to return? Janet wondered silently for at least the fiftieth time. What was there for her really, especially with Morag here in the past? A job she was probably going to get fired from? An empty apartment in Cleveland she rarely saw?

There was no man in her former world who was special to her. No family either for that matter. Her parents had been dead for over five years, killed in a diving accident three days before Janet's twenty-second birthday.

Neither did she boast any real friends in the future save Morag—Morag whom she was still yet to see. She was beginning to worry that she'd never see her a—

"Janet!"

Wide-eyed, Janet whirled on her heel at the sound of that very welcome voice. Smiling brightly, she continued to clutch Glynna's pudgy little hand as she opened her arms and giggled when her best friend came bounding into them. "Morag!" she laughed.

"Oh Janet!" Morag hugged her tightly. "I was so verra worried for you!"

"I'm fine," she promised, hugging her back. "But what about you? How are you?"

Morag released Janet and stepped back a bit. It was then that she noticed Glynna for the first time. She smiled down to the little girl. "And who is this?"

"Glynna," Janet answered.

"Euan's daughter?"

"Yes."

Glynna smiled, displaying neat white teeth. "Hallo, milady," she whispered very sweetly in Old Gaelic.

"Hallo," Morag answered back with a grin, apparently having learned about as much of the tongue as Janet had. "You are verra pretty, Glynna."

"Thank-ye."

Janet's brow furrowed. Obviously Morag had learned a bit more of the tongue than she had. She reverted back to English. "How did you know those words? And how did you know Euan's name?"

"Stuart."

"Stuart?"

"Yes Stuart," Morag responded. Her cheeks pinkened a bit as she cleared her throat. "My, uh . . ."

"Husband?"

She nodded. "I tried to tell you that day in the forest but—"

"It's okay," Janet said wryly, "I pretty much figured it out for myself."

"Among other things, I'd wager."

Janet shook her head. "What's that supposed to mean?"

Morag chuckled. "We were in the same boat as you and your husband, you know, even if the men would no' let us see each other until we docked."

"And?"

She grinned. "Your man was doing more than a wee bit of moaning from what I could hear all voyage long."

Janet's face flushed with heat. She couldn't hold back the small smile that tugged at the corners of her lips though. "So glad I was able to unknowingly provide entertainment," she murmured.

Morag smiled, chucking her playfully under the chin. "Quit blushing. You have the look of a turnip."

Janet happened to glance down just then and noticed that Glynna was watching a little girl across the room play with a doll. The look in her eyes was one of unadulterated longing, a child desperately wanting to play, yet she made no move to dislodge herself from Janet's side even though it was obvious she'd rather be doing little girl things.

Good lord, Janet thought, she'd never met a child so in control of her naturally playful and exploratory nature. Not a good thing at the age of six, to stand off to the side rather than indulge. She turned to Morag. "Do you know the word for 'play'?"

"Hmm." She thought that over a minute, then threw a word at Janet.

Janet nodded her thanks then turned back to Glynna. "You may play now if you would like." She smiled down to her.

Glynna's return smile was so big as to border on bursting. Janet now understood that when Euan had first brought the little girl to her side, he must have instructed her to remain with Janet unless told otherwise. Good grief how boring for a six year old!

"Thank-ye, mum."

Janet's back stiffened. She hadn't been expecting such an endearment so soon, if at all, and she was confused as to how she should feel about it. It was frightening. And yet heartwarming at the same time. Realistically she knew the little girl was probably only calling her by the name she'd been told to use, but it didn't keep her heart from swelling up just a bit. "You're welcome," she said softly, scooting her gently away from her skirt. "Go play now."

Morag chuckled as the little girl bounded away. "She is a verra pretty wee thing."

"Mmm yes. She is."

The conversation turned then as they caught each other up on all that had transpired since they'd been separated. "I love it here." Morag waxed nostalgic as she spun around in a circle and took in the massive great hall and its bustling activity. "Stuart might be a bit high-handed at times, but he's good to me, gentle with me. No' at all a tyrant as my damned brothers were."

Janet didn't know the first thing about Stuart, but she could agree with that bit about Morag's brothers. She shook her head, bemused. "Are you telling me you don't want to go back to the future?"

Morag sighed, then shrugged. "I really don't know, Janet. I was no' thrilled with my life back in Nairn, hated it in fact. I would have gone crazy had I no' had you for a friend."

"I know what you mean," Janet murmured, her catlike green eyes straying to absently watch Glynna play dolls with her friend. "But I can't imagine life here will be easy either." Her brow wrinkled as she considered something. She glanced back toward Morag. "Do you even know where we will be living once we leave the castle? Are Euan and Stuart sort of like, I don't know, soldiers to the big guy here or something?"

Morag's mouth dropped open. "You mean you do no' know?"

"Know what?"

Morag chuckled. "Janet lovie, Stuart is a soldier to the big guy as you so aptly named him, but Euan *is* the big guy."

Janet's eyes blinked a few times in rapid succession. She wasn't exactly sure what Morag . . . oh my.

Janet's eyes strayed across the hall to where her husband was instructing a man to send a message from him to another laird. She couldn't eavesdrop on much of the conversation—they were standing too far apart—but she did manage to make out the last sentence he'd uttered. *Tell him Mac Dhonuill nan Eilean sent ye.*

Mac Dhonuill nan Eilean?

Janet's breath caught in the back of her throat. She swallowed roughly as her eyes darted back toward a grinning Morag.

"That's right," Morag nodded. "You married the Mac-Donald of the Isles."

Chapter Ten

EUAN GAZED DOWN AT the slumbering form of the woman sound asleep beside him. He'd loved her hard this eve, ridden her sweet cunt twice and her wanton mouth once before he'd felt sated enough to leave her be.

'Twas little wonder, he thought with more than a wee bit male pride, that his lady wife was snoring louder than Auld Sheumais did when he'd been hitting the ale overlong. Of course, he conceded in a rare flash of amusement, her snoring was also making it difficult to fall asleep.

Reclining on his elbow, Euan ran his fingers through Janet's shiny mane of curls, brushing a few stray ones back from her hairline. 'Twas hard to believe that a woman so finely made was his. 'Twas not just her plump breasts and woman's hips that tempted him so, nor even the way she gave herself over to him so willingly.

'Twas her heart as well. The way she was with wee Glynna, taking to her these past few weeks as if she'd birthed her herself, spending time with her and making her feel important.

'Twas also the way Janet made him feel. When he held his wife in his arms and made love to her, or simply when his eyes clashed with hers from across a chamber, he felt . . . alive. Whole and content. 'Twas the first he'd felt this way in—well mayhap in forever.

Euan bent his neck to kiss Janet softly on the lips. He hadn't been expecting it, but was pleased when she woke up, blinked a couple of times as if coming out of a daze, then smiled slowly before pulling his face down atop hers to kiss him more thoroughly.

They kissed for a few minutes, softly moaning into each other's mouths as their tongues swept back and forth over the other's. After a bit more of this languid loving, Euan raised his dark head and gazed down into Janet's eyes. "Ye're awake," he murmured.

"Yes." She nibbled on her lip for a moment. "Plan to do anything about it?" she whispered, her cheeks tinting scarlet as the words tumbled out.

Euan couldn't help but to grin, something he found himself doing quite a bit of lately. And now that his wife understood his tongue almost as well as he did, he'd discovered much to his delight that she had a wondrous sense of humor. She never bored him. Never a dull moment at the keep with Janet about.

'Twas not her words that caused his grin this time, though, but the fact that her cheeks were pinkened. As many times and in as many ways as they'd loved each other, it never failed to amuse him when Janet would suddenly turn shy on him. "And what," he murmured, "would ye have me tae do aboot it, vixen?"

She grinned at his endearment, having never thought of herself in such outrageous terms before. Or at least not before meeting Euan. She'd been telling herself for weeks not to form a deeper attachment to him, not to let herself fall any more in love with him, until she knew with stark clarity just what it was that she wanted. Did she want to remain in the past or try to find her way back to the future?

But as usual where Euan was concerned, the moment he gazed into her eyes with longing she brushed her concerns aside and refused to deal with them. It was wrong, she knew, but she couldn't seem to help herself.

"Hmm," she teased, pretending to think his question over. "Perhaps you could read to me by the fire or—"

Euan half growled and half grinned as he came down on top of Janet and settled himself between her thighs. She giggled, running her hand along the strong line of his jaw. It was always good to see the proof of him feeling carefree and lighthearted. Since arriving, she'd quickly discovered that such common things were contrary to his nature, most likely born of his position in life. From a young age, he had ruled many. Not only that but he'd been responsible for the rearing of his brothers as well.

He entered her welcoming flesh in one long thrust, gritting his teeth as he did so. 'Twas like a bit of heaven on earth, being deep inside of her. "I've got a treatise ye can ponder o'er, lass."

Janet's eyes widened on a laugh. She'd never heard him crack a joke before. He'd done it fairly well for a novice.

"Oh do you now?" She grinned, wrapping her legs around his waist. "Anywhere near as good as *The Odyssey*?"

"Much better, I'm thinkin'." He rotated his hips and thrust deeply to underscore his words.

"I see," Janet gasped. "And what is the name of this treatise?"

Euan slid into her flesh again, causing his wife to suck in her breath. He ground his teeth, beads of perspiration forming on his brow. "I call it *Mac Dhonuill nan Eilean Falls in Love.*"

Janet stilled. MacDonald of the Isles falls in . . . love? She had been expecting a witty return, not a declaration of his feelings. Her eyes darted up to meet his, rounding when she saw the affection in his gaze. She realized at once that her husband was deadly serious. *He loved her.*

"Oh Euan," she whispered, "thank-you so much for telling me that." *It made her decision so much easier.*

He grunted a bit, hopelessly attempting to conceal the rising color in his cheeks. "Have ye nothing tae say back tae me, wife?" He glanced away, wishing he hadn't asked as much.

It dawned on Euan that for the first time in his life he was feeling quite vulnerable. He quickly decided he didn't care much for the feeling, but also realized there was naught to be done about it. "Forgive my tongue," he said gruffly, "I should no' have—"

"Euan," Janet murmured, clutching his face between her hands as she searched his eyes.

"Aye?"

She smiled. "I love you too."

The heat in his face went from pink to crimson, endearing him to his wife all the more. "Of course ye do," he grumbled under his breath. "Let us speak of these silly things no more, ye ken?"

She grinned. "But I really love those silly things."

He sighed like a martyr. "Did I know ye were tae be so bluidy demanding, I mayhap would no' have stolen ye, Janet mine."

She slapped him playfully on the rump for that. "Oh really?"

Euan grinned, then shook his head slightly as he studied her features with a serious expression. "That's no' the truth," he murmured. "I would have stolen ye no matter the circumstance."

"Why?" she whispered.

He kissed her softly on the lips. "Because I love ye." The dimple on his cheek popped out as he added teasingly, "Daft wench."

Chapter Eleven

*L*ACK OF TV—NOT a problem. No electricity—who cares? Non-flushing latrines made of stone—kids' stuff.

Janet breezed around the keep for the next couple of days feeling drunk on giddiness. He loved her. Handsome, virile, sexy Euan was in love with mousy Janet Donald nee Duval.

So it was much to her chagrin when Morag squirreled her away in an alcove on the second day following Euan's pronouncement of love, wanting to escape.

"I can no' stand to be with Stuart, Janet." Morag threw a lock of red hair over her shoulder. "Did I say he's no' as bad as my brothers? Ha! He is a thousand times worse!"

Janet cleared her throat. "What did he do?"

"What didn't he do is more the question needing to be asked," Morag huffed. "He tells me what to do, orders me around like a bloody personal servant, he . . ."

Janet listened with half an ear as Morag detailed the longish litany of her husband's sins. She knew Morag—and her temper—well. Even though her best friend didn't realize how she got when she was in a pique, Janet understood implicitly that she'd change her mind about wanting to leave Stuart once she cooled down a bit. She knew Morag loved him. It's just that Morag always became agitated whenever a man displayed even a hint of behavior that smacked of her brothers'. A fact Janet could hardly blame her for.

"So are you with me or no'?" Morag finished her tirade with a definitive nod of the head. "Or do you plan to make me find passage back to Nairn myself?"

Three years of experience enabled Janet to deal with the potentially explosive situation pragmatically. She knew Morag would change her mind once she let off a bit more steam. It was just a matter of distracting her until then.

Janet pretended to turn the matter over a bit. She narrowed her eyes and gazed thoughtfully toward the ceiling. "I don't think we should discuss this here. Let's go take a walk outside," she whispered.

Morag's blue gaze rounded as if she hadn't expected Janet to capitulate in the slightest and, in fact, had been hoping she wouldn't. That only confirmed Janet's initial suspicion—Morag just wanted to vent. "Y-You want to discuss it outside?"

"Of course." Janet shrugged. "This is hardly the sort of thing we can talk about in here."

Morag was so taken aback it didn't occur to her that there was no reason they couldn't talk within the castle walls because nobody would understand them anyway. "Well . . ." She scrunched up her face and cocked her head. "You want to leave Euan?" she squeaked out.

Janet decided not to bother playing games. Clearly, Morag had no desire to leave. Not deep down inside at any rate. "Not any more than you want to leave Stuart." She held out her hand and smiled. "Come on. Why don't we go outside and take a nice brisk walk and you can tell me all about what a jerk he is and then you'll feel tons better and more ready to confront him."

Morag chuckled. "You know me too damn well, lovie."

"Lucky for you." Janet grinned. "If I was any other woman we would have been halfway to Nairn by now."

"I DINNA KEN HER problem," Stuart growled, his sword clashing against Euan's. They were sparring in the lower bailey, honing their skills.

Euan disarmed him almost immediately, then pointed the tip of his sword just under his brother's chin. "Ye best figure it out, mon. 'Tis affecting your concentration." He released him and resheathed his weapon.

Graeme, who had been watching from the sidelines, chose that moment to amble over and do a little grumbling of his own. "At least ye have a wench tae moan o'er, Stuart. I still can no' believe Auld Sheumais let wee Elizabeth get away from him." He threw his hands in the air dramatically. "All the mon had tae do was watch her whilst I took a piss!"

Stuart found a grin at that. "He'd been hitting the cups again, no doubt."

Euan snorted. "As always." He shook his head, then rumpled Graeme's hair affectionately. "'Tis tae young ye are tae worry o'er a wench, boy. Ye'll get another. I'll find ye a betrothed myself come Michaelmas when a few of the clan leaders come tae sup."

Graeme shivered at the notion. "I can scarcely contain my excitement, brother. Will ye betroth me tae that MacPherson wench who possesses a face with a frighteningly close resemblance tae that of a pig, or will it be the dowered daughter of the MacInnis with the over-large teeth?"

Euan and Stuart couldn't help but to chuckle. "Well," Stuart teased, "what is your preference? A pig face or over-large teeth?"

Graeme didn't see the humor in the situation. He sniffed at such a choice. "Ye best save your ill-wit for one who can appreciate it. Since I dinna care for it and since your lady wife is planning tae run away from ye, one must wonder—"

"Back up, whelp," Stuart interrupted. His smile faded abruptly. "What do ye mean Morag plans tae run away?"

Graeme's eyes widened. "Well," he stammered out, "she was mayhap no' serious. Mayhap she was just grumblin' aboot because she was mad at—"

"Graeme," Stuart ground out, "tell me what ye heard."

"Aye," Euan rumbled, his thoughts turning to Janet and her close friendship with Stuart's wife. "Tell us."

Graeme sighed, thinking the scene he'd witnessed this morn not worth the telling of it, but eventually he gave in with a shrug. Why not? "I dinna ken most of what she said for she was mutterin' tae herself in that foreign tongue of hers, but after ye stomped off from the great hall this morn she grumbled under her breath in Gaelic that she was off tae find Janet and leave this place forever."

A chill of foreboding coursed down Euan's spine. Janet had never even confessed to him from whence she'd come. If she got away, he wouldn't have the foggiest notion where to hunt her down to.

"Damme!" Angered, Stuart cursed up a mild storm before turning back to his brothers. "I best go see what the wench is aboot."

"I'll come with ye," Euan murmured.

Stuart's eyes rounded comprehendingly. He nodded. "Let us go."

Chapter Twelve

MORAG TWIRLED A FRESHLY picked bluebell between her fingers and smiled as they walked alongside the perimeter of the wall that led toward the waters surrounding Skye. "You were right," she admitted with a grin, "I feel a lot better now. Sunshine and sea breeze was just the thing."

Janet tossed a tawny ringlet over her shoulder and smiled. "It is quite beautiful here, isn't it?"

"Mmm. Like a dream."

Janet stopped when they came toward an area of the wall with a hole in it. Gliding up to it, she put her eye against it and looked to what was beyond the stone structure. "Wow. Morag come look at this. The beach out there is about the prettiest thing I've ever seen."

Morag tried to oblige her, but wasn't able to see anything. "I'm shorter than you by a good three inches and you are standing on tiptoe. I canna see a blessed thing."

Janet chuckled. "Too bad. It's so pretty."

Morag thought that over for a second as she surveyed the wall. "We could try to climb to the top using these holes as footfalls."

Janet wrinkled her nose at that. "What if we fall? No thanks!"

Morag sighed. "Janet, we may love our husbands but let's face it, there is no' a damn thing to do in this time. If we fall, so what. At least trying to climb the wall gives us something to do for the next fifteen minutes!"

Janet half laughed and half snorted. "True."

Five minutes later the women had gotten no more than halfway up the wall when the thundering sound of horses' hooves came rumbling from the castle bailey charging toward them at top speed.

Morag crinkled up her face, glancing over her shoulder without letting go of her hold on the wall. "Is that my Stuart?"

Janet used one hand to shield her eyes from the sun's glare. "Yep. And that looks like Euan with him too." She winced when she heard Stuart's cursing. "Wonder what's got him so upset?"

Morag's eyes widened. "You do no' suppose we are under attack?"

Janet wasn't given the opportunity to answer. Twenty mounted men came to an abrupt halt at the wall just then, all of them staring straight up at the women from below ground. They looked distinctly uncomfortable, Janet thought, which seemed a bit odd. But then again, Stuart was cursing loud enough to wake the dead. That would make anybody uncomfortable.

"What are you bellowing over now?" Morag screeched, her nostrils flaring as she glanced defiantly down toward her husband.

Stuart didn't answer that. He didn't bother. Janet thought his face looked red enough to start a campfire off of. "Get," he said distinctly, spacing out his words evenly, "down from there now."

Morag chose that moment to contradict him. "No," she sniffed. "I will no'."

A tic began to work in Stuart's jaw which Janet found curious. He really seemed to be overreacting to the situation if indeed she and Morag's excursion up the wall was what had set him off.

"Morag!" he bellowed. "Running away will do ye no' a bit of good. I will find ye every time. And punish ye just as I will when I get my hands on ye!"

Morag rolled her eyes. "Oh sure, like I'll come down now," she said dryly, "knowin' you plan to punish me and all." She sighed. "I mean really Stuart, you—" She broke off as she glanced toward Janet. Confused, she threw her a baffled look before doing the same to her husband. "Wait one moment. What do you mean aboot running away, Stuart? I was no' running away. We were but climbing the wall to get a look at the beach on the other side."

A few muffled laughs rose up from the soldiers on horseback, inducing Janet to wince. Geez but she couldn't blame them. She knew for a fact Morag was telling the truth, but climbing a wall to look at the beach? It truly did sound like a lie, and a weak one at that.

"Climbing a wall tae look at the bluidy beach?" Stuart laughed mirthlessly. "How lackwitted do ye think I am, woman?"

When Morag opened her mouth to speak, Janet forestalled her by coming to her defense. She was afraid that, as angry as her best friend was, she might have chosen to actually answer Stuart's question thereby getting herself into hotter waters with him. "It's the truth," she said with a nod, gazing down at her brother-in-law. "She wasn't running away. We were just bored and we wanted to—"

"Enough."

That one word, uttered quietly yet icily from Euan, was enough to send a shiver up Janet's spine. She flicked her gaze down toward her husband, swallowing roughly when she realized how angry he was. But there was more than anger in his expression. There was something else. Something that looked remarkably like . . . pain.

Oh no! she thought in a flash of realization, Euan actually believed that Morag had been trying to run away. And worse yet, Janet now understood that he believed her to be guilty of the same crime. Her eyes rounding, she implored her husband to listen. "You don't really think I was trying to run from you do you?"

He said nothing. Merely stared at her.

"Do you?" she asked shrilly.

Euan was wearing his mask again, Janet noted with more than a little trepidation. His black gaze was boring holes into her, the line of his jaw stubborn and un-bending. Her eyes widened nervously.

After what felt like an eternity, Euan broke his harsh gaze from hers and threw a command at one of his men. "Get her down from there," he said with seeming indifference. "And lock her in my bedchamber."

Chapter Thirteen

JANET'S CHEEKS PINKENED WITH mingled anger and embarrassment as Euan's man Niall escorted her back to her sleeping chamber. Her only consolation was that the gruff warrior looked as though he felt sorry for her. In fact, just before he locked her inside he turned to her and mumbled sheepishly, "For the record, milady, I do no' think ye were tryin' tae escape."

And then he was gone, leaving Janet alone to stew. She was angry. Very angry. But also quite frightened. The final look Euan had thrown her way before galloping off had been laced with promises of retribution. She could only wonder at his punishment.

One side of her, the indignant half, wanted to stay right where she was and await his arrival so she could rage at him for treating her like this, for not believing her when she'd told him the truth. But the other side of her, the pragmatic half, wanted to bolt. Janet had no clue as to how her husband planned to punish her for her alleged sin, but she conceded rather gloomily that none of the scenarios she was coming up with in her mind boded well.

Janet paced back and forth in the bedchamber, uncertain as to what she should do, what she should say, when Euan finally saw fit to make an appearance. Just then the door came crashing open, causing Janet to whirl around on her heel and dart her eyes nervously toward her husband.

He looked angry. Very, very angry. For some reason or another she wasn't afraid of him any longer though. For some reason or another rather than cowering as most would have and she probably should have, she found her eyes narrowing acidly and her lips pinching together. "Go away," she seethed, turning around, giving him her back. "I have nothing to say to you."

It took Euan five long strides to reach her. When he did, he whirled her around to face him. "I'm certain ye are verra angry with me," he gritted out, his nostrils flaring, "for putting a stop tae your grand plan. But ye will do as I bid ye regardless."

That was too much. She thumped him on a steely arm, not that the big ogre so much as flinched from it. "This is ridiculous!" she screeched, raising her voice to him for the first time since they'd met. "I wasn't trying to run," she fumed out, "and I resent the fact that you don't believe me!"

His nostrils were still flaring as he searched her gaze. He looked like he wanted to believe her but was afraid to hope. And then the vulnerability in his eyes was quickly masked and the steel replaced it. "Take your clothes off," he ordered her.

Janet's eyes widened. Her chin went up a notch. "No."

"I said," Euan repeated icily, "take your clothes off." A tic was working in his cheek now.

"I heard you and I said no." She crossed her arms defiantly over her breasts.

Apparently he didn't care for that answer for the next thing Janet knew he was lifting up her skirt and removing her dress himself. She struggled, indignant now. "How dare you!" she sputtered as the dress went over her head and sailed towards the other side of the room.

"I am Euan Donald, Mac Dhonuill nan Eilean," he said arrogantly. "I dare what I will." His black gaze raked her body insolently. "Go lie on the bed."

"Are you deaf?" she screeched. "I don't wish to speak to you let alone have sex with you! You didn't believe me when I told you the truth and I have nothing more to say to you!"

A vein in his neck began to pulse as his face stained red with anger. "Ye expect me tae believe ye were climbing up the wall tae see the beach!" he roared.

"Yes! I expect you to believe it!"

Euan growled like a trapped animal, the need to believe his wife warring with rational thought. He didn't know what to think in that moment, just knew that he needed to be inside of her. *"Get on the bed,"* he bellowed.

Her chin lifted impossibly higher. "No!"

He slashed his hand through the air. *"Now."*

Janet's eyes widened at the unadulterated pain laced in that one word. It was that knowledge, and not the order itself, that sent her legs gliding toward the bed. Climbing up on top of it, she sat there on her knees and waited, uncertain as to how she could convince him she had been telling the truth out there on the wall. It was paramount that she convince him. She didn't want him hurting inside.

"Why did ye run?" he asked as he took off his clothing and joined her on the raised bed. "Did ye really think I'd let ye go?" He ground that question out through a clenched jaw as he came down on his knees in front of her and took her breasts in his palms. "Ye should have known better, *Seonaidh, leamsa.*" Janet, mine.

She met his tortured look unflinchingly. "I did not run from you."

His black gaze softened somewhat, but Janet could tell he wasn't yet totally convinced. He was beginning to believe her, though, which gave her new hope.

And then Euan was massaging her nipples, rubbing them between his thumbs and forefingers and Janet found her lips parting on a breathy sigh under the sensate assault. "Ye have beautiful thick nipples," he said gruffly as he plumped them. "I want them pokin' straight up in the sky for me tae suckle of."

Janet gasped as his lips closed around one diamond-hard nipple. He slurped it into his mouth, closing his eyes as if to savor it, rolling it around between his tongue and teeth. Liquid desire shot through her, dampening the flesh between her legs and elongating her nipples further. She ran her fingers through his hair and mashed his face into her chest. "Yes, Euan," she breathed out. "Oh yes."

He drew from her hard then, sucking on her nipples incessantly until she was panting for air and he was primal with the need to fill her up with his cock and his cum.

"Whether ye want me or no'," Euan rasped out in a moment of unveiled vulnerability, as he pushed her down onto her back and settled himself between her thighs, "I will always want ye. I will always need ye."

Janet's eyes closed briefly, saddened as she was by the pain in his voice. Her eyes opened and clashed with his. "I love you, Euan. I swear to you," she promised softly, "that as ludicrous as my explanation might have sounded back there at the wall, it was the complete and total truth." She wrapped her legs around his waist. "I will never run from you. I love you."

He lay poised above her, his eyes searching hers frantically for the truth, hoping against hope that he could believe what he'd been told.

"Tha gaol agam ort, a Euan." *I love you, Euan.*

He impaled her in one long stroke, inducing Janet to gasp as he filled her. "I love ye tae," he rasped out, his teeth gritting at the exquisite feel of her tight flesh enveloping him, sucking him in.

Janet clutched his buttocks in her hands and stroked them soothingly. "Do you believe me then?" she whispered. "Please tell me you do. Even if it's a lie. I couldn't bear it if I thought you believed Stuart."

Euan kissed her lips gently, sipping at them. "I believe ye, my love. And that's no' a lie."

Janet had no time to respond to that pronouncement, for within the next breath her legs had been thrown over his shoulders and Euan was drawing himself up to his knees.

His callused fingers digging into the flesh of her hips, he held her steady and impaled her to the hilt.

"Oh yes."

"Mmm," he said thickly as he began to rock in and out of her cunt in long, deep strokes, "ye feel so good tae me." He thrust harder and deeper, his strokes becoming faster and more penetrating.

"Oh god."

The sound of her vagina sucking up Euan's steely flesh was as much of a turn-on to Janet as her husband's primal pumping. She bore down on his cock, meeting his thrusts, loving the deep mounting he gave to her when her legs were splayed wide over his shoulders. *"Faster."*

Euan's jaw clenched tightly, his muscles cording and tensing, the veins on his neck and arms bulging. Grabbing her thighs, he pounded into her slick flesh.

Faster. Harder. Faster still.

"Oh yes."

And then Janet was coming, her back arching and her head falling back in ecstasy as she moaned wantonly for him, her nipples stabbing upwards as her sopping flesh contracted around the length and breadth of him. *"Yeeeeessssss,"* she groaned, gyrating her hips at him as her cunt sucked every bit of pleasure from him that she could.

"Janet." Euan used his fingers to clamp down on her jutting nipples as he thrust into her once, twice, three times more. Throwing his head back, he made a guttural sound as his orgasm ripped through him, spewing into her flesh.

Both of them dripping in perspiration, Euan held his body over Janet's while they both steadied their breathing.

He kissed her softly on the lips, then eased her splayed legs from off of his shoulders. Coming down on the bed beside her, he drew her into his arms. "I love ye," he murmured, kissing her temple.

She smiled contentedly. "I love you too."

They were silent for a long while, enjoying the simple pleasure of basking in each other's embrace. Eventually it was Euan who broke the languid quiet. "I was wondering aboot something," he said, stroking her thigh as he spoke.

"Mmm. What about?"

"Ye are no' of the clan Hay."

Janet grinned, sensing the question that was coming. "No I'm not."

"Where did ye come from then?"

"It's a long story."

"We've plenty of time."

She smiled up at him, running her hand across the impressive width of his chest. "True. But before I tell you that story, I have something else I'd like to tell you first."

Euan cocked a black eyebrow. "Sounds intriguing. And ye sound mischievous. Should I round up a tankard of ale before we talk?"

She grinned. "You might need two."

Epilogue

EUAN DONALD, LORD OF the Isles, master of all he surveyed, swiped an unmanly tear from his eye as he
watched his beautiful wee Janet suckle their hour-old son,
Alistair. Bonny Glynna was sitting next to them on the
bed, grinning down at her new baby brother as she held
onto one of his tiny hands.

He thought back on that eve several months past when
first his wife had told him she was carrying his bairn. She
had been right, he thought with a grin, he had needed more
than one tankard of ale. Though not from the announce-
ment of his son's conception but from the tale of how Janet
had come to be with him in the first place.

Odd, but Euan had believed every word, having decided
after that day at the wall to never doubt his wife again. He
wasn't a man given to trusting others, yet Janet he trusted
both implicitly and explicitly. 'Twas a good feeling, having
another in the world he knew he could always rely upon.

"Look da'," Glynna giggled, "he's all red and wrinkly."

Janet laughed. "I'm sure he'll grow out of it, sweetheart."

Euan grinned at his wife and daughter as he strode toward the bed to join his family. "Let's hope so. Otherwise he might no' be verra popular with the ladies."

Janet and Glynna giggled at that, warming his heart.

It occurred to Euan as he sat down and gathered his wife and children closer to him that a year ago when he'd first set out to steal a bride, he had never anticipated finding such bliss. Fate was a funny thing.

Thank the saints.

Adam 483:
Man or Machine?

RUTH D. KERCE

Chapter One

ABOARD THE MINERAL FREIGHTER, HCS *Jenway,* Tyree Samou sat in her quarters, studying the MW-12 star charts. The computer contained all the navigational information needed but she enjoyed the challenge of mapping the ship's path by hand.

Her talent at charting, more than a hobby, came in handy whenever their data system blipped or went off-line. Once she had even maneuvered them safely past an asteroid field, after the nav computer had shut down because of a power drain.

She often felt born into the wrong century. Fantasies of navigating the high seas, before technology had taken that thrill out of man's hands, haunted her dreams.

Even more enticing, in her seafaring fantasies she indulged every eroticism she craved. Sexy-as-sin pirates took her body and soul to sexual heights she'd never experienced.

If only those fantasies were real . . .

A harsh buzz snapped her thoughts back to reality. Rarely did she work or even relax uninterrupted these days. The burden of a senior officer's rank, she supposed. Her time as strictly a navigational officer with less responsibility had come and gone long ago. She pressed a button on the edge of the desk, unlocking the door. "Come."

With a light swoosh, the panel opened.

The medical officer, Lieutenant Sheera Roiya, strode inside. "Captain."

Tyree's gaze returned to her charts. "No need for such formality, Sheera. We're alone."

"I'm here on business."

Tyree paused and sat back in her chair, her interest captured. "Business? Is there a problem? We lifted off from Jenway Station without incident. The ship and crew checked out perfectly."

"While docked, your newly assigned, personal security bot came aboard."

Tyree frowned. She hated the idea of some pre-programmed robot following her around. But in the last month, ore smugglers had made three attempts on her life. After finding out about it, her brother, the Ambassador of Jenway and the one in charge of her expedition, insisted upon sending along personal protection for her.

A heated argument had ensued when she'd heard his decision. "I don't want a shadow dogging my every move." She'd made her opinion clear before leaving Jenway.

"Don't sound so disgruntled. A lot of senior officers use

them." Sheera stuck her head out the door. "In here. The Captain will see you now."

The doorway filled with a large presence, and Tyree's breath hitched. "It's a male."

Sheera looked at her as if she'd lost her mind. "Of course. A male looks more intimidating to any aggressors lurking nearby and intending harm when you're off-ship."

Tyree stood and rounded the desk. She examined her new guard. Though a robot, she still felt uncomfortable with a male. Especially since regulations dictated he stay inside her quarters.

He stood over six feet, with dark wavy hair, deeply intense eyes, broad shoulders, a square jaw and something she couldn't identify. He held himself differently than other robots, almost proudly. "He's Cyborg?" she ventured warily, because Sheera was a friend who Tyree felt would admit to the truth.

"Of course not!" the woman responded quickly, sounding full of astonishment. "You know Cyborgs were outlawed five years ago."

"That doesn't mean the Governing Council eradicated them all. This bot is not standard issue. He looks too . . . real." She preferred the days when a robot looked like a mechanical. At least she always knew who and what she was dealing with.

"Isn't that the idea, to blend in?"

"Perhaps, but this situation leaves a bad taste in my mouth." She circled him. Strong shoulders, tight butt. Nice. She stepped in front of him again and glanced between his legs. What started as a casual look, ended with her captured attention. He possessed a *very* noticeable bulge. Her body responded with an automatic rise in temperature.

"He seems capable, don't you think?" Sheera prompted.

At the sound of the woman's voice, Tyree gave herself a mental shake. "Mmm." *Capable of what?* She attributed her carnal reaction to simply being too long without a man, dismissed the feelings and raised her eyes to his.

He returned her stare without wavering.

A shiver raced down her spine. That direct look, as if he knew her every thought, intimidated her somehow. But she held her ground.

"What are you called, bot?"

"Adam 483," his voice rumbled in response.

If she didn't know better, she'd swear a look of humor entered his eyes. "Adam? How original." The human imagination never ceased to amaze her.

"Your brother said Adam was preprogrammed to serve you, so the installation of your personal computer chip isn't necessary. I checked him out. He's functioning fine."

Tyree waved her hand toward Adam. "I don't want a security bot. Shuttle him back down while we're still in range."

"You don't have a choice. The orders were clear. Ambassador Samou will cancel our mission if you refuse."

Her brother was more stubborn than a frozen engine coil. "Fine," she huffed. "Leave us then. I'm weary and not prepared for an argument tonight." She'd dispose of him, herself, later. Stick him down in storage somewhere.

"Yes, Captain. I'll report to the Ambassador that Adam is in position," Sheera replied. One eyebrow rose slightly with her direct stare. "And doing his duty."

Tyree sighed. Her gaze switched from Sheera to Adam and back again. The woman knew her too well. Fine. "I will humor my brother in this, for now. But next time we set down on Jenway, he goes back."

Sheera nodded. "As you wish." She turned to leave, then slowed her steps, worriedly glancing at the bot on her way out.

She probably feared he'd be scrapped as soon as the opportunity arose. The idea held appeal.

The door whooshed closed.

Tyree studied Adam from head to toe. Tentatively, she touched his cheek. The skin felt like living tissue. Stubble even grew on his face. When he leaned into her touch, she jerked her fingers back.

And something else disturbed her. "You have body heat."

"All circuits and engines generate heat."

"Hmm, yes, of course." She pulled a knife from her belt. "Give me your hand."

He obediently complied.

"Palm up."

Again, he obeyed without hesitation or change of expression. His large, strong hands and thick fingers caught her attention—the type of hands that made her fantasies soar.

The thought of him intimately probing her with those fingers made her blood run hot. His powerful, masculine aura aroused desires in her too long denied. With her curiosity now piqued, she felt like ordering him to drop his pants, so she could steal a look, and more, at what appeared from the bulge to be a rather large cock.

Instead, she took the knife and sliced open the skin of his hand. His fingers curled in reflex, but he said nothing. Circuits popped and crackled as they became exposed. *Okay, definitely not human.*

So why the uncomfortable feeling that something about him wasn't as it appeared? She felt the need to ask again, "Are you Cyborg?"

"Cyborgs were outlawed in 2178."

"That's not what I asked." His voice held too much inflection for a standard robot. He was some sort of advanced design she hadn't come across before. Her brother ran various test facilities for advanced weapons and electronics research, so the possibility existed that he was a product of some secret research project.

She turned and secured the knife in her weapons' case. She wasn't in the mood to deal with the bot tonight. After working nineteen hours straight, she wanted rest. "I'm going to shower. Allow no one into my quarters." Not that anyone would come in without permission, but she felt compelled to issue some sort of order.

She also needed a specific place on-ship for the bot and again contemplated the storage units on the bottom deck. She only really required his presence for off-ship protection, to watch her back. She didn't want him located inside her quarters. Damn the regulations. "You processed that, right?"

"Yes, Captain. No one will enter."

She shook her head at the delayed response. Long ago, she'd learned to trust her instincts, but she would shelve her doubts for now. Her brother had sent this bot. Sheera had checked him out. He was completely safe and top-of-the-line, according to them.

Exhaustion and frustration with her current assignment was probably just clouding her reason. She wanted more of a future than ore recovery provided. Each day, she grew wearier of this in-space life.

She couldn't even remember the last time she'd had any real fun.

Needing to wash off the sweat of the day, she disappeared into the private bath.

Adam let out a sigh of relief. He examined the cut on his palm and started repairs. No major circuits damaged, so the fix was easy. When he heard the shower turn on, he glanced toward the bath. The Ambassador's sister was smart.

Beautiful, too. Her appearance had taken him by surprise. Porcelain skin, chestnut hair pulled back into a bun, sharp green eyes, and a lush body—not a stick figure like many of the commissioned women he knew.

This assignment turned more interesting by the moment.

Serving the Ambassador on Jenway had become more dangerous the last few months—too many suspicious people on staff and visiting the station each day. The unstable military situation with Jenway's sister planet added to the problem and kept everyone on edge day and night.

Up here, he could survive. And not end up terminated

like other Cyborgs, just because a few went berserk. Well, maybe more than a few.

He was more man than machine anyway. In his opinion, he didn't deserve to die. And neither did she. He glanced at the bath door again. Tyree's mission to find and bring back valuable ore attracted every criminal and scavenger in the sector, according to the Ambassador.

Samou had insisted he confide in Tyree about his true identity, but he wasn't convinced and asked the Ambassador to keep his identity a secret for a while longer. She didn't want him here. He needed to prove his worth first.

Unknown even to the Ambassador, he'd hacked into her private text records before coming on board, so he knew her secrets. His specialized training gave him the advantage of offering her a variety of services she would find hard to refuse.

When she'd studied his mouth, his hands, his package, and then touched his face, he'd seen her interest in him beyond that of a mere robot. The softness of her skin against his almost spurred him into an action worthy of an arrest for sexual excess and time in a detention cell. He wanted between her legs badly. He allowed a rare smile to grace his face.

Tyree's brother said his sister needed to feel safe and happy. Perfect. He intended to see to those needs—*all* her needs.

Tyree barely glanced at Adam as she stepped from the bath. He stood in front of the main door as appropriate to her order.

She pulled her robe tighter, then silently chastised herself. If she walked around naked, it wouldn't have an impact on the bot. She actually wondered what his response, if any, to such an action would be, and almost laughed at the thought of testing it out.

She sat on her bunk and towel dried her hair. One of these days, she was going to hack off the long strands, which were more trouble than they were worth most of the time. But the soft waves reminded her of her feminine side, and she hesitated to rid herself of that small bit of vanity.

The porthole next to her bunk drew her attention to the vast loneliness of space. Even after a three-day layover on Jenway, she still felt tired and every muscle in her body was clenched tighter than an iron vise. She tossed the towel aside and rolled her shoulders, trying to ease the tension.

What she needed was . . . what? She didn't know. Something out of the norm, for sure, to relax her.

Strong hands settled on either side of her neck.

She jumped up and spun around, breaking the touch. Adam stood close, too close—an impassive expression on his face. "What are you doing?" she demanded, backing away a step, and almost stumbling over her service boots on the floor.

He reached out and steadied her. "You looked tense."

"So?" She shrugged off his hand. Not the best retort, but the most manageable at the moment.

"I have been trained in relaxation massage."

Tyree laughed. "You? Why would a security bot receive relaxation training?" She dragged a hand through her tangled hair and retreated another step, feeling penned in by him.

His gaze momentarily focused on her hair, then eased back to her eyes. "On Jenway, I received full personal pleasure training, in addition to security and communication training, to serve you better."

"Pleasure training?" She took advantage of eroti-bots from time to time. Impersonal robots seemed easier than dating—no emotional entanglements after the sex. Though she barely remembered the last time she'd indulged in bot sex. Robots weren't overly satisfying, so she'd sworn off. Maybe this one's programming included spontaneous touching coded in as a prelude to something more physical if he met with no resistance.

"No offense"—as if a bot ever took offense, she thought— "but robots don't do it for me when it comes to sex." She wondered if her brother ordered Adam's training and flushed in embarrassment at the thought.

She grabbed a comb off the corner chest and pulled it through her hair. With the strands hanging loose, she felt less like an officer, the commander of this vessel, and more like a vulnerable woman fighting her attraction to some new man. She glanced at Adam, feeling his eyes on her. "What?"

"No sexual programs were pending, Captain. Do you wish to choose an erotic fantasy for me to fulfill?"

"Didn't you hear me? I'm not interested in having sex with you." Okay, she lied, but better not to make the attempt. He must have faulty programming to have misunderstood. Just what she needed, an erotic bot.

Erratic! She meant erratic. *Geez!*

Her hand shook. Because of a mechanical? She tossed

down the comb. She had to quit responding to him as a human male. She needed a drink.

She turned and fixed herself a StarGin from her personal bar. As a perk of her rank, her quarters contained a private bath that utilized filtered and recycled water, a fully-stocked bar, and even a cooler for snacks. She took a sip of the sour liquid, and grimaced. She set aside the glass with a plunk.

A drink wasn't what she really needed. She'd been in space too long. That was the truth of the matter, and short layovers weren't helping. She wanted a real vacation on a green planet with white, fluffy clouds and lots of water and open land. She closed her eyes, imagining how stress-free that would feel.

A muscled arm slipped around her waist from behind, and Adam's hand, warm and strong, squeezed her shoulder.

Tyree's eyes popped open. Her body froze, but her voice came out without hesitation. "Why are you touching me again?"

The bot's programs needed tweaking or shutting down. His actions were too unpredictable and unsettling.

Tense moments passed as she waited for his answer. Or his next move. He should explain without hesitation.

Too much time ticked by.

A frisson of alarm raced through her. She tried to pull away, but he held tight, drawing her close against his frame. Why did his body feel so good? Steady and all male.

A bot going against his programming was unusual. Suddenly, she wondered what exactly his programming consisted of.

As if reading her mind, he responded, "My programming indicates a bodily need, despite your words and actions. So I have chosen an erotic fantasy at random for you." He nuzzled her ear. "Relax, Captain. Do not fight me." Boldly, he glided his tongue down the side of her neck, then back up again.

"Ahh." Her uneasiness faded next to the thrill that skittered down her spine. His tongue felt wet and warm, not like a scratchy, damp washcloth, as was her experience with other eroti-bots.

He sucked at the sensitive skin below her earlobe.

"Um . . ." Geez, he had great lips.

His voice rumbled low and sexy in her ear. "I can lick and suck other places that will please you more."

Her heart pounded against her ribs. They'd definitely improved bot programming since she had last indulged, at least in the sensual stimulation area. She admitted she was intrigued by what he could do. But Adam was still just a machine.

He reached inside her robe and cupped her bare breast.

She squirmed in his embrace. "Hey, what are you doing?" His hand felt warm and even slightly callused. She slapped at his fingers, now caressing her skin. She couldn't believe he was actually fondling her. He seemed to know just how to touch her body for the best response. Every feminine part of her came alive.

"I'm fulfilling your fantasy, Captain." He rubbed his thumb back and forth across her hardening nipple, mindless of her swats and protests.

Her knees suddenly felt weak. His touch excited her

more than she ever thought possible. "I did *not*—" He pinched the bud. "Oh!" She shuddered, unable to deny the pleasure coursing through her body. Too much time had passed since her last orgasm, and even that hadn't been overly satisfying—the lack of intensity a definite let-down. She really needed to come long and hard. Her body ached for the release.

But that's all her reaction was. Built-up sexual tension. Otherwise, she'd be immune to the bot's touch. He did have great hands though, for a piece of machinery.

He turned her around in his arms and tugged roughly at one shoulder of the robe, fully exposing her breast. She pushed at his chest, but he was immovable. His fingers squeezed the plumpness, and he again pinched the nipple, slightly harder this time.

Tyree bit her bottom lip to keep from crying out at the pleasure. *This is exactly what I need. And he knows it.*

His other hand slid into her hair, and he tilted her head back. "Stand still. Look at me." For several heartbeats, he simply stared into her eyes.

She saw intelligence and emotion in the dark, almost black, depths. *No.* She was mistaken about the emotion part.

He thumbed her nipple and pulled her closer, nudging his knee between her thighs. "Order me to suck your tit, Tyree. I will make you come."

She opened her mouth to protest, but then snapped it closed. She hadn't expected such words and actions from a bot. She didn't know what to say, an odd feeling for her. She wanted to blast him for his audacity, but not, if that made sense.

No way could he make her come simply by sucking her. Bots didn't have the kind of sucking power required. Their mechanics weren't that advanced yet. Still . . . the thought of him trying intrigued her.

Adam wasn't like the other eroti-bots she'd been with. He knew more, knew how to excite her. His security training made him more aggressive than a regular eroti-bot. Maybe that's what threw her off balance, and what made her hot at the same time.

The bots and men whom she had associated with in the past were too accommodating and not very exciting. Men always seemed intimidated by her position of power and relation to the Ambassador. Bots always needed to be told what to do, and how to do it.

Adam didn't wait for orders, nor was he intimidated by her. In fact, *she* felt intimidated, and aroused, by *him*—a combination she wasn't used to dealing with.

"Tyree . . ."

Her name, spoken in his deep, rich voice along with the intimate brush of his knee, caused moisture to gather between her thighs. Her whole body hummed with awareness. She wanted him to toss her on the bed and take her, despite the doubts she still harbored about him.

"Submit to me." Adam lowered his head and lightly brushed his lips against her mouth.

She jerked back from the tender kiss.

He cocked his head.

She'd surprised and confused him, but didn't explain. He didn't need to know how she felt about kissing. That would be too personal for a bot. As far as submitting . . .

Oh, how tempting to finally allow a man complete control of her body. But then, Adam wasn't a man. And a bot simply responded to his programming and orders. He didn't make demands, not in life and certainly not in bed.

His gaze dropped to her exposed breast, then returned to her eyes. "Let me suck, lick, and bite your nipple. I want to pleasure you, Tyree, with my mouth and my cock. Your body needs fucking."

At his explicit words, she simply gaped. At the same time, she knew what he said was true. She did need fucking. Desperately.

The tone of his voice deepened. "Let me between your thighs, up your . . . gorgeous ass"—he hesitated as if letting the words sink in—"between your breasts, and deep inside those luscious lips. I want it all, every part of you."

Her body throbbed at the image of him and his cock working her over. Yes . . . He said all the right things to make her hot and needy and unable to resist.

The intercom buzzed.

Not now. She stared into his compelling eyes. She wanted to go for it—all of it.

The intercom buzzed again, its intrusive sound drawing her out of the sensual moment. A denial tempted her, but she knew her duty.

"Damn." Shrugging her robe up, she pulled away and stalked to the table beside her bunk. He let her go without protest. She clicked a button. "Yes?"

"You're needed on the command deck, Captain," a male voice announced.

Well, that put an end to the sexual encounter. For now.

Perhaps the interruption was for the best. She needed some think time. "I'll be right there."

Without a word, she stalked past Adam and into the bathroom for her uniform. Work was her priority. Her emotions and needs would have to wait until later.

Chapter Two

TYREE STUDIED THE MILITARY-grade black freighter off their port side. The plasma screen displaying the ship flickered and the transmission turned to fuzz. She punched a vid-button and adjusted the reflector, reestablishing and stabilizing the image.

"No apparent heading—they're drifting. No appearance of life from the portholes. Everything's dark over there. The ship looks abandoned. Communications?"

"None," Corporal John Hanson, the Engineer and Mechanical Specialist, reported.

"High ore concentrates show in their storage tanks," she observed, the blood thrumming through her veins. She wasn't sure if the rush was from the possible salvage or from the residual effect of Adam's words and touch.

"Shall we board, Captain?" Analyst Mick Ridgeway asked, excitement in his voice.

"Don't be so eager, Corporal. Any life detected?" She

wasn't boarding a ship without knowing for certain whether the crew still controlled the vessel or not. She only salvaged ore from abandoned freighters, unlike space pirates, who also trolled the area.

"Checking now," he grumbled. Ridgeway activated the sensor reads. A multicolored bar chart of elements popped up on his panel. "Analyzing."

Her crew always expected to collect any ore they came across. A large part of their pay came from a percentage of the take. She understood their desire for profit but carelessness wrought problems, especially from taking on an inferior load. Less room in their tanks meant less room for a larger profit if they came across a better find. Her earnings weren't based on a percentage, so she stood in the best position to make an educated decision about each salvage.

This freighter, drifting past the control deck viewers, loomed almost as large as her own. Normally, the abandoned ships they came across were small, with crew quarters of eight or less.

The control deck's lift door slid open.

Mick Ridgeway jumped from his seat.

Tyree's hand automatically settled over the knife on her belt. When she saw who stepped out, she waved her hand dismissively. "It's all right." She turned and studied Mick's rapid breathing. "Relax, Ridgeway. That's Adam 483, the security bot Ambassador Samou put aboard."

"Security bot? The crew wasn't informed. And a new assignment hasn't been logged."

"You're informed now, and with barely more notice than I received myself. I'll post a log entry later." Ridgeway reseated himself but Tyree noted that he studied Adam from the corner of his eye. She couldn't blame him. She did the same.

"Do you have the information I asked for, Corporal?"

His gaze shifted back to his monitor. "One moment, Captain."

Adam strolled around the command deck. Tyree noticed he didn't touch anything or purposely distract anyone from their duty. One of the female crew couldn't seem to ignore his presence though. Corporal Ellen Pratt, looking a bit smitten, explained the sensor functions to him as he stood by her station. He simply nodded in response.

Tyree wondered what he, as a bot, thought. If he even had thoughts, or just processed information.

"Completed, and no life forms register, Captain," Ridgeway reported. He flipped on the intercom. "Attention, crew, prepare for salvage."

Tyree's head snapped toward him. "Hold up!" Irritation grated along her spine. She stalked over to the man's station and, with a sharp snap, shut off the ship-wide channel. "Last I checked, I was still Captain of this vessel, Corporal. When I decide we board for salvage, I will give the order. Do you understand?"

Mick's eyes narrowed. He didn't acknowledge or refute her words. The anger in his gaze spoke plainly enough though.

The heat of a body directly behind Tyree drew her attention. Adam. She didn't need to turn to know he stood there.

"Do you understand, Corporal?" she repeated.

"Yes, Captain," he said this time.

Somehow she doubted he complied because of her order, especially since his narrow-eyed gaze remained locked behind her the entire time. He'd been just shy of subordination ever since he'd come on board. This was his second mission under her command. A couple of months ago, he'd replaced Lieutenant Samantha Nikor, a close friend of Tyree's, after the woman had become ill and passed away suddenly.

Tyree felt Adam move away, giving her space. She also noticed Ridgeway visibly relax at the bot's departure. "What's the freighter's atmosphere?"

"Oxygen, nitrogen," Mick answered, turning back to his panel. "No detectable breaches on any deck. Habitable without life support equipment."

"Very well. We'll shuttle over a crew to check things out."

He abruptly turned back toward her. "Request permission to serve on the team."

"Denied." The man took too much for granted. She didn't trust him. His enthusiasm and constant presence every time she turned around made her nervous. "I'll go. Hanson, you'll accompany. And Adam, you'll come too."

"You're taking a robot instead of me?" Ridgeway protested.

"That's right. You have a problem with my decision?" Even though no life forms were detected on board, it *was* Adam's job to protect her off-ship. She didn't feel the need to reiterate that to the crew.

"No, Captain," Ridgeway answered tightly, his mouth forming a grim line. "No problem."

Mick wasn't flying any more missions with her. She'd already put in a request for his transfer. She didn't like the man or the way he questioned her orders.

The next time he defied her in any way she planned to punch him in the nose and toss him into a detention cell. "Gentlemen, let's go."

ADAM GLANCED OUT THE pod's side porthole. The black freighter they approached looked like a ghost ship in the emptiness of space. He checked his weapon, making sure of a full charge.

The pod descended through the landing port and into the freighter's expansive bay. Smoothly, the capsule set down on the deck.

The engine hummed, vibrating the pod's interior. The power slowly decreased, then faded into silence. The air lock popped and the hatch opened.

Adam exited the pod first, his laser pistol in hand. Only the pod's landing lights gave off any brightness, so he switched on his infrared visor and scanned the deck. No organic life forms detected but robots might be aboard and operational. In the immediate area, he picked up no movement or threat. "All clear."

Tyree exited, followed by Hanson. She secured the hatch and coded the security lock, as regulations dictated. "Before we salvage, I want to know what happened to the crew," she announced. "Let's head to their command deck."

"Aye, Captain," Hanson agreed, scanning the area around them.

They crossed the bay, keeping watch for any crew members or other signs of life. Adam made sure Tyree stayed between him and Hanson for maximum protection. They entered the lift, which still maintained power, making things easier than climbing levels by hand.

Adam pushed up his visor and discreetly studied Hanson. He wondered about the trustworthiness of the man. He'd already decided Ridgeway was an ass. He didn't like the way the Corporal's eyes followed Tyree's every move.

On the silver panel near the door, Tyree pressed a green button. The lift rose smoothly.

Fully functional. Good. Though he stayed alert for signs of a glitch, just in case.

Moments later, the lift stopped and the door slid open. Adam stepped out first. The command deck sat dark and abandoned. He moved aside. "It's clear."

Tyree and Hanson stepped out of the lift, joining him.

"Check the logs, Hanson," Tyree ordered. She led Adam to an operational panel. "What do you think?"

He looked over the navigation controls and power readings. "Their engines are toast."

"Toast?"

He inwardly cringed at the casual term. Tyree was a senior officer and not easily deceived. He needed to be more careful in his speech patterns. He would pretend not to notice his mistake. Any other reaction would only further fuel her suspicions of him.

Deep down, she already knew he wasn't what he pretended. He saw it in her eyes. For some reason, she kept doubting herself though and hadn't acted on her suspicions.

She just continued to question and test him. She was probably looking for solid evidence before she made a definite decision on what to do. He'd take care not to give her any.

"The controls are not even functional enough to prevent drift. This ship is not going anywhere on its own."

She double-checked the panel readings. "Agreed." She flipped a few switches. "Overheated, from the looks of the readings. Like they were trying to outrun someone."

"I've pulled up the logs, Captain."

Tyree moved across the deck. Adam followed.

"They were boarded by a patrol ship. The Commander reported that the security team was searching for someone but no details were entered."

Adam's heart rate increased. He shared a glance with Tyree. When her eyes narrowed, he schooled his features. They both knew patrols only stopped vessels when looking for a criminal or Cyborg stowaway. "What does the log say happened to their engines?" he asked, switching his gaze to the data screen.

"It doesn't say anything about the engines or anything else. That was the last entry. No indication of mechanical trouble noted. Or that they tried to outrun the patrol. Nothing about the crew off-loading either."

"Strange."

"I don't like it." Tyree glanced from Hanson to Adam. "Let's get a salvage crew over here. Get the ore and get out. I'll file a report with Space Patrol Command. If they want to follow up, they can. That log entry isn't legitimate. It's too incomplete. Whoever boarded them wasn't a patrol team. If they were and arrested the crew, they wouldn't leave the freighter out here. They'd have hauled it back to impound. If pirates boarded, the ore would be gone and the crew dead. A Sector 6 slaving vessel, I suspect, overpowered them, which would explain the disappearance of the crew and the fact that the ore wasn't touched. Slavers don't have the proper storage tanks on their ships for anything other than human or humanoid-type cargo."

Adam nodded. Tyree was correct. Slaving vessels from the neighboring star sector often ventured into this area of space, looking for easy pickings. They might even still be in the area. He'd stay alert, make sure they got the ore and got out of there, as Tyree ordered. Safely.

Tyree finalized the salvage report and shut down the computer. "We got a good load today," she told Adam, who stood stationed by the door, back ramrod straight and hands behind his back. His black outfit, with three silver bars on each shoulder, identifying him as security, made him appear even more mysterious and powerful.

"You should let your crew handle the takes on salvages. The ship could be a trap, rigged to blow when boarded."

She leaned back in her chair and studied him. He had a good point. Normally, she'd think that a bit paranoid but, after being attacked more than once in recent months, perhaps not. "I'm not one to sit around and watch others work. It makes me uncomfortable."

His hands casually dropped to his sides. "I make you uncomfortable."

Very perceptive. "That, too."

"You can trust me more than anyone on this ship."

"Maybe." He was programmed to protect her from smugglers and space pirates and anyone else out to harm her. But was she safe from *him*?

He cocked his head. "Would you like to continue the erotic fantasy we started earlier?"

Surprised laughter escaped her. Her heart began to race and she rose from the chair. Earlier, she'd taken a shower to wash off the ore's grime and dust, and she automatically tightened the belt of her robe—because it was loose or as a protective measure, she wasn't sure. She'd also taken a short nap before starting her reports and felt revived now, enough to confront him about his actions. "Why are you so intent about sex between us?"

"You need it."

"Your assignment is not to get me off."

"Consider it an added perk."

Too human, the words echoed in her head. She'd done a bit of research while online. A classified, robotic experiment, funded by her brother, took place a few years ago. No other information was available, but Adam could be a product of that research. She intended to find out his secrets. She chewed at her bottom lip, then released the bit of flesh. Her gaze raked his body, so well put together.

"All right," she breathed in a barely audible whisper. "Let's see what you can do." So much for not getting personal, but it was not as if she'd picked up some stranger from an outpost tavern. He was just a machine, like a glorified vibrator. Besides, he'd been trained to provide the service. And getting up close would give her the perfect opportunity to check him over more thoroughly.

"Booting up erotic fantasy now."

Booting up? Was that a joke? She swore a twitch of a smile caught one corner of his mouth. A moment there, but then gone. Like on the other ship, when she'd thought she detected worry on his features.

"I'd like to choose a standard missionary position fantasy." Not her favorite, but the safest way to go.

"I have chosen the fantasy. You will comply."

Her mouth fell open. "Excuse me?"

He stepped forward and stopped directly in front of her. "We will continue from earlier. Where were we?"

"Wait, wait, wait . . ."

His voice lowered to a husky tone. "Quiet, Tyree. I am in control."

How did he do that with his voice? The tone vibrated right down her body. She shouldn't be nervous, but suddenly she was. Not fear. When she looked into his eyes, she instinctively knew he wouldn't harm her. No, this was nervous excitement she felt.

"Ah, I remember." Adam pulled one side of the robe off her shoulder, as he'd done earlier, only he moved slowly and gently this time. "All day, I have wanted a taste of this." His head lowered and his tongue flicked at her nipple.

"Oh!" At the moist contact, fire spread throughout her body. He definitely possessed more tongue control than a normal eroti-bot. Her fingers curled around his muscular upper arms. She needed something solid to hang on to. Her legs felt wobbly. "That's decadent."

"And just a preview, Tyree." He squeezed her breast, lifted it and sucked the nipple into his mouth.

The feeling was incredible. Tyree gulped in air as he drew on her flesh. The muscles in her vagina contracted. She *was* going to come from him sucking her, just like he'd said he could do.

Adam increased the pressure and showed no signs of letting up. His full lips sucked her nipple deeply. He groaned, and his seeming enjoyment of the act increased her pleasure even more. She knew he didn't really possess emotions, if he was what he said, but her mind conjured up a vision of such.

He yanked the robe from her other shoulder.

At the abrupt and unexpected move, Tyree's heart hitched. *Yes!*

Both breasts were now exposed to him. He worked her other nipple with his fingers—tugging, rolling and pinching—until it was rock-hard. "I'm going to come!"

He released her nipples and stepped back.

"What—" Tyree looked up at him in shock and wobbled backward. Disappointment flooded through her. She'd been so close. "Why did you stop?" She should have expected as much. In a way, it made her feel better. Only a robot, something with no feelings, would have stopped.

He had no concept of desire. She started to shrug her robe back up, feeling too vulnerable, half-exposed with him silently staring at her with those dark, penetrating eyes of his.

"Stop, Tyree." He stepped forward. "We are not done yet." He yanked hard on the robe's tie. The material fell open.

"What are you doing?" She reached for the sides.

"No," he ordered. "Do not cover yourself."

The way he looked at her was unsettling. Exciting. Commanding. She couldn't help feeling turned on by his aggressive actions. She let the robe hang open.

"Good. You will obey me."

"Obey?"

"Yes." He stared at her bared body. His gaze rose and met hers and his expression hardened. "I'm going to thrust my cock inside your pussy, Tyree. As deep as I can get it in."

Her breath caught, and her heart hammered.

"Lie on your bunk. On your stomach. Now."

She looked at the bunk, feeling shell-shocked. Slowly, she leveled her gaze on him and regained her temporarily lost composure. She intended to retake control fast, before this got out of hand. No matter her true desires, she'd never trusted anyone enough to make herself that vulnerable.

"Sorry. I turn my back on no man . . . or machine. Never order me around again. On this ship, I'm the one who gives the orders. Don't forget your place. You will do as I say. If we fuck, it will be my way, not structured by a preprogrammed sex code written by some horny gear-head."

Chapter Three

ADAM KEPT FROM SMILING, kept his face from revealing any feelings at all. Tyree wanted to test him. Fine. She was one strong-willed woman. But he was equally determined. *You're in for a surprise, lady. I love a challenge.*

He noticed she did obey his order and left her robe open. She was aroused by him and his actions whether she admitted it or not.

From her psychological profile, he'd discovered that commanding an ore freighter and the responsibility of a crew were constant weights on her shoulders. A weight she didn't particularly enjoy. He'd also read her online journal of personal fantasies. He shouldn't have invaded her privacy to that extent, but his life was on the line, and he needed every advantage. Through those intimate entries, he'd found out her need to relinquish control and feel free.

She spoke a strong game but, now that he knew her true desires, he was only too happy to fulfill them. He imagined few men in her life had ever really demanded compliance from her—sexually, without force and solely from her need to submit. That was about to change.

Adam grabbed a handful of her robe and stepped so close that he felt her breath, fast and excited, on his skin. His other hand reached between her legs and cupped her curls, so silky soft.

"Oh!" At his bold move, she tried to move back but his grip on the robe was too tight. She clamped her hand around his wrist. "Move your hand."

"Aye, Captain," he practically groaned. Slowly, he pushed a finger between her moist folds and burrowed deep.

Her eyes widened and she gasped. "That's not what I meant." She clung to him, leaning closer.

"I know." His voice lowered to a rough whisper. "On your bunk, Tyree. On your stomach. Ass up—place the pillows under your hips. I want you to offer your wet pussy to me. Beg me to fuck you, Tyree. Long and hard, until you scream in ecstasy. I want your cream flowing over my cock and down onto the sheets as evidence of my sexual dominance over your body."

"How . . . how dare you speak to me like that?" she sputtered, still clinging to him.

He wasn't fooled or deterred by her words. "I will dare whatever it takes to make you ache for the pleasures I intend to give you."

She chewed at the corner of her lip, and her grip on him tightened. Telling actions. Oh, yes. She was going to be one hot fuck.

He needed her facing away from him when he plunged

his cock into her. He couldn't take the chance of her seeing his expression change too much. He'd also have to pull out before he climaxed. That would be the hardest part. He wasn't ready to reveal his true identity yet, not until she was fully satisfied with his services.

He felt her tremble and he pushed deeper, curling his finger inside her.

"Oh!"

He stroked her internally, wanting to add a second finger, then a third up her tight pussy. *Enjoy it, baby*.

Passion mixed with indecision crossed her face. He loved watching her reactions to being sexually stimulated. "Let go, Tyree. Do as I say. You have no reason to be afraid of me." He pulled his finger almost completely out of her, then inserted a second finger, slowly pushing deep, stretching her to accommodate him.

She stiffened, and a gasp of pleasure escaped her. "I'm not afraid of you."

"I think you are. At least a little." Adam again curled his fingers and stroked her until she whimpered. Before she climaxed, he withdrew both fingers and stepped back. Three fingers would come later.

Disappointment crossed her face, and she reached out for the top of the dresser. Her trembling fingers revealed just how much his touch had affected her.

Before she switched from sexy woman mode back to ship's officer, he pushed his advantage. "I am not an erotibot, Tyree. I am more highly trained than that." He sucked the moisture from his digits. "I will make you come many times, until you are so sated you cannot move. I will not let you deny your true desires or needs, no matter what they are. We will do unspeakable things together, yet so sexually satisfying you will never want another man or bot."

She leaned against the dresser and pressed her thighs together. "Whoever programmed your line—the Adam robot series—coded in more human-like responses than I'm used to in a mechanical." She pulled her robe closed but didn't tie it. "Eroti-bots always say they will satisfy me but haven't in a very long time." She raised her chin a notch. "What makes you think you'll be able to? Highly trained or not, I have my doubts."

"Like I said, I am not an eroti-bot." He'd obviously put her off balance. He knew from her responses that she had enjoyed what he'd done and yearned for more. "And you do not doubt my ability at all. You are scared to death that I will give you the best fuck of your life."

She stared at him, but said nothing. Even so, the flush that crept over her features told him what he needed to know.

Tyree was a strong, confident woman in her job, but he suspected she craved a more submissive position in her bed. And that suited his desires well. He strode forward and scooped her up in his arms.

"Hey!" She locked her arms around his neck.

He set her gently on the bunk, on her back. He needed her trust. The robe fell open to each side, exposing her naked body to his eyes.

She was gorgeous. Her long, wavy hair flowed down over her shoulders. He itched to feel those strands draped across his naked body. Her full, firm breasts with fat nipples—delicious for sucking, which he already knew from personal experience—jutted toward him. Dark, thick curls protected her pussy. His. The possessive thought struck hard as he stared between her long legs. Her slit glistened, wet and slightly open, weeping for a good fuck. His gaze slowly traveled back up her body to her face. "My internal programs are able to monitor responses."

Her eyes narrowed. "Meaning?"

He pushed her knees apart and knelt between her legs. His fingers trailed up and down the inside of her thighs. He felt the muscles contract at his touch. "Meaning, I can tell what pleases you. I cannot be fooled by your words, Tyree." He scooted back, then leaned over and kissed her slightly rounded stomach, just below the navel. Her skin was incredibly soft. His hands skimmed her hips, perfectly shaped for cradling a man's body. His nose picked up the scent of her sex, hot and ready for him.

He sat back on his heels and dragged his shirt over his head. Her eyes dilated with desire as she stared at his bare chest. He unhooked his pants, but didn't remove them. After a moment of watching her response to his actions, he spoke. "You are uncharacteristically quiet, Captain."

TYREE SWALLOWED HARD. ADAM'S eyes had filled with such desire, or what her mind perceived as desire.

When he pulled off his shirt, his perfectly sculpted chest drew her attention. A sprinkling of dark hair covered his pectorals, narrowing to a thin line as it made a path down his flat stomach and into his half-open pants.

The bulge between his legs seemed even more pronounced now. She itched to get inside those pants and let his cock free.

She had no idea how to relate to Adam. Here she was, naked and vulnerable with her robe open, and him hovering over her, determined to penetrate her body. And her soul, she feared, despite her protests. Even so, she believed he'd never force her to comply, if she really didn't want him.

She recalled him sucking her moisture from his fingers. Bots couldn't taste. So why would he do that? A coded move? Programmed in to psychologically stimulate his partner.

He lowered himself over her until he was settled comfortably within the span of her hips. She felt the bulge in his pants press against her, and she squirmed. Bots weren't usually so well-endowed. Not that she'd had sex with every product line, but she wasn't a novice either. Adam's cock felt large enough to satisfy even the most jaded woman.

His arms rested on either side of her, supporting his weight. He leaned forward and she knew he intended to kiss her.

She turned her head. "No kissing."

For several moments, he said nothing. Finally he ventured, "Why will you not allow me to kiss you, Tyree?"

She turned back to him. "I don't like the synthetic taste of bot. We don't need to kiss." Actually, her reasons went deeper. She didn't enjoy lip-locks of any kind, nor understand the attraction of the activity, even with human males. That simple skin against skin contact had never excited her.

"Yes, we do need to kiss."

His answer surprised the heck out of her. She studied his features but, before she could question him about it, he continued.

"How about we negotiate a deal?"

"Negotiate?" She couldn't hold back her laugh. "You are insolent, bot."

"Adam. My name is Adam. Say it."

He almost sounded hurt. "Okay." She'd play his game, whatever it was. For now. "Adam," she whispered in compliance.

"Do not call me 'bot' while we are being intimate. Agreed?"

She sensed the importance of this to him. "All right, Adam. I won't." Intimate wasn't something a robot would say. Uneasiness crept down her spine.

At the same time, she noticed he never used contractions in his speech, as a human or Cyborg would. He was an enigma, to be sure.

If she hadn't already sliced his palm, she'd have definite doubts about him being a machine. But he was just a product of her brother's advanced research or some other highly specialized programming. Nothing more. If he were otherwise, Sheera would have found the evidence during her exam. She would take a look at his internal databases herself after this was over. Her curiosity was too great not to check into his coding.

"Here is the deal. You allow me to kiss you, open mouth, with full tongue, and I will kiss you here"—his hand slid between their bodies to rest on her mound of dewy curls—"open mouth, with full tongue."

Her body reacted instantly, and she pushed against his hand. The ecstasy of his fingers inside her, the erotic memory of him stroking her intimately, returned with full force. The thought of his tongue licking her almost sent her over the edge. By sheer willpower alone, she forced herself to stop moving and lie still. She couldn't remember ever feeling this wet and achy. "I can order you to do that without agreeing to your deal."

"True. But I am apt to do a better job with my tongue if you do agree."

Tyree pressed her lips together. His meaning was clear. She supposed she could suffer through a kiss or two. Normally, she'd just say forget it and send him away. But she was stuck with him, and too worked up to open his control panel and tweak his circuits now.

She needed his tongue between her legs more than she wanted to admit. Once she experienced some sort of sexual release, even a mild one, she'd be able to think more clearly. "All right, Adam. You can kiss me. Anywhere you wish."

Adam was pleased with the victory, both with the kiss and with her use of his name. He brushed his lips along hers, nibbled at one soft corner, then the other. When she sighed, he settled his mouth fully against her slightly parted lips. His tongue slipped inside and he explored her with slow and deliberate ease. She tasted good, like heat and spices. He teased her tongue, hoping for some response.

After a moment, she began to kiss him back. Tentatively, she pushed her tongue into his mouth. *That's right, Tyree. Show me what you need.* He encouraged her with a low groan and angled his head to give her better access.

She wrapped her arms around his neck and explored his mouth, flicked his palate, sucked on his tongue. Her little moans of pleasure, and the undulation of her hips against his, made him feel like super stud of the universe.

She'd been truthful about the metallic taste of bots. He knew that. But he wasn't a bot. His mouth and tongue were completely human, and she was responding like a woman desperate for an intimate connection. He wondered how long it had been since she was truly kissed well. He used all the skills he knew to make her crave his mouth, and more.

When he finally pulled back, he almost laughed at her shocked expression. "Advanced construction," he offered as explanation. "I take it you like the way I taste."

She blushed, and that show of vulnerability in her softened his heart.

"It won't do any good to lie to you. You know I did. It was nothing like I expected. I mean, I've never—" She shook her head.

He kissed her cheek but didn't prompt her to finish her admission. More important activities were pending. He whispered low in her ear, "Now for my end of the bargain." When she squirmed, he couldn't help but push his advantage. "Spread your legs wide for me, Tyree. Open your pussy."

A hesitant look entered her gorgeous, green eyes.

As he suspected she would, she resisted. Too used to giving orders instead of taking them, he supposed, even though she ached for the sexual release.

He registered a faster heartbeat from her and a rise in

blood pressure. She wanted this, needed it. He slid down her body and pushed her thighs apart, until her knees bent and she was fully exposed to his mouth and more-than-eager tongue. "So stubborn," he murmured. "But that makes your submission to me even sweeter."

Tyree took a deep breath, waiting for the feel of Adam's mouth. He kissed the inside of her thigh and she practically jumped out of her skin. She'd never been this sensitive to a male's touch. And his kiss, their kiss, had shaken her to the core.

"Relax," his voice rumbled so close to the juncture of her thighs that she felt his warm breath stir her curls.

Adam's tongue lapped once at her moist folds. She jerked and moaned at the contact. "More," she begged, unable to stop herself. One simple swipe of his tongue had pushed her right to the brink of coming.

"Yes, ma'am. I will lick you over and over again, if that is what you need." He pushed his tongue into her pussy and lapped at her creamy center—long, wet strokes, then rapid flicks against her swollen clit, using the tip of his tongue.

"Ahh!" Tyree's back arched. Pleasure raced through her body and intensified with each intimate lick.

Adam sucked the fleshy bud into his mouth and she exploded. The orgasm he gave her was more powerful than anything she'd ever experienced.

A cry she barely recognized as her own tore from her throat. Waves of ecstasy rolled over her, cresting then ebbing, then cresting again, until finally she collapsed, completely spent.

Adam rose to his knees. He wiped his mouth while he

studied Tyree. Her eyes were closed and she looked totally limp. He could eat her several times and still want more. He moved up beside her and gently turned her onto her stomach. She murmured something when he dragged the robe off her body. He didn't understand her words and thought they probably didn't matter much, as long as she wasn't protesting.

His hands slid down her bare back to her ass. He caressed the round flesh. Firm, but soft at the same time. He stroked his finger slowly down the crack. She moaned and pushed back against his hand. He gently spread the fleshy mounds.

"What—"

"Shh." He leaned over and tongued the delicate, puckered skin in the center.

"Oh!" She jerked and twisted on the mattress.

"Stay down." He eased the tip of his tongue just inside the rim of her asshole.

"Adam! Ah." She slapped the mattress.

He lightly tongue-fucked her ass, enough to get any woman hot—circling the rim, then stabbing his tongue deeper. He pulled out and sucked at the surrounding skin. "Soon, Tyree, my cock is going up that hole. And you will love every thick inch of it. But right now, I want your pussy. Do you want my cock?"

"Yes! Fuck me, Adam. Fuck me, now!"

With jerky movements, he pushed off his pants and stretched out beside her. The urge to come inside her was so strong that he had to force himself to go slow or it would be over too soon.

"I want to see you." She tried to turn over.

"No." Using a tender touch, he eased her against his body, until she lay on her side, her back to his front. "Not this time." He lifted her leg over his hip and eased into her pussy from behind, one inch at a time. He gritted his teeth, but couldn't keep from groaning at the snug, wet fit. Up to now, she hadn't questioned his groans of pleasure, but he felt he was pushing his luck.

Tyree gasped and jerked forward.

He held her tightly. He needed to make this good for her. "Easy. I know I'm big."

"Yes." Her voice sounded shaky. "Big. Feels good." Her hand fisted in the sheet. "Deeper. Need it. Deeper."

He cupped her breast, squeezing lightly, and pushed deeper, until he was all the way in. They fit together perfectly. He moved his hips slowly back and forth.

"Oh, yes! Thick, and so long."

He nibbled at the sensitive flesh between her shoulder and neck. "Move against me, Tyree. Fuck me back."

When she pushed against him, he moaned her name. "Yeah, that's perfect." His hand slid from her breast, down along her side, and he curled his fingers around her hip. Holding her steady, he changed his rhythm and moved his hips in short fast strokes, slapping hard against her ass.

"Yes, yes, yes!" she cried.

Tyree liked it hard. Good.

The aggressive fucking took him too high, too soon though. Fighting for control, right on the edge of losing it, he pulled almost completely out of her pussy, then pushed back in, slow and deep.

"No. Fast. Hard. Like before."

He tugged on her nipple and whispered in her ear, "Just concentrate on the pleasure, Tyree." He was controlling this fuck, not her. When it came to sex, he'd give the orders and she would follow.

"I need more," she pleaded.

"You'll get all you can handle. Believe me."

The intercom buzzed. Tyree cursed at the interruption. "Not now!"

Knowing she couldn't see his face, Adam didn't bother to squelch his smile. "Reach over and answer it."

When she didn't move, he plucked lightly at her nipple. She moaned, until he soothed the hard bud with his palm.

"If you refuse, someone will come looking for you. We can invite them in to watch me fuck you, if you want, but I am not letting you out of this bed until you come to my satisfaction."

"Dream on. I don't do group sex." To reach the button, she had to roll onto her stomach.

Adam rolled with her, staying inside her. He watched her bite her bottom lip as he pushed in to the hilt. When she hesitated to reach for the button, he reached over and punched on the intercom for her, taking the decision out of her hands.

"Captain?" Corporal Hanson asked. "Are you there?"

"Y-yes."

Adam pumped his hips.

Tyree sucked in a sharp breath.

"We need your navigational input, Captain."

Adam whispered in her ear, "You're not going anywhere

until I fuck every last drop of cum out of you. I mean it, Tyree." He plunged into her again, harder this time, making his point.

She buried her face in the mattress, muffling her moan. "Captain?"

He gathered her hair behind her and licked at her ear. "Answer him."

Tyree raised her head. "Take the information off the computer, Corporal," she ordered in a ragged voice. "I entered it earlier."

Adam released her hair and pinned her hands to the bed. He moved slowly but continued pushing into her hard, grunting low in his throat with each deep thrust.

"Shh," Tyree attempted. The sound came out as more of a whimper.

The totally submissive position she allowed him to put her in worked him up more than he'd ever imagined it would. The possibility of discovery by the crew added to the erotic mix.

"Are you sure, Captain?" Mick Ridgeway's voice broke in. "You usually give the coordinates personally."

"Don't question me!" she growled. She tried tugging her hand free to flip off the intercom.

Adam held her immobile, circling her wrists with his fingers. He nuzzled her ear. "No." He wasn't letting her off so easily. "Leave it on. If you come, everyone on the command deck will hear. Does that excite you? Do you want that?"

She shook her head, though she didn't speak. Nor did she fight it.

Damn, she was sexy as hell and loving every minute of his control. He continued fucking her, very slow and as deeply as possible. He could tell by the way her body was trembling, the way her pussy clenched his cock, that he had her right where he wanted her. "Hold your pleasure. Until I say."

"Bastard," she whispered under her breath, but her voice held no real contempt.

He licked her ear. "I know you, Tyree. Maybe better than you know yourself. I will control you in bed." He pumped his hips a little faster—not hard, just thoroughly deep strokes. He continued to speak quietly in her ear, low enough so he knew his voice wouldn't carry over the intercom. "The crew can hear your excited breathing, Tyree, and know you're getting fucked. And they wonder if I'm the one pumping your pussy."

"They can't hear me," she whispered.

True, but his sexually charged words were turning her on. He registered the internal changes as she experienced them. Faster heart rate, raised blood pressure, increased perspiration. "They're all gathered around the intercom, listening, waiting to hear you scream from the orgasm I'm going to give you. And jealous that my cock is the one inside you, instead of one of theirs."

"Adam . . . Please."

He smiled at the sexy way she drew out his name, the way she begged. She was ready. He reached over and flipped off the intercom. "But I'm not here to give them pleasure. This is between us, just you and me. Now come for me!" He thrust into her once more—this time hard, and as deeply as he could go.

Her body tensed. "Adam!"

He felt the spasms rack her body, rolling through her as she thrashed wildly beneath him. *Yeah, come.* Three more hard thrusts caused her to cry out and orgasm again.

"Oh, yes! Don't stop!"

I don't intend to, baby. Keep coming for me. Keep coming. A few more good plunges up her pussy, then he'd pull out, before—

The climax raced through him and shattered his body before he expected it. He stiffened, shouted Tyree's name and spilled his seed inside her. He felt her spasm and come a third time, milking his body more completely than any woman ever had.

After long moments of mind-blowing pleasure, they collapsed together. *Shit.*

Adam sighed and tried to control his breathing. He'd blown it. He'd let himself go too far. He also realized he'd forgotten to control his speech patterns after he started pumping her. But, damn, her pussy had felt incredible gripping and squeezing his cock! No man would have been able to control himself or think straight.

He felt her tense beneath him.

"Get off me, Cyborg," she ordered on a tight breath.

"Hell." He rolled off. "I—"

"Don't say anything." She scrambled off the bed, not bothering to cover herself. "Bots don't climax."

"Advanced programming?"

"You lied to me."

"Yeah, Tyree. I did. But you knew I did. You knew from the beginning. Don't tell me you didn't." Adam took in her image. Naked, hair tangled, a blush tinting her skin. No woman had ever looked more beautiful. She stalked toward the bathroom.

"Tyree . . ."

She stopped, her hands on each side of the door frame. She didn't speak, just stood there, her back to him. Her hair flowed down behind her and her shapely butt drew his attention, giving him erotic ideas he shouldn't be having right now.

"What?"

"If you take me in, they'll kill me."

She didn't respond, nor move.

"Please." His life was in her hands. There was nowhere up here he could run should she turn against him. Even if he stole a pod, Tyree would probably hunt him down.

She turned her head but didn't quite look over her shoulder. "Come into the bathroom. Get yourself cleaned up . . . bot."

Chapter Four

TYREE STOOD UNDER THE shower, letting the warm water soothe her aching muscles. Too bad her jumbled emotions weren't eased as simply.

Why she let Adam off after his deception, she didn't know. Maybe she'd done so because he gave her the best orgasms of her life. Cyborgs were dangerous, apparently *in* bed as well as out.

The thought disturbed her.

Was she really that shallow? Or did her feelings run deeper? They'd just met, but she felt like he understood her better than any other.

She'd known from the beginning that he wasn't a robot, just like he'd said. She had simply refused to accept it.

He affected her, clouded her judgment and made her yearn for impossible things. No man had ever caused her such emotional turmoil.

If she were no longer able to do her duty properly as an officer, she should resign her commission and get the hell out of space. Okay, maybe that was a bit drastic, but that's how confused she felt over this situation.

She vaguely registered him hovering near the shower door. Did her brother know what he was, what he'd sent her? Certainly he must. Her brother would never do anything to endanger her. If he trusted Adam, shouldn't she?

Adam opened the door and stepped in behind her. He had balls, that's for sure. She stiffened, but didn't turn around or say anything. He pressed his chest against her and drew her hips back. His body felt warm and firm against her skin. He caressed her shoulders, her arms, her hips. Her muscles slowly relaxed under his ministrations.

Strange, after all they'd done, she still hadn't seen him fully naked. He always kept her back to his front. To hide his facial responses? Well, that need was past, now that she knew what he was. Even when she'd jumped out of bed, he was half-covered by the sheet. She turned, needing to finally see him, all of him.

His dark eyes, burning with desire, caught her attention first. True emotion. She averted her gaze, afraid he'd see more emotion in her eyes than she wanted revealed.

Her fingers skimmed his broad shoulders, strong and dependable. She leaned forward and licked a drop of water from his throat. He growled, but didn't move.

Her hands fluttered across his lightly tanned chest and her nails grazed his flat nipples. He tensed, but still didn't move to touch her. She admired his control.

Gradually, her gaze slid down his body to his cock. She

gulped. Even longer and thicker than she'd imagined. And growing hard right before her eyes. That impressive dark purplish head and long shaft had been deep inside her body. She trembled. She needed him inside her again.

She reached down and fingered the cock and balls she'd yet to explore up close and personal. She pictured using her tongue on them instead of her fingers, and she licked her lips at the image.

"Tyree . . ." he groaned.

The erotic sound of her name sent a thrill down her spine. She fantasized all sorts of intimate, physical acts with him. He was so damn sexy. Unfortunately, she couldn't separate the emotional connection that went with the physical. She cared. And he seemed to care about her too, at least a little.

"Follow your heart, Tyree."

Could he read her mind? No. That was crazy. He was simply observant, keying in on her feelings, and he sensed her indecision. Anyone would have been able to do that, at this point.

If she were smart, she'd lock him inside her quarters, go to the command deck and then turn him in to the nearest security outpost.

When he reached out and his hands cupped her sensitive breasts, her eyes fluttered closed. He caressed the round flesh, flicking her nipples with his thumbs. Each touch from him made her feel less in control. She chewed at her bottom lip.

"Do you want to come again, Tyree?"

Her heart jumped, and she opened her eyes. "Trying to bribe me with sex?"

"Consider it the last request of a condemned man."

"Man?"

"Yes, Tyree. I am a man. Never doubt that." His fingers slid down her stomach and one hand cupped her pussy.

The warmth of his palm seeped into her and felt so right.

"Keep me around and I'll get you off whenever you want, however you want. I'll do anything, fulfill every fantasy you've ever had. I'll protect you on and off this ship. And I'll hold you close when you feel lonely or sad."

That last part got to her. Up until right then, she wouldn't have had any problems tossing him to the space patrol. Well . . . okay, that wasn't true. She only wished it were. Things would be much easier that way.

Was she really willing to commit a crime to keep him with her?

He burrowed his fingers inside her.

A moan of ecstasy tore from her throat.

He slowly circled her clit, teasing her with light strokes. His other hand gently caressed one breast. "So soft." He leaned forward and licked her ear. "You need to come."

He was trying his best to please her. Her own personal sex slave. There were worse fates for a man on the run, she supposed. "I could lose my commission if I keep you on this ship and don't report you. If you're found out."

"Your brother gave you that commission. And he knows what I am."

So, she was right. Her brother did know. "I *earned* my commission. Nobody gave it to me."

He gently eased her around, so that her back was against his chest and the water rushed over her sensitive breasts. He slid his arms around her middle and rested his hands on her stomach. "Forgive my too-quick words." He kissed her neck, her ear, her temple. "You're right, Tyree. I'm sorry." He sucked her earlobe into his mouth.

She trembled, her body ultrasensitive to his every touch. He actually did sound sorry, and her heart softened. "I'll need to contact my brother to verify your story."

She felt him stiffen, and he released her lobe.

"Don't. Your communications could be monitored." He nipped at her shoulder and widened her stance by pushing her feet further apart with his. "I'm here to protect you, Tyree. There will be no more lies between us."

"I don't trust you." She said the words but wasn't sure what she believed at this point.

"You trust me." He knelt behind her and caressed her ass. "Lean forward a little."

She leaned into the water, placing her palms on the tile in front of her. The force of the water continued to beat down on her breasts, specifically her nipples, sensitizing them even more. His tongue touched her from behind. She moaned and pushed back against his mouth. "Oh, yes, lick my pussy."

He flicked her several times. Then he opened her wide, spreading her wet folds with his fingers, and pushed his tongue deep inside her.

"DAMN. *I* SHOULD BE LICKING that cunt."

Ridgeway watched the monitor in his quarters. Everyone on the command deck had known something was going on between those two when they'd heard the transmission from her room. He'd made an excuse to leave his station, and had come back to his room to check it out.

He'd arranged an onboard assignment, after drugging the former officer's drink at a tavern on Jenway, then had secretly set up video surveillance in the security and docking bays to gather sensitive information for his superiors. One video camera, hidden in Tyree's bath, was placed as an afterthought. The cam had paid off.

"Yeah. Tongue-fuck that uppity bitch." He opened his pants and his cock sprang out. He pumped his aching dick while he watched the action.

He had watched her do herself in the shower once or twice but this was better. Definitely more stimulating.

When the Devron Council sent him undercover to cause havoc within Ambassador Samou's regime, he'd decided to start with the man's sister, Tyree. Psychological blows from loss of family were the most devastating. Once she was neutralized, with the Ambassador mourning and unable to effectively command his troops, Devron would take first advantage. Eventually, they'd shut down Jenway Station and the weapons research plant there that Samou thought was so cleverly disguised as a retreat for soldiers on leave. Then they'd destroy the Ambassador and all who served him. He had no doubts about their victory.

Tyree came hard against Adam's mouth, and Mick groaned. "Man, I'd love a taste of her cream." His dick twitched and spurted. "Oh, yeah!"

• • •

ADAM PULLED THE COVERS over Tyree and held her close. He'd given her another orgasm in the shower, wearing her out completely. She fell asleep immediately upon hitting the mattress.

He'd jacked himself off while lying beside her, his hand gently caressing her ass, not wanting to wake her just to service his needs. But he knew he'd need her again before morning. At this pace, he would wear them both out. But that was fine with him. He'd never enjoyed being with a woman so much. He even liked arguing with her.

He still wasn't sure what was going on in her head. But he knew she needed him. She needed his protection. And he needed a place to safely exist. They could help each other and, if they could enjoy the added perk of hot sex, why not?

He stared at her beautiful features, and his heart softened. Emotionally, he realized he was in trouble. He knew that with a quiet certainty and wasn't afraid to admit it—to himself, anyhow.

Even after the short time they'd been together, Tyree had touched something deep inside him. But telling *her* that, well, it scared the shit out of him, so he intended to keep his mouth shut, for now.

He eased away from her and sat up on the side of the bunk. He raked his fingers through his hair and pushed to his feet. Tyree would probably sleep until morning. Normally, after sex he'd be out for hours, but he couldn't settle down. He plodded into the bathroom.

His contact was probably wondering about his status by now. He should check in. He'd hidden a communication device behind the toilet. Having a friend on ship was a major plus. Hopefully, their connection wouldn't be discovered. If Tyree changed her mind and decided to turn him in, he might need help in escaping.

He felt bad about the deception, especially after promising no more lies, but at least for now, he had to be extra cautious. After he was certain of his safety, he'd reveal everything to Tyree, apologize, and do whatever he needed for her forgiveness.

"What are you doing?"

He spun around. "I thought you were asleep."

"And I thought you were." She glanced down his body. "I need to get you a robe."

He smiled. He enjoyed not hiding his expressions from her anymore. Though he'd still have to play bot with the crew. "Why? Don't you like what you see?"

"Too much. That's the problem."

His hand grazed his cock and it started to grow hard again. "It doesn't have to be. I'm sure we can take care of this bad boy if we keep trying. Wear him down until he's no good for at least a week."

She rubbed her brow and chuckled. "Don't distract me. I need to know some things, so I can decide what to do. Why weren't you destroyed?"

"Do we really need to talk about that now?"

"Yes. Now."

He turned serious, his heart pounding in a dull thud against his ribs. "All right, Tyree. Your brother hid me and then helped me escape before my true identity was discovered."

"Why?"

"We're friends."

"That simple?"

Tyree was definitely a determined woman. He knew he wouldn't be able to put her off on this, so he gave her the much abbreviated version. "There's a history. It's not important."

When that's all he said, she huffed out an exasperated breath. "I want to know more than that, Adam. Tell me."

He supposed she did deserve the truth. Or, at least, as much as he could remember. "Before I was Cyborg, I was in an accident. Your brother felt responsible and repaired me, turned me into a cybertronic, so I could live."

She waited for more, but again he said nothing else. "And? I need to know details."

"Details are overrated." He didn't like remembering—the pain, the months of uncertainty over what he'd become. Not knowing what to expect from his body and brain.

"Not if your life hinges on them."

He studied her a moment, worry trickling through him. Then she lightly touched his arm, and a smile tugged at his lips. He saw the decision in her eyes. His heart expanded and soared. "You're not going to turn me in."

She blinked as if surprised by his words. "What makes you think not?"

His fingers grazed her cheek. "Because you're intrigued by me, and I think you care too much about what happens to me. I can see it in your eyes, Tyree." His cock hardened so much it was painful. He needed relief. "Go wait for me in bed. I need to fuck you again."

She raised her chin defiantly. "You give too many orders. Did anyone ever tell you that? Submissive is not in my nature. And you changed the subject. We were talking about your accident."

His smile widened. "Submissive is in your fantasies, my beauty. You know it, and I know it." He peeled the robe off her body.

"Um . . . wait a second."

He slid the tie from the loops, then dropped the garment.

"Okay, what are you doing?"

Stepping behind her, he grasped her wrists and pulled them behind her back. He locked them together in one of his large hands.

"Hey!" She tugged against his hold.

"Quiet." He draped the tie over his shoulder and slapped her ass with his palm. She immediately stiffened but stayed silent, so he didn't repeat the punishment. He wasn't concerned that his actions were out of line. If she really didn't want this, she'd be fighting like a space-devil.

He secured her wrists with the tie. His gaze dropped to her ass. Beautiful and so sexy. He wondered if she even realized how much. He wanted to bend her over and push his cock up that soft ass so badly, especially with her bound and at his mercy. But he wanted something else even more. He stepped in front of her. "On your knees, Tyree."

Her shocked expression was priceless. "You heard me. Use the robe as a cushion. Go down on your knees. Now."

After a moment of hesitation, she complied.

Good. He had read her right. He held his cock in one hand, and the back of her head with the other. "Lick the tip. Slow. Don't speak. Just do as I say." He needed to come again, needed her to submit to him.

Her tongue eased out and curled around his cock. She licked the head—around the rim, the underside, then she pressed her tongue against the tip and flicked back and forth.

"Damn, that's good. Yes . . ." The image of filling her mouth with his seed hit strong. The ultimate turn-on. His fingers tightened in her hair. "Slide your lips over my shaft and suck me off, Tyree. I want you to swallow every last drop of cum that I shoot into your mouth."

MICK RIDGEWAY WATCHED THE monitor as Tyree slowly took Adam's cock into her mouth. He was one big fucker. She barely managed more than the head.

Why bother though? A bot couldn't feel.

He was surprised she'd let him bind her. Intriguing. He wondered what else she sexually enjoyed. His imagination ran wild at the possibilities.

Too bad he wouldn't be able to taste her sexually himself before disposing of her. He doubted he could work his plan to that advantage.

He'd lucked out spotting them in the bathroom again. She was an insatiable whore, that one.

Restless and unable to sleep, he'd gotten up to take a leak and saw them on the monitor. Adam actually looked like he was enjoying himself, though he knew that was impossible for a robot.

He tipped forward in his chair. "What the hell?"

Oh, man. He couldn't believe it. Adam just shot a massive wad right down Tyree's throat. What a camera angle! He could see her sucking it down. A trickle escaped one side of her mouth, another lined her chin.

Realization hit hard. This was too good. Adam was not a bot, after all.

The man was Cyborg!

And Tyree knew. Otherwise, she'd have jumped back at getting a mouthful of cum.

He could collect a bundle for turning in a Cyborg. Then with Adam out of the way, he'd have free access to do whatever he wanted with Tyree.

If she didn't want to go to jail for harboring a cybertronic, she'd have to do as he said or he'd tell the authorities that she'd known all along. They'd believe him, especially if he produced a computerized copy of this little sex act here. Cyborg-hunting and conviction of those who illegally harbored them was big business. Bounties had been set high.

He knew what he needed to do. And it was the perfect plan.

LYING ON HER BUNK, Tyree stirred against Adam's chest. She yawned and glanced up at him. He stared at the ceiling, not looking happy. It couldn't have been the sex. She hoped. A streak of insecurity raced through her. She tugged on his chest hair. "Hey, don't you sleep?"

He looked down. "Not much tonight." He tightened his arms around her body.

"What's wrong?"

"Nothing."

"You're frowning. Was it something I did? Or didn't do?"

He relaxed, and a smile tugged at his lips. "No. Of course not." He rubbed her back. "I'm picking up some heightened electrical activity and I can't pinpoint it. It's communication-oriented. My internal sensors are picking it up."

"Hmm." Tyree rolled away from him. She punched on the intercom. "Corporal Pratt, are we transmitting?"

"No, Captain," came the immediate response. "Is there a problem?"

"No. Just checking." She turned back to Adam. "It's not ship-to-ship."

"Don't worry about it. I'll figure out the source." He smiled and gathered her into his arms. "How do you feel?"

"Sore, but good." She snuggled against him, completely satisfied. He was the best lover she'd ever had. He seemed to know and understand all her desires. "Adam, how much of you is cybertronic?"

He was quiet for so long she thought he wasn't going to answer. She didn't like the idea of secrets between them.

When he finally did answer, his voice lowered to a near whisper. "Part of my brain."

She gasped, and her stomach clenched. *No!* Anything but that.

"Don't worry. I won't go berserk. I have an implant control. It's experimental, but effective."

She relaxed, though tendrils of concern still clung to

her. She intended to find out everything about him on record, as soon as possible. He could get her access to the classified documents. "What else?"

"My hands."

"Hands. Yes, I knew that, from when I sliced you. So you can't really feel me then?" Disappointment flowed through her. His talented fingers weren't flesh and blood. At least she knew she hadn't hurt him with the knife.

"Skin sensors transmit impulses to my brain. It's not the same as real hands but it's fairly close."

"Anything else?"

"My legs from the knees down. And pieces of my spine to help support my frame."

"How did the accident happen? I'd really like to know."

"My original training was in engineering and computerized circuits. I got caught in an explosion on Jenway, while repairing an experimental weapon."

"I'm sorry."

"Your brother saved me. But it was getting too dangerous for me to continue working at the station. I was just going to jump in a ship and take off. Hiding never set well with me. I couldn't live as a recluse on Jenway, without going stir-crazy. But before I left, your brother asked me to board your vessel instead to help protect you. I owed him, so I agreed."

"And what? You figured keeping me sexually satisfied would guarantee your safety? If you could make me come hard enough, then I wouldn't turn you in, once I learned what you were?" She couldn't keep the edge from her voice.

"It's more than that. You know it, Tyree."

"Do I?"

"You can trust me. I don't fuck women as a bribe for keeping my secret." He caressed her back, then sucked his finger into his mouth. He lowered his hands to massage her butt, lightly teasing her asshole with his lubricated finger.

She squirmed.

"Stay still." He penetrated her just barely, and she mewled. He pushed deeper, then began an in and out motion. "I know you like this. Don't you?"

"Yes," she breathed out, unable to deny the pleasure.

"You're special, Tyree. I wouldn't be in your bed otherwise, doing these things to you. I'd have stolen a pod and left long ago, if I didn't want to be here."

"And I'd have tracked you down."

"I know. But I still would have tried to get away."

"So much for owing my brother."

"I only promised him that I'd board and check out the situation, then make my final decision." He pulled out his finger and rolled her over onto her back. "Now, I want to make love to you, Tyree. Soft and real slow this time."

The sincere look in his eyes had her believing him. And her heart and emotions turned to mush. She just hoped she wouldn't come to regret giving her trust to a man she barely knew—a Cyborg. Not only was her career on the line but her crew's safety, as well as her own, could be in jeopardy if his presence were discovered or, worse . . . if his circuits became compromised and he went berserk, like so many Cyborgs in the past.

Chapter Five

TYREE SLAPPED ADAM'S HAND as he reached for her ass. "Stop it." She yanked down the cotton shirt she wore, which barely covered her nakedness. She should have grabbed her robe when she slid out of bed earlier, at least until she finished with her business. She flipped on the intercom on the side table. "Corporal Pratt?"

"Yes, Captain."

"I won't be up on the command deck for most of the day. Don't disturb me unless there's an emergency."

After a brief hesitation, Pratt asked, "Is there a problem, Captain?"

Her crew was well-trained and knew this behavior odd for her. "No, I'm just not feeling up to it." Okay, she lied, sort of. She *didn't* feel up to working but not because she felt sick.

She again slapped at Adam's wandering hands. The man never got enough. She would be upset, but his hunger translated to her pleasure. She grinned at the memory of their recent heated, sexual encounters.

"Do you want me to send Dr. Roiya down to see you?" Pratt asked.

"No. It's not that serious. I'll be up later."

"Very well, Captain."

Tyree flipped off the intercom, then spun around. She forced the smile from her face. "Can you *not* feel me up while I'm talking to the crew?"

Adam chuckled and wrapped his arms around her waist. "You love it."

"Don't be so cocky, or I'll have to exert my authority."

"Ooo, baby."

Unable to maintain her serious façade, she laughed at his playful tone. "Eat your sweet pocket." She nodded toward the desk where breakfast waited.

"I'd rather eat your sweet pocket," he whispered suggestively in her ear.

She smacked his arm. "That is so terrible. Everyone probably realizes why I'm staying in my quarters, you know."

"Do you really care?"

She didn't hesitate in her response. "No, actually, I don't. But we do need to talk about things, Adam."

"Later." He tightened his hold on her and nibbled at her lips.

She pushed at his chest. "Now! Stop distracting me."

With a sigh, he released her and walked over to the desk. He plopped down in a chair and took a bite of the fruit-filled sweet. "What's to talk about? You know I'm Cyborg. You're not going to turn me in. I'm here as your per-sonal security bot . . . and eroti-bot, as far as the crew is concerned. And that's that."

"How can you be so unconcerned about the danger this presents to all of us? I have a lot of questions for you. There are still things I don't understand."

"There's no danger as long as you don't say anything. If I ever think you or your crew is in jeopardy because of me, I'll be out of here. The authorities won't be able to find me. And you shouldn't try either. I'll make sure you're not im-plicated in any way. I won't endanger anyone, Tyree."

Somehow the thought of him taking off didn't sit right with her. Danger or not. What if she couldn't find him? A panicked feeling hit and grabbed on. "Promise me you won't just disappear unless you talk to me first."

He stood and walked over to her. "Don't worry so much about this. Let the problem alone, at least for a few hours. Then we'll talk everything out."

"You didn't promise me."

He smiled down at her. "I know."

"Adam—"

"Shh." He pressed his finger to her mouth. "Later." His mouth lowered to hers, swallowing any further protests.

Knowing she was beaten, she wrapped her arms around his neck and kissed him back, letting the matter drop for now. She enjoyed the feel of his mouth against hers too much to push him away again and indulge her worries, when what she really wanted was his cock inside her. She never thought she'd feel so turned on by a kiss. She pulled back and licked his lips. "You taste like asterberries. My favorite."

He brushed some stray tendrils of hair from her face. "So, will you allow me to guide you in this tentative relationship we've started here?"

Tentative. At least he realized she still harbored some doubts. Not about him personally, but about how she intended to deal with him and their situation, and maintain her responsibilities at the same time. "Is 'guide' a polite way of asking if I'll let you sexually dominate me?" After all the intimacies they'd shared, she understood him better than he knew. The thought of giving in to her submissive fantasies with him soaked her vagina, and a tremble ran through her body.

"Ah." He smiled. "You have me figured out."

"I'll take that to mean yes."

He turned serious. His eyes hardened, reflecting need and desire. "How about *my* question, Tyree? What's your answer to that?"

"I've never allowed a man the kind of control you're asking for."

"I want your answer."

"My answer is . . . yes," she breathed out in a mere whisper. She wanted to submit.

A smile tugged at one corner of Adam's lips. His head lowered and he covered her mouth in a demanding kiss. When she opened her lips, his tongue slipped inside to duel with hers. At the same time, he held her like she was the most precious possession in the universe.

She leaned into him, pressing her breasts against his bare chest, giving him everything he wanted.

His hand tangled in her hair and he gently tugged her

head back, breaking the kiss and exposing her throat. He nibbled at her pulse point, then his tongue swiped back and forth over the tender spot.

"I love that." Each stroke of his tongue increased her pleasure, until she thought she'd melt to the floor.

Adam released her and backed up to the desk chair. He snapped open his pants and sat down. "Take off that shirt."

Her gaze traveled over his bare chest and followed the thin line of dark hair down his stomach and into his slightly gaping trousers. "Whatever you want, Adam." Slowly, she grasped the hem of the shirt and pulled up the cotton. She peeled it off of her body and dropped the garment to the floor.

Adam sat staring at her. He didn't say anything. He just looked at her naked body.

She began to feel self-conscious and wondered about his thoughts. Did he find her lacking in some way? She rarely questioned what someone thought of her. But with Adam, his opinion mattered. How he'd gotten under her skin so quickly, she didn't know. Somehow, already, they'd connected emotionally as well as physically. She wanted this relationship to work between them. With her job and schedule, long-term commitments in her life had never been successful. This time she wanted a different outcome.

Adam's hands rested on his lap. His fingers slowly clenched and unclenched. His eyes darkened with desire. "Caress your tits."

She exhaled a breath of air she wasn't even aware of holding. He didn't find her lacking. The realization made her feel desirable and feminine. Her hands covered her breasts and she began massaging them. The sight of Adam watching her, enjoying what he saw, caused her pulse to race.

"Pinch your nipples."

Tyree smiled and slowly licked her fingers. She slid her hands back over her breasts and tweaked her sensitive buds, trying not to let her pleasure show on her face too much. Even though she loved the idea of submitting to him, she needed to take this a step at a time, so he didn't assume complete control. She needed to make certain he understood that her submission was only during sex. Otherwise, she was very much in command of her own life and didn't intend for that to change. She'd welcome less stress and responsibility, if the opportunity arose, but she made all decisions concerning which path her life took.

When he abruptly stood, she backed up a step. Something in his eyes looked so primitive that the move was automatic.

"Get on the bed," he ordered. "Face down. You're taking my dick up your ass."

She gasped.

"Do it, Tyree. Now."

She scrambled onto the bed and flopped onto her stomach, then cringed at how eager her immediate compliance must have looked. So much for "a step at a time." She glanced over her shoulder at him. "Adam?"

"What?"

"Only in the bedroom will I follow your orders."

"Mmm-hmm." He disappeared into the bathroom, leaving her lying there waiting and in need.

Her heart thudded dully in her chest. She wasn't sure what to make of his response. Later, she'd talk to him about it and make sure that he did understand. She didn't want their relationship to start out based on any misunderstandings.

After what seemed an eternity, he returned with something wrapped in a towel.

"What's that?" she asked, her curiosity too great to keep quiet.

He simply looked at her. His gaze locked with hers and, for a long moment, he said nothing. Then he smacked her ass. "Don't ever question what I do to you sexually."

"Hey!" This wasn't what she'd had in mind when she'd imagined submission. He'd spanked her once before in the bathroom, but not as hard. She hadn't said anything at the time, thinking it a one-time event. "Do you really think spanking me—"

"Quiet." He smacked her ass again.

Her pussy contracted and pleasure swept through her. She hadn't expected to feel anything but anger. She held her tongue this time, not knowing what to make of this new experience.

"Your safeword is Cyborg. Understand?"

"Um, yes." Good. He realized that she might need to take back control if she felt too uncomfortable with his domination of her.

He set the towel down on the side table next to the bed. "Turn your head away."

He wasn't going to let her see what the towel hid or what he intended to do. Figured. She turned her head on the pillow and peered toward the bathroom. An image of them making love in the shower popped into her head. She relaxed and smiled at the memory. He'd been the perfect combination of forceful male and gentle lover. She trusted him completely with her body. It was herself that she didn't quite trust, especially where her jumbled emotions were concerned.

"Have you ever had anal sex, Tyree?"

Her pulse jumped. "Yes." At her admission, she sensed him pause in whatever he was doing.

"Did you enjoy it?"

Only once when she was much younger had she allowed a man that kind of entry. "Yes."

"Tell me about it."

"Tell you?" His request took her by surprise. Men didn't generally care to hear about previous lovers.

He slapped her butt. "Don't question."

She squirmed on the mattress.

"Now, tell me. Who was he?"

His hands touched her hair, then slipped down to her back. His fingers caressed her softly. Slowly, he glided his hands lower, toward her ass. She answered quickly. "He was a mechanical engineering assistant in my father's personal transport repair center."

"How old were you?"

"Seventeen."

His hands stopped at the small of her back and he brushed his fingers lightly back and forth across her skin. "So young. How old was he?"

"Twenty-five."

"Where were you two when he stuck his dick up your ass, Tyree?"

His language kept the atmosphere in the room sexually charged. She wondered if he did that on purpose or if that was just the way he talked about sexual matters.

"In the repair center after hours."

"Not very romantic."

"No, but hot."

"Were you two a couple?"

"Not before that, and after it didn't work out."

"Tell me about the fuck." His hands moved down to her ass.

She jerked, but he simply massaged the fleshy mounds. She cleared her throat, hoping her voice remained steady. "He'd just finished repairing a personal transport. I came in because I saw the light. I'll admit . . . I flirted shamelessly with him. I wanted it, and he knew it. Without a word, he grabbed me, turned me around and pushed me over onto the hood of the transport. He flipped up my skirt and ripped off my panties. Then I felt something cool and moist on my ass. I still don't even want to know what he used. He kicked my feet apart and his finger stabbed inside me, along with the gooey substance. I heard him open his pants. He pressed his cock against my asshole and pushed it right in. I came immediately. He came immediately. And that's about it. Short, definitely not sweet, but a good memory on cold, lonely nights."

Adam's voice softened to a caress. "When I'm up your ass, I won't come immediately. And you'll come more than once. That's a promise. Then you'll have a new memory, and one that hopefully we can share for a long time."

She simply nodded, not sure what to say to that. Did he want this to be a long-term relationship as much as she did?

"What ever happened to him? Why didn't it work out between the two of you?"

"A few days later, my father sent him out to a mining colony to do transport repairs and he got killed by some falling boulders during a landslide."

"I'm sorry, Tyree. Really. I wouldn't have asked, if I'd known."

She shrugged. "That's okay. It's terrible what happened to him. But we wouldn't have made it anyhow. As bad as it sounds, he was one of those guys who, well, was a great fuck, but not much else."

"And what am I?"

"A phenomenal fuck . . . and much, much more." Her voice lowered at the admission of her feelings.

His voice lowered in kind. "I feel the same about you." He leaned over and gently kissed each of her ass cheeks.

Tyree swallowed hard. His soft voice and touch seemed completely at odds with his earlier demanding nature, and made her, even more so, want to give him whatever he wanted.

"Fuck me, Adam."

"In the ass?"

"Yes."

He pushed a pillow under her hips. "I'm going to clip something onto your clit, Tyree, so you come harder."

She rose up on her elbows. "What?" *Clip?* That sounded uncomfortable.

"Remember . . ." He pushed her back down, slapping her ass at the same time. "Don't question me."

He had a definite spanking fetish. She relaxed on the mattress, unexpectedly enjoying the warmth of the sting. She needed more info about this clip thing though. "Will it be—" *Oops. No questions.* "I'm not into excessive pain." *There. That was clear enough.*

"You'll be fine. You'll love it. If not, you know what to do."

Her heart raced. Yes. She had her safeword. Maybe Adam would show her pleasures she'd never dared. Her excitement mounted at the possibilities.

His tongue touched her pussy from behind.

"Mmm."

The sound of pleasure filled her ears. She wasn't sure if it came from her or him. Maybe it had come from both of them.

"I want you really wet, Tyree."

"I am. Soaked. Need to come."

"Not quite yet. Don't move. I'm going to clip you. Try to stay relaxed."

She bit her bottom lip, not knowing what to expect. She felt him press something cool along her pussy, as his fingers held her open. Metal. It brushed her clit and she tensed.

"Easy."

Then she felt the pressure as it closed around her sensitive bud. Her fingers grabbed the sheet.

"Okay?"

She swallowed hard and nodded. The sensation was intense and intriguing. "Where'd you get that thing?"

"I made it earlier while you were sleeping." He slapped her ass.

She gasped. *Oh, yes*. She was definitely getting into this spanking thing. She felt a tugging sensation. A thrill raced through her.

"That's the attached chain. I pulled on it. It gives me complete control of your clit." He tugged on it again, a little harder. "Does that feel good?"

"Y-yes." Her clit throbbed and seemed to swell, making the flesh extra sensitive.

Adam stared down at Tyree, naked and waiting for his cock, her ass perched on the pillow, like an erotic offering. He tugged again on the clit chain.

"Oh. I'm going to come."

"Let it happen, Tyree." He reached beneath her, released the clip and grazed his thumb across her moist clitoris.

"Ah!" With a shriek of pleasure, she came, and her cum coated his fingers.

Man, he loved getting her off. He pulled his hand away. One hand tangled in her hair. He held the other to her lips. "Lick my fingers clean."

Her tongue eased out and, one by one, she lapped her essence from his digits.

"Good. I'm going to re-clip you now."

She groaned as he reattached the device to her clitoris.

"You did well, Tyree. Time for the lube." He almost wished she'd ask something, just so he could smack her ass again. He wanted her to learn to enjoy it as much as he did. He could slap her ass anyway, but that would go against the pattern they'd established. If she enjoyed getting spanked, she knew how to get him to do it. Earlier, she'd said she wasn't into excessive pain—interesting that she didn't just say pain. Something else for him to explore.

He grabbed the tube of jelly he'd brought from the bathroom and popped the top. "Your ass looks like a perfect fuck, Tyree. It's the ultimate submission, you know that, right?"

"Is it?"

He smiled and slapped her ass. Then he chuckled. She'd asked that one on purpose. Or so he hoped. "Well, it's in the top three, I'd say. Do you have any other questions?" He heard the excitement in his voice. Would she take the dare?

"I know what you want to do, Adam. Do I have to continue asking silly questions to get the proper spanking you're itching to give me?"

He choked on her words, not expecting her to say anything close to that. She pleased him like no other, knew his thoughts and needs. He coughed and cleared his throat. "No, baby, you don't. Are you sure you can really handle what I want to do?"

"I wasn't at first, but now . . . I want it."

He set the tube down. His hands caressed her cheeks, as his heart pounded hard in his chest. "You'll like it. I know you will."

"Do it."

He raised his right hand and brought it down on her left cheek, then her right. He paused, waiting for her reaction.

She made a low sound of pleasure.

"Damn, you're sexy, Tyree." He slapped each cheek again, a little harder this time. His cock strained against his half-open pants. "Again?"

She nodded.

He repeated the action, not stopping this time, nor asking permission. He spanked her thoroughly. The sharp sound of his bare hand connecting with her ass filled the room. She squirmed and her bottom turned a nice, rosy shade that he couldn't tear his eyes from.

"Fuck me up the ass, Adam. Now!"

His pulse skyrocketed. He stepped back and ripped off his pants, then smeared some jelly along his cock. He squished a glob on her ass and finger-fucked it into her asshole.

"Your cock, Adam." She raised her ass. "Stick it in," she pleaded. "Hurry."

He crawled up on the bed and spread her ass cheeks. He massaged the puckered skin around her hole. "Relax." He grabbed the clit chain and wrapped it around his wrist, so it would tug while he fucked her.

Positioning himself, he pressed the head of his cock against her asshole.

She pushed back against him.

"Slow, Tyree." With a groan, he eased the head just barely inside her. The erotic sensation and sight made his cock ache.

Tyree clenched her ass and he about lost it. "Damn!" He tugged on the clit chain.

She gasped. "Fill me up!"

He pushed in deeper. She was so fucking tight. He clenched his teeth.

"Oh, yes!" She came fast and kept coming. "Adam!"

"Yeah!" He pumped her ass, teetering on the edge of losing it himself. He knew she'd be good but he hadn't expected this. Back and forth, the pleasure along his cock intensified. His balls tightened. He wrapped his arm around her waist, stilling his movements, and held her tightly.

"Don't stop."

"Just catching my breath. Extending the fuck, baby." He pushed his dick a little deeper, careful not to go too far or hurt her. "Is that good?" It was damn fantastic for him.

"Yes! Come up my ass, Adam. I want to feel you spurting into me."

Her words pushed him over the edge. He squeezed one of her ass cheeks, pumped his hips and spewed. "Ahh-hh!"

Tyree came again, thrashing beneath him. She didn't scream this time, only made little whimpering noises that sounded sexy as hell.

Her ass clenched him tightly, holding his cock inside her, and he groaned her name. Finally drained of cum, he collapsed across her back. She relaxed, and he slipped out of her body. That was, by far, the best fuck of his life.

He rolled off her, unclipped her clit and dragged her into his arms. "Are you all right?"

"Completely satiated."

"Me, too."

Chapter Six

TYREE SAT ON THE COMMAND deck, filling out reports on an electronic, handheld data pad. She normally did entries in her quarters but, if she stayed in her room, she'd end up in bed with Adam. Or on the floor, or bent over the desk, or any other place he wanted to fuck her.

Making love with him was better than anything she'd ever experienced, but sex was not conducive to work. Even now, concentrating on mundane, operational reports proved difficult when images of him lying naked in bed, waiting for her, played through her mind.

He'd shown her things about ecstasy and her body that she'd never thought possible. Including some acts she suspected *must* be illegal in more than one star sector. A grin crossed her face.

The memory of her submission to all of his sexual demands almost shocked her. But the pleasures she experienced were phenomenal.

Their last encounter, before duty finally called, readily came to mind. He'd found her vibrator in the bathroom and immediately put it to good use. He'd tossed her on the bed, tied her wrists and ankles to the side supports, then teased her clit mercilessly, not allowing her to come until, practically mad from unfulfilled desire, she'd begged him for release.

Once he let her climax, he'd given her orgasms she thought would never stop—first with the vibrator pressed against her clit and three fingers pumping deep inside her pussy, then he'd replaced the vibrator with his talented tongue and licked her through two more massive climaxes. Finally, he substituted his cock for his fingers and used the vibrator on her nipples, all the while saying wild, sexy things to her, encouraging her to come harder and longer with each orgasm.

After she was completely spent, his cock remained hard as steel. If he hadn't come inside her pussy, up her ass and down her throat multiple times already in their affair, she'd have questioned if his cock was even real. He had exceptional staying power.

Once she'd somewhat recovered from her own orgasm-a-thon, she'd crawled on top of him and ridden him like a wild animal, determined to work his cock hard. He came then, his shout of pleasure so loud she was surprised that crew members hadn't busted in to investigate.

He'd promised her something extra special tonight, extra-kinky with specially designed toys he planned to fash-ion himself. She could hardly wait.

What he didn't know was that she had erotic plans of

her own. After she finished with him and his cock, he wouldn't walk for a week. And he definitely wouldn't seek pleasure outside her body or bed ever again.

"Captain?" Hanson interrupted from his station.

She looked up. "What?"

"A patrol ship is coming up on us from behind. They've opened communications."

Tyree immediately went on alert. Her heartbeat increased, and her pulse began to race. She set aside the electronic pad and stood, looking toward the monitors. "Confirmed patrol ship?"

"Yes. I have a visual." He brought it up on his screen for her to see.

The compact ship sported the silver, yellow and orange colors of an official patrol. "Okay." She turned toward Corporal Pratt. "Put them on speakers."

"Yes, Captain."

A moment later, a male voice filtered onto the control deck. "This is Space Patrol Ship 1-1-4. Prepare to be boarded."

"This is Captain Tyree Samou, salvaging for Jenway's Ambassador Samou. What is this about?"

"We have reason to believe you're harboring a male Cyborg on board. As such, we have authority in this sector to board and search your ship."

Tyree gasped. Adam. No!

"Incoming pod, Captain," Hanson informed her in a low voice.

"There is no Cyborg on this vessel." Raising her chin a notch, she fought to keep her voice steady. She didn't want them suspecting her of deception.

"We will make that determination. We're coming aboard. Our pod is docking in your bay now. Any resistance will be deemed a criminal act and result in the confiscation of your freighter."

"Cut communications." She raked her fingers through her hair, pulling the bun from its neat coil. "Shit!"

"Captain?" Hanson asked with concern in his voice. "Your orders?"

She glanced around the command deck. Each crew member looked at her expectantly. But suspicion knifed through her at what she didn't see. "Where's Ridgeway?"

"I . . . don't know," Hanson answered. "He left about fifteen minutes ago, and didn't say where he was going."

"Accompany me to the docking bay."

"Yes, Captain."

After a short, silent, but tense ride in the lift, Tyree and Hanson arrived at the freighter's docking bay. They spotted Ridgeway already there, talking to the space patrol team. Tyree was so mad she expected steam to come out of her nose. "Ridgeway, what are you doing up here?"

At the sound of her voice, the group of men standing next to the official hunter green pod turned toward her. The large yellow and burnt orange star painted on the side served as a reminder of just how much trouble awaited her.

"Captain," Mick greeted. He glanced at her loose hair. She flipped the long strands behind her back.

"I'm doing my duty and following regulations, Captain. Let me handle this situation. We'll talk later."

Had he just issued an order to *her*? *Talk later, my ass.* "Excuse me, Corporal?" If the patrol weren't here, she'd grab him by the collar and jerk the insubordination right out of the idiot. "What the—"

"Captain." The patrol leader stepped forward, his face a mask of concentration. "My name is Lieutenant Stanton. My team will search this ship now." He didn't wait for her permission but simply moved forward, leading his men.

She rushed to follow. "This is completely unnecessary."

"Then there will be no problems," he answered over his shoulder.

She glanced around for Hanson. He'd disappeared. What the hell was going on around here?

She could tell from the smirk on Ridgeway's face that he was the one who had alerted Space Command. She wondered how long he'd been in contact with them, and if the communication Adam had picked up had anything to do with this.

Damn! She couldn't even get a message to Adam. To warn him. Not without the patrol knowing. It would look too suspicious if *she* suddenly disappeared.

"He's probably in her quarters," Ridgeway offered. "I'll show you the way. The Captain doesn't know anything about this. He fooled us all. I just recently found out myself."

They all crowded into the lift and descended. Tyree elbowed Ridgeway in the ribs when he pressed his groin against her butt in the close confines.

What was Mick up to? And how had he figured out Adam's identity? No way could Adam fool the space patrol. Their instruments would register his human side and his cybertronics.

Instruments . . . Wait! Sheera. She'd said she examined Adam. She had to know he was Cyborg. Her medical equipment would have picked up his human tissue.

The lift glided to a stop, the door slid open, and they all piled out.

Where was her brain? Adam had totally screwed up her thinking. She should have connected everything before now.

Her friend had betrayed her and told Ridgeway. There was no other way he could have known. A sick feeling clenched her stomach.

Ridgeway easily opened the door to her quarters and the space patrol team ran in. A tremor ran through her. He knew her entry code. Tyree's heart beat so hard it hurt.

The patrol searched the bathroom, closet, under the bed, and even looked for hidden panels in the floor and along the walls. The room was empty. So, where was Adam? Hiding places on the ship were practically nonexistent. The odds of him evading the patrol weren't good.

"Spread out," the patrol leader said to the other three team members. "Search the entire ship."

They rushed out, leaving Tyree alone with Ridgeway. The team leader must have believed Mick when he'd told them she had no knowledge of Adam's Cyborg status, otherwise they would already have placed her in custody. Or maybe Mick was working with them, as an undercover patrol agent, and intended to take her in himself. No, she mentally shook the thought aside. He wasn't smart enough for an agent, only a lowly informant.

"I expect appropriate payment for protecting that sexy ass of yours, Tyree."

What? The scum-sucking leech wanted money?

"Come to my quarters tonight after you get off duty. Oh, and don't wear any panties. You need a *man's* dick up your hairy cunt. Not some subhuman's."

With an enraged shriek, she turned and punched Ridgeway in the jaw, sending him tumbling back into the bar. A glass fell and broke, spilling its liquid on the floor. Tyree wished it were Mick's blood instead. "I'll see to it that you never see the light of a real sun again, you fucking bastard!"

"Captain?"

She spun around, her hand throbbing. She ignored the pain.

Hanson stood inside the open door, pistol in hand.

Her pulse raced faster. "Are you on his side or mine?" She fingered the knife on her belt. She would attack anyone who stood in her way. She needed to find Adam, before the patrol team did. She knew this ship better than anyone. She might be able to shuffle him from place to place unseen. If located by the patrol, he'd be killed, no questions asked.

Hanson, looking wary, kept his eyes on her as he strode across the room. He bent down and checked Ridgeway. "He's out cold. I'm on your side, Captain. Always. I'll secure him so he can't cause more trouble. Go to the command deck. When the space patrol can't find Adam, they'll go there."

"You know where he is then. Where?"

"The less you know right now, the better. Keeps you from getting caught in a lie."

Frustration rolled through her like an electromagnetic

space wave. "I don't like this, Hanson. I want some answers. You disappeared on me in the docking bay. And now you expect me to trust you?"

"You have to trust me."

"No, I have to—"

"You're running out of options, Tyree. Don't blow Adam's only chance."

Damn! She didn't know what would be the right thing to do. Obviously, Hanson knew, too, that Adam was Cyborg. Too many people knew now. But if she went searching for Adam, it might look suspicious to the patrol and seal his fate, as well as hers. She needed to appear unconcerned. Not involved, and not guilty of the accusations. It could be the only chance to save them both.

NONE OF THE CREW said a word to Tyree when she stepped onto the control deck. They only waited, the tension in the air palpable. She paced in front of the engineering panel, feeling guilty and rethinking her decision about leaving Adam to fend for himself.

Finally, as Hanson predicted, the space patrol leader stepped out of the lift. She turned toward him, making sure she looked composed and in command.

"My apologies, Captain. It seems the tip we received was wrong. My men are preparing to return to our ship. I'd like to speak to Corporal Ridgeway before we leave."

Relief spread through her. They hadn't found him. Then a shaft of panic hit. Had Adam somehow escaped the ship undetected in a pod? No, he couldn't have. Even if he'd managed to block sensors, he'd have been caught on visual. He had to still be on board somewhere.

"I don't appreciate the strong-arm treatment, Lieutenant." She glanced toward the docking bay panel to make certain all pods were present and accounted for, but she was too far away to see the readings.

"I do apologize. However, all Cyborgs must be destroyed, as you know, for everyone's protection."

The door to the lift swooshed open and Hanson stepped out.

Tyree still didn't know for sure whether she could trust the Corporal or not, even though he'd been on several missions with her and had always done his job well. Trust was hard for her to come by these days. Like he'd said though, she didn't have a lot of options.

"Hanson, do you know where Ridgeway is?" She hoped he had some sort of plan and was truly loyal to her; otherwise, this was the end of the line.

"He's up on the docking bay. I found him trying to plant an explosive device on the space patrol's pod. Here it is. Deactivated." He handed a tiny, metal panel to the team leader. "He must have fabricated the story about a Cyborg to get you aboard."

Stanton suspiciously examined the device handed to him. "We *have* had several boarding team pods blow up upon reentry to our main vessels, as I'm sure you've heard."

"Yes, space chatter travels fast," Hanson confirmed.

Tyree was aware of the chatter, too. Some unknown organization was systematically trying to destroy Space Command, starting with all teams currently on patrol in this sector. Already, more than fifty officers had suffered injury or death due to bomb plants. The device Hanson handed Stanton was a standard explosive panel used to blast through titanium plates and other alloy-based materials. They carried a supply on the ship. His story held merit and might buy them some time.

"Has Ridgeway served you long, Captain?" Stanton asked.

"No. This is only his second mission with me."

"I see. We'll take him back with us for questioning. I'm sorry for any inconvenience or delays we've caused." He turned to Hanson. "He's secured?"

"I turned him over to your men. He's denying everything of course. But I have him on disk."

Tyree shifted nervously. Disk? That wasn't possible. Hanson's story was certainly a lie.

He took a silver disk from his pocket and handed it over. "The picture is grainy, but still visible enough to tell what's going on."

"Thank you for your assistance. We'll get to the bottom of this, Captain."

She nodded and watched the team leader leave the deck. She noticed Hanson's nervous twitching out of the corner of her eye, but she didn't move until the patrol pod redocked on the other vessel, and the ship disappeared from view. "Maintain our position for now. I'll plot new coordinates and feed them into the computer from my quarters," she ordered.

Hanson whispered in her ear. "We need to go to medical."

She didn't question or even acknowledge his words, only turned and followed in silence. Her mind raced, unsure of what to believe at this point. She kept her hand near her knife, just in case. She needed answers. Fast.

WHEN TYREE AND HANSON entered the medical unit, she was fuming. Hanson had refused to answer any of her questions in the lift, insisting she wait until they arrived at medical. Sheera greeted them.

"Tyree. John."

"Where is he?" Tyree asked, dispensing with pleasantries. Her heart was pounding against her ribs and she felt ready to jump out of her skin.

"Here."

At the sound of Adam's voice, she spun around. Instant relief flowed through her. He was okay! And still on board, like she'd thought. The urge to run and throw her arms around him almost overwhelmed her. But she resisted in front of the other two crew members. "Someone better tell me what's going on."

Adam stepped forward hesitantly, as if still not sure of his position with her. "Sheera is an old friend. She, unfortunately or fortunately, depending on your point of view, spilled the beans to Hanson about me. He came to your quarters and got me after the patrol boarded. Sheera hid me in the medical supply cold storage unit. It's impenetrable to instrument scans when locked up."

She stared into Adam's eyes, seeing a variety of emotions in those dark orbs. He was uncertain and wary. He didn't think she'd planned to turn him in, she hoped. She nodded almost imperceptibly. He picked up on the movement, for his body visibly relaxed. A grin tugged at his lips. She smiled slightly in return, then looked over at Hanson. "Why would you help him?"

"I'm loyal to you, Captain. Like I said. Besides, Sheera convinced me that Adam wasn't dangerous, due to his advanced design, and he was worth saving." When his gaze drifted to the other woman, his eyes softened.

Ah. More than likely he was in love with her, and that's why he'd done it. Men often did things they wouldn't normally consider for the love of a special woman. Tyree looked at Sheera. "You lied to me about Adam. And I asked you straight-out."

"Sorry, Tyree. Your attitude at the time would have been dangerous to his safety."

"How did Ridgeway find out about Adam?"

"I wondered about that, too." Hanson held up a small device. "And this is the culprit. After you went back up to the command deck, I found this hidden camera in your bath. I figured a video plant was the only way he could have known, so I did a sweep. Nothing was in your main quarters, but this small cam was embedded in the ceiling close to your shower."

Mortification filled Tyree. The things Ridgeway must have seen!

"I've destroyed the drive inside, so no record exists of anything. I didn't watch it."

Tyree nodded, breathing a sigh of relief. Sheera and John really were true friends to her and Adam. "How did you get a disk of Ridgeway sabotaging the patrol pod? He didn't really do that, did he?"

"No. I programmed the images onto the disk." He smiled, revealing a rarely seen dimple in his left cheek. "If they try, they can discover it's a fake. But I think they'll be more interested in locking up someone for the recent bombings, just to satisfy their own command, if nothing else."

Tyree wasn't so certain of that.

"Even if another incident occurs, we should be okay, since the space chatter is that a network of people planted the devices."

"And when the device you gave them doesn't match the others?"

He shrugged. "Maybe we'll get lucky and different devices were used. I don't know the details on that. The lieutenant didn't flinch when I handed him the explosive panel, so let's not borrow trouble."

"I suppose." She stared at Adam, her tense muscles finally relaxing. She slowly regained her composure and thoughts. They needed a plan. "What am I supposed to do with you now?"

A smile crossed his face. "Well . . ."

"I'm serious. You can't continue to fool the rest of the crew. They're probably already suspicious, especially with the patrol team coming aboard."

"I fooled a lot of people for a long time on Jenway Station. I'll keep a low profile."

"It's too dangerous." There had to be a way to keep him safe—and keep him close. "How about we tell people you're really human, and we only pretended you were a robot to make you more intimidating?"

"Won't work. Any sensor or monitor within a hundred meters will pick up my electrical circuitry. I can pass as robotic easier."

"Monitors would also pick up your human organs."

"True, but how often do you scan for human tissue when surrounded by humans, unless you're a medic? Even patrols only monitor for dual existence when following up on a specific tip. They don't generally scan for the heck of it. Full scans take too long, and filtering out one hundred percent human profiles uses up too many portable energy packs."

"Good point."

"If you're thinking of sending me away, or hiding me out somewhere, forget it. I'm not running and leaving you vulnerable."

Tyree's heart softened. "I don't want you to go. But I want you safe."

"I have a suggestion," John offered.

"What?" Tyree asked, willing to listen to any ideas right now.

"We set down on Wetran. Stay there. The four of us." His gaze drifted to Sheera, who actually blushed in return.

Hanson's suggestion surprised Tyree. "Just disappear?"

"Why not?"

"Wetran is a deserted planet. The climate is too volatile for normal colonization."

"Which makes it perfect."

Her thoughts raced, mulling over the possibility. "Why

the four of us? Why give up your careers for us?" Her gaze switched from John to Sheera and back again. She could tell the two were in lust, but leaving their assignments seemed a drastic move.

"I could use a change." Hanson raked his fingers through his mop of brown hair. "Besides, I'm an explorer at heart. I'd love to discover that planet's hidden secrets."

"It's a green planet, Tyree," Sheera added. "Water, dense foliage, as well as open land. Everything you've ever wanted. And it's perfect for my research on natural healing."

"And there's no military presence in that sector either," Adam tossed in. "It's an interesting idea."

"But unrealistic. I can't just disappear. My brother would send his men to find me, and he's not one to give up."

"So, tell him," Adam said. "He's not going to turn us in. We have the last salvage. Let's head directly back to Jenway as if nothing's wrong, dock, tell the Ambassador what's going on, pick up some supplies, and then head back out."

After some thought, Tyree nodded. And finally she smiled as hope filled her. This could actually work. She hadn't felt excited about her future in a long time. Now, finally, the freedom she craved was within reach. All she had to do was take the chance.

"Okay, let's do it. Hanson, go to the command deck, tell the others I've decided we're returning to Jenway, then head us home. Adam and I will prepare the salvage for transfer and do the reports, so nothing looks suspicious. Sheera, put together whatever we have on board here that we'll need, anything that would look too suspicious to re-supply. I don't want our departure to look like we're not coming back. We'll move to a smaller, more manageable ship when we dock. I have my own personal ship at the station. After we leave, we'll send a false distress signal, then cut communications. Everyone but my brother will think we exploded, or drifted into the Corian asteroid field or something else equally deadly. We'll be declared dead and the case will be closed. This might really work."

Sheera emitted an excited squeal.

Adam and John did some sort of male, hand slapping ritual. "Yeah!" they said simultaneously.

"We welcome your help and company," Adam told the man. "Thanks for what you did for me and Tyree."

"I did what I thought was right."

Tyree smiled at Sheera. "Well, I see we're all in agree-ment. I owe you my thanks, Sheera. You're a good friend."

The woman glanced briefly toward John, her green eyes sparkling. "I'm looking forward to the adventure."

"Okay, then. Let's move it."

Epilogue

YREE LAY ATOP HER bed, snuggled into Adam's arms. "Everything is ready and in place. Do you think that fake evidence on Ridgeway will really fool the Space Patrol?"

"No, not for long. They'll come back looking for us once they figure out we lied. But, with the Ambassador's help, I think your plan will work."

"I'm sorry tonight didn't turn out as we arranged." She rubbed his bare chest, tugging lightly at the hair there and pressed her breasts against him. Her nipples immediately hardened, and she sighed at the incredible feeling. "I was looking forward to those kinky toys."

"Ah." Adam chuckled. "Well, me, too." He kissed her lips tenderly. "But I don't think tonight's the time for that. I do still want to make love to you, Tyree. Soft and slow. I want you close to me, in my arms, warm and safe, all night."

"I'd like that, Adam. Um . . ." Confessions weren't normally her style but she felt safe with Adam, physically and emotionally. She wanted to let him into her thoughts. "I was so scared when the patrol stopped us. I figured for sure you'd be—"

"Shh . . . Don't. It's over."

She nodded, her emotions still raw. "You thought I was going to betray you, turn you over to them. Didn't you?"

"Honestly, I wasn't sure. I'm sorry I doubted you."

"You never have to doubt me." She chewed at her bottom lip. Time for another big step in her life. After a hesitant moment, she spoke again. "Adam?"

At her uncertain tone, a frown crossed his face. He caressed the back of her head. "What is it, sweetheart?"

Her heart pounded. She'd never said to a man the words she needed to say to him, here and now. "I'm . . . I'm falling in love with you."

His eyes widened, then they gradually darkened with compassion and desire. He pulled her tighter against his body. One hand tangled in her hair and he kissed her gently, brushing his lips along hers. "Show me," he whispered.

She smiled and leaned down to kiss and lap at his neck. She actually felt a tremor rack his body when her tongue touched his skin.

He didn't say how he felt about her. But he must care, otherwise, he'd have taken off after the patrol left, to ensure his safety. He could disappear a lot more effectively without her than with her.

"Get on top of me, Tyree. Now."

She crawled on top of him and slid over his rock-hard

cock. "Oh . . ." His penetration of her body felt like coming home, as if their joining was meant to be.

Steady and sure, she moved on him. Their gazes locked and held. He looked at her as if she belonged to him. And she liked how that felt. Her pussy tightened, hugging his cock.

"Tyree," he whispered, his hips surging upward. His fingers curled around her thighs. "Ride me, baby."

She never took her gaze off his as she increased her rhythm. She could see the pleasure in his eyes. He loved being ridden. "Your cock feels great inside me."

His fingers tightened. "Tell me. Everything you're feeling."

She glided her hands slowly up her body and massaged her tender breasts, then tugged on her nipples. "You make me feel sexy, decadent—"

"Hot?"

"Yes." She closed her eyes and bounced faster on top of him. "Oh . . ."

"Open your eyes, Tyree." He groaned. "I need to see your beautiful eyes. Squeeze my dick with your muscles again."

Her eyes fluttered open and she followed his instructions, needing to please him more than ever. All these feelings were so new to her. Her pussy held his cock tightly.

"Oh, yeah, that's great! Tell me you love me, Tyree."

Her pulse jumped. He knew the truth. She wasn't falling in love with him, as she'd said. She had already fallen—hard. And she wasn't going to deny it now. "I love you."

"Again." He pumped his hips fast and hard, pushing deep inside her.

"I love you." She was close to losing control. Her pleasure escalated, coursing through her body.

"I'm going to come!" He groaned, and his semen shot into her.

"Yes!" She came hard, her body trembling with wave after wave of sheer ecstasy.

Adam pulled her down against his chest, holding her close to his heart. After their breathing returned to semi-normal, he whispered in her ear. "Tyree . . . I love you, too."

What air remained in her lungs whooshed out of her, and moisture welled in her eyes. She couldn't stop the tears from rolling down her cheeks. The words she'd longed to hear from him, he'd finally said. Nothing else mattered.

"This is going to work between us, Adam." He made her happier than she'd ever been in her life. Even if they had to run forever, he was worth it, as long as they remained together and he was safe.

"Yes. I'll see to it, Tyree." He held her close. "I won't ever let anything tear us apart. I give you my word. Now, go to sleep. Late tomorrow we'll arrive at Jenway Station and a new adventure begins."

Tyree snuggled in his arms. Resting her head on his chest, she looked out the porthole into the vastness of space.

Soon Adam's slow and steady breathing indicated he'd fallen asleep. She didn't know what the future truly held for them, but she knew she'd made the right decision.

Adam 483, whether man or machine or a combination of both, had captured her heart.

Bachelorette

SHERRI L. KING

Cash refunds and charge card credits on all merchandise
are available within 7 days of purchase with receipt.
Merchandise charged to a credit card will be credited to
your account. Exchange or store credit will be issued for
merchandise returned within 30 days with receipt.
Cash refunds for purchases made by check are available
after 12 business days, and are then subject to the time
limitations stated above. Please include original packaging
and price tag when making a return. Proper I.D. and
phone number may be required where permitted.
We reserve the right to limit or decline refunds.

Gift cards cannot be returned for cash, except as required by law.

The personal information you provide is confidential and will
not be sold, rented or disclosed to a third party for commercial
or other purposes, except as may be required by law.

HALF PRICE BOOKS

RETURN POLICY

Prologue

CATHERINE STOWE GLANCED DOWN at her watch. As usual the time had flown away from her while studying. Her term paper on the Impressionist movement, due the very next day to her art history professor, was finished but not quite up to her exacting standards just yet. However, she'd promised her dorm mate Norah that she'd go to a party with her tonight, and she couldn't let her friend down. After disappointing Norah by backing out of so many other frat get-togethers, she just didn't have the heart to cancel once again. The term paper would have to be submitted as it was, even though it was still a lot less than perfect.

Oh, how Mike would tease her about that when he learned of it. She, arguably the greatest perfectionist in the world, was going to let something slide in order to attend a party. For a brief moment she considered calling him, to invite him along, but then she remembered he'd mentioned needing to study late tonight. It was an understood thing between them that she not disturb him while he studied. He was so scatterbrained at times that the smallest interruption could distract him from getting anything accomplished.

Catherine smiled. She always caught herself smiling when thinking about her fiancé. Even though they'd been sweethearts since the eighth grade, she loved him now at the age of twenty-one just as passionately as she had in her teens. Her world revolved around him. Sure, she was a little disappointed that they hadn't married after graduation. But Mike had pointed out that a lengthy engagement during their college years would only strengthen the bond between them.

Besides, it was cheaper to live in the dorms separately than to rent an apartment together. As there were no co-ed dorms at Piedmont University of Liberal Arts, they couldn't live together on campus. They both had decent grants that covered living expenses, so it just seemed wiser to wait until after college before they tied the knot.

Still, Catherine sometimes felt she would have been able to see more of Mike if they'd gone the way of apartment renting. And she would have been willing to work to make ends meet. She'd even recently been offered an evening intern position as assistant makeup artist at a small local television station. She had her design professor to thank for the job offer—Ms. Brooks had dropped her name several times to her friend, the head of PR at the station. The income from that position would easily have kept them afloat had she and Mike chosen to move in together.

But Mike was always the decision maker between them. She was content to let him have his way. After all, it was only four years before college graduation. What were four years when compared with a lifetime together? Not much, admittedly. And since three of those years had already passed and they were both now junior classmen, it seemed moot to dwell over it anymore. They'd be together soon enough, and she would have to content herself with that knowledge.

Catherine sighed and tidied up her desk. The door to her shared dorm room opened and Norah, ever punctual, bounded into the small space in a cloud of designer perfume.

"You ready?" Norah asked without preliminaries.

"Hello to you too. Just let me grab my purse and we can go."

Norah studied her from head to toe and tsked. "You can't go like that."

"Why? What's wrong with me?" Catherine looked down at her white button-up shirt and blue jeans. She thought she looked fine. It was only a frat party after all and not a formal dinner, but Norah was looking at her like she was a wet dog.

"You wore that to your classes today. People have *seen* you in it. Wear something else. Something new, and less drab."

"I don't have anything new."

"Good grief." Norah strode over to the closet they shared between them. Delving into Catherine's side, elbow deep, she muttered impatiently. "Don't you own anything besides jeans and sweats?"

"Well excuse me for preferring comfort over vanity." Catherine laughed when Norah turned and shot a horrified look over her shoulder. Norah was never anything less than impeccable in her attire, and expected everyone else to be the same.

After several moments of searching Norah huffed and gave up hope. "Here." Norah reached into her own section of the closet and grabbed a black sheath dress. "It'll be a little baggy on your frame"—Norah eyed Catherine's B-cup breasts pointedly while thrusting her own 36C endowments forward—"but it's black and cut to fall straight so it shouldn't matter too much. Just hope no one's looking closely."

Catherine quickly donned the dress, fluffing her long dishwater-blonde hair out from beneath the collar carelessly.

Norah cringed. "You're hopeless, girl. If I had hair as thick as yours I'd take better care of it." She fingered her own fine auburn hair while eyeing Catherine's thick mass of waves enviously.

"I brush my hair when it gets tangled. I wash it when it gets dirty. That's really all it needs," Catherine chuckled. "And that's all the patience I have for it."

"Well here, let me pull it back." Norah used an oversized alligator clip to gather the weight of her hair. "That way you can at least see where you're going. And people can see your face better. You never go out anymore so some people might not recognize you," she teased. "There. You look good. Not great but good. Now let's go par-*tay*."

Norah hooked Catherine's arm with hers and together they left, smiling and laughing.

THE PARTY WAS LOUD and raucous. The booze flowed freely as it was wont to do with Norah's crowd. It had been so long since Catherine had ventured out into the frat scene that it was jarring at first, but after quickly downing an ice-cold beer she was feeling much more relaxed. The music blared, the laughter roared and everyone seemed to be having a wonderful time.

Norah dragged Catherine from group to group, like a butterfly flitting from one meadow to another. She was the life of the party. Everyone knew her. Everyone envied her. Everyone wanted to be her. Catherine, more comfortable observing in such a crowded gathering, merely let her friend direct their way through the crushing melee of drunken revelry. Sometimes Catherine wished she could be as bold and outgoing as Norah was, but those times were few—she was comfortable enough with herself not to want to change. And she doubted Mike would care for her to do so.

She might not be the most social, or the most charismatic of people, but she was engaged to a fine man who loved her. Her future was destined to be a comfortable one. After graduation she'd settle down, raise a family, and probably find work as an art teacher at an elementary school. Not the most exciting prospect one could have, but then she just wasn't meant for the highlife. And a demanding career just wasn't something she was interested in. She was happy to look forward to marriage and a family of her own. They were the most important things to her, and had been ever since she was a little girl.

What girl didn't dream of growing up to meet the perfect man? To love and nurture the children they would have together? These had been Catherine's goals ever since she could remember. Since her own family had been a dysfunctional one at best, she was determined to be the perfect wife and mother. She loved her own mother and father, but they drove her crazy with their constant bickering and neglectful attitudes. She would have none of that when she began her own family.

And Mike was the perfect man to share her life with, Catherine was sure of it. She loved him so much it was like a constant ache in her heart. From the first moment she'd seen him, playing basketball for the home team at a long ago school function, she'd known he was the one for her. Beyond infatuation, beyond any schoolgirl crush she'd experienced before then, her love for him had been instant and all consuming.

She couldn't wait to begin their life together.

"Snap out of it, Catherine." Norah nudged her none too gently. "You haven't heard a word I've said, have you? Fix your hair, dear. There's something over here I want to show you. Something you need to see." Norah grabbed her arm in a vise-like grip.

Beer sloshed over the rim of her cup and onto her hand. Not wanting to chance getting her borrowed dress stained, she looked around frantically for a napkin. Busy cleaning up her dishabille, she didn't immediately see what Norah was up to until it was too late.

When her eyes rose she couldn't have hoped to escape the scene that unfolded, nor was she in any way prepared for it. There, on a couch before them, nestled between the thighs of a half-dressed, reclining strumpet was her fiancé. Mike was lying between the woman's splayed legs, dry humping her, squeezing her plump breasts and kissing her so deeply Catherine wondered that the woman didn't gag on his tongue.

"Hello, Mike. Look who I've brought over to see you." Norah's voice was catty and spiteful. For a panicked moment Catherine wondered if Norah had staged this meeting for her own personal amusement. It wouldn't be unheard of—Norah was famous for her spite when wronged. But they were friends—why would Norah do this to her in so public a place?

Catherine felt as if someone had punched her in the stomach. She felt faint, breathless. She felt her heart swell and burst, bleeding out her love in a torrent of pain and betrayal. A few of the surrounding people seemed to sense an impending scene, scenting out the perfume of scandal like a pack of jackals. The voices around her grew quieter. The onlookers waited for the explosion, prepared to feed on the backlash of emotion.

Finding a strength she didn't even know she had, Catherine straightened her spine proudly. Her voice was clear and calm when she spoke, and no one was more surprised about it than she. "Mike? When you're finished creaming your pants, I'd like to talk to you in private."

Her fiancé started at the sound of her voice and jerked violently away from the woman beneath him. "Baby! I didn't know you were here," he said lamely, chuckling ruefully and blushing with guilt.

"Clearly." Catherine was a rock, steady and unfeeling. Her heart had gone numb. She felt no anger, no pain. Not then. But she was completely aware of the eyes that watched her raptly. She vowed not to cause more of a scene than was necessary. "Come outside with me."

"Honey—" he started, clearly sounding as though he was actually about to try to placate her.

Catherine could hardly believe it. "*Now,*" she bit out

unflinchingly. Turning, she caught the tiny smile that played about Norah's mouth. "You too, Norah. Outside."

Norah started but readily obeyed. Without looking back to see if Mike followed, Catherine led the way out of the house and into the darkness of the yard beyond. When she was certain they were out of earshot—if not completely out of sight—she turned around to face them. Now that they were afforded a small amount of privacy she began to feel again. Inside she was shaking, but was relieved to find the strength to keep her pain hidden, if only a little.

Dreading the answer, but needing to hear it anyway, she addressed Norah first. "Did you know about this or did you only just find out that Mike was fucking around?"

Norah fidgeted uncomfortably, flushing and averting her eyes. "I knew."

"How long?"

"Since the first week of our fall term."

"This fall?" How she hated this. Why hadn't Norah warned her? Why had she sprung it on her like this?

"No." Norah swallowed, looking decidedly nervous now. "Since our freshman year. When you and I first roomed together."

Catherine was completely stunned by Norah's unexpected response. "*All this time*?" She looked at Mike's face, saw the truth there like a stain on his boyish good looks, and felt a large portion of her heart die inside. "He's been doing it this whole time? And for this long you've known and you never told me? *Why* didn't you tell me sooner?" She turned back, addressing Norah.

"I didn't know how. It was a difficult thing for me to

think about, so I let it slide for a while. I wanted to tell you. I swear I wanted to, but you're always so absorbed in your studies—"

"Ask her how she knows, Catherine." Mike sneered hatefully at Norah.

Her breath hitched with alarm. Oh, God, she knew where this was going, but why, why, *why*? Why was this happening? "H-how did you know, Norah? How did you find out?" Just a few short hours ago her life had been perfect. Her entire life had been mapped out, comfortable and assured. How could it all change so fast?

Norah reached out pleadingly, but Catherine flinched away from the grasp of her friend's perfectly manicured hands. "I wanted to tell you. I just didn't know how. I wouldn't have done it if I had given it any thought, but I was drunk and then it was too late to undo it."

"Wouldn't have done what?" She already knew the heart-wrenching answer.

"Well, I slept with him, *okay*? It was before we were really friends, you and I, that first week at school. It was at a party and I was drunk. It was a mistake. I knew that right away. And then you and I became friends and I didn't know how to tell you. After that I saw him with lots of other girls, at nearly every party I went to, but it's gotten worse during this term. Why do you think I've been asking you out to parties for the past six months? I wanted to show you what he's been up to, to let you see for yourself. I'm sorry, but what was I supposed to do?" she rushed on, but Catherine had heard enough.

She turned back to Mike. "How have you found the *time* to do all this fooling around?" It was the first thing she could think to ask him.

A grin appeared on his lips, the one he used when he knew he'd made a mistake and sought to make amends. It was the same boyishly charming grin Catherine had so loved all these years, but now she found it despicable. "What can I say? I don't need to study all the time like you do. I keep my grades up, no problem. And there's a lot more to college life than sitting around with your nose buried in a book all day and all night."

"So when you tell me you're studying, that you can't be disturbed . . ." She couldn't finish.

"Yeah," he chuckled sheepishly. "I just told you that to keep you satisfied. You're so possessive about spending all of our free time together. I just need time now and then to have a little freedom. But don't worry, baby," he hastened to add, "none of those chicks mean a thing to me. To us. I mean, I know you're mad now and that's understandable, but try to remember that these are my last days as a bachelor. It's better that I get my fun over with now before I settle for having the same woman every night."

Catherine reeled. He actually sounded like he believed in his own selfish reasoning. He was smiling at her as though he'd merely been caught with his hand in the cookie jar—instead of beneath another woman's bra. She took a deep, calming breath, determined not to cry as her last girlish dreams were crushed so ruthlessly by the two people she'd most trusted in the world.

"Are you a complete idiot?" she asked, surprised at the levelness of her tone.

Mike started, surprised. But he quickly rallied himself and actually had the temerity to appear angry—at *her*. "It's not as if you're the best piece of pussy in the world. Did you think I was so whipped that I wouldn't play the field? Grow up, Catherine. Not everyone is as obsessed with marriage and family as you are. I *will* marry you like I promised. I'm a man of my word and I *do* love you. I'm just living a little before we get leg-shackled, that's all. Don't get all bent out of shape over it. I'm sure you'd rather I did it now and not after we're married."

Catherine pried the tiny diamond engagement ring off of her wedding finger—a ring she'd help pay for as Mike was just as poor as she—and threw it at him. "I wouldn't marry you now if my life depended on it! What the hell is wrong with you? You're not the man I thought you were. You're some kind of—some kind of *monster*," she sputtered disbelievingly.

Mike flushed angrily. "Don't think you didn't have this coming. I have needs of my own. You only see me as a safety net or as someone to take care of you. Like if you marry me your life will be perfect from then on out. All you cared about was a white picket fence. You didn't care how I felt. You're so selfish, all you ever think about is what you want."

"What!" she exclaimed, incredulous. "How could you think that? I see you as a person, as someone I loved. We've been together for *seven years* and you never complained before. I never forced the marriage issue. *You* proposed to *me* at prom. I even agreed to wait until after graduation." She felt the traitorous tears fill her eyes, even after fighting so hard to keep them at bay. "How could you do this to me? And for so long." She looked over at Norah, who was fidgeting uncomfortably, clearly not enjoying being party to this public quarrel. "And with my best friend."

"She wasn't your best friend at the time."

"Is that supposed to make it better?"

"I warned you that she was a bitch from the start but you wouldn't listen. You thought she was *so* nice. I can't help it that you have poor judgment."

"You're a pathetic waste," Catherine bit out. She looked at Mike and Norah, really looked at them. And she loathed what she saw. Loathed that she'd been so dependent on their love, on their friendship. Loathed herself for not seeing this faithlessness in Mike sooner and for not seeing the codependent weakness in herself.

How foolish she'd been. How naïve.

Without another word she turned and walked off into the night.

"Wait! Catherine!" She didn't stop and Norah was forced to trot to reach her. "Don't get mad at me. I just didn't know any other way to tell you."

Catherine rounded on her. "Of course you didn't. You're so self-centered you didn't even think for a moment how painful such a discovery would be for me. You *should* have told me—but not like that. In front of all those people, with the proof of his infidelity right there in front of me. It was like being stabbed. What were you thinking, Norah?"

"Everyone knew he was cheating on you. I know you've heard rumors about it; even you aren't that oblivious to the world around you. A weekend hasn't gone by without Mike getting naked with a girl in some public place. It was almost like he *wanted* you to find out, he was so open about it. And you'd have to be stupid not to see the warning signs even without the gossip."

Catherine continued walking, feeling the blessed rush of anger warm the cold regions of her shattered heart. "Of course I didn't hear about it. How could I? I barely talk to anyone besides you and Mike and my professors. And if my trusting him made me stupid, then I guess I'm stupid for not suspecting his every move. But, it doesn't matter now. Oh, Norah. You knew. My god, you even fucked him! But you never said anything. Not one word."

"I already said I didn't know how to tell you, so I just showed you. Besides, you're so dense about Mike that I figured you'd need to see it to believe it. I may be your friend but he was your *soul mate*," she sneered hatefully. "You would have believed him over me without proof, any day. You're really stupid about him. You always have been."

Catherine gritted her teeth, dug in her heels and faced Norah down with all the rage and pain she was feeling. "You know what? I don't need friends like you, Norah. Three years this has been going on, but you said nothing. All this time I thought you and I were close, but I was wrong. You don't care about anyone but yourself."

She laughed but it was a bitter sound, even to her own ears. "All this time you've complained about my appearance, about my study habits and my mannerisms. I always thought it was because you cared about me personally, because you hated seeing me work so hard and have no fun.

But it was for your own benefit wasn't it? By pointing out my faults you felt better about yourself. You kept me around to have someone to help you study, to get passing grades when you'd otherwise fail, and to have someone to talk to when there weren't any parties to attend. Well I won't have it anymore. You're a user, Norah. I see that now, and I don't need you anymore. Go back and enjoy your party. I'm getting the fuck outta here."

"Fine then, *bitch*. And while I'm at it, I think I'll just go offer Mike a little comfort. See how you like that." Norah's usually lovely face turned red and blotchy with her anger.

Catherine turned away, this time for the last time. "Be my guest," she muttered. Putting one foot before the other, she walked further away from the deadliest blow she'd ever been dealt, and once she'd reached her dorm she could have sworn she was made out of stone.

Nothing would ever have the power to hurt her like this again. No lover, no friend, no one. She was on her own now, and she'd learn how to prefer it that way. She had to.

Chapter One

Six years later

*N*O ONE EVER NOTICED the makeup artist—or as some in the field preferred to be called, the cosmetic technician. Beyond the perfunctory greeting and occasional small talk from their employers they were pretty much ignored. They were paid to do a job. If they were good they were paid very well, but they were hired for their skills, not their personalities. They were paid to be invisible.

Catherine was good at being invisible when the occasion warranted. In fact, she rather liked that part of her job because it gave her a lot of time for quiet introspection. And she liked to watch the people around her, to see how they behaved, how they interacted with each other on and off camera. If anyone ever asked she'd have quite a story to tell, even after a mere six years on the job.

Well, being asked by the tabloid papers didn't really

count. And they did ask—often. She'd never sell her secrets to a rag mag, though, no matter how much money they offered her. They offered quite a lot—more and more each time they managed to contact her. But her employer, Don Garrison, paid her far better to keep her mouth shut and her makeup brushes moving along the handsome planes of his face.

Catherine had been lucky enough to get assigned to Don during the early stages of his career as a soap opera star. Back then she'd been employed by the network station, a job she'd accepted on her college professor's insistence. Not long after the betrayal of her longtime fiancé, she'd dropped out of school, unable to face him and her former friend any longer. Norah and Mike had hooked up almost immediately after the party, but Catherine suspected it was more in an effort to hurt her than due to any mutual romance on their part.

Their petty plan had succeeded. Wounded beyond even that first moment of catching Mike in the act of betrayal, she had left school and taken the job at WCON's station in Chicago. She'd embarked on a new life, in a totally different direction from any she'd ever planned to take. Remaking herself in an entirely different image. And she'd never looked back.

Now Don Garrison was an up and comer, gaining star status from his roles in several critically acclaimed dramas. Though still technically only a B-actor, he had his own following of fans, and a growing portfolio of work in the business that would take him quite far before it was all said and done. Catherine had seen the potential in him early on and focused nearly all of her attentions on him instead of the dozen other clients she'd had at the time.

Her hard work had paid off. Don had sworn then as he did now that he couldn't live without her in his entourage. He hired her as his personal makeup artist the minute he'd left the station some five years ago.

There was no real prestige in the job, unless one counted appearing in the credits of Don's films. And it was hard work. But the money was good, the contacts were lucrative and the travel was extensive.

It was the travel that Catherine really loved. All the new lands full of new and interesting people—there was far more adventure than she'd ever envisioned for herself when she'd been with Mike.

Invisible and silent, she worked her magic on Don's appearance as they prepared for his newest scene. As the lead role in this, a religious film with quite a bit of controversy behind it, he now had the opportunity to become a full-blown star in Hollywood as never before. Catherine would use every ounce of expertise she possessed to help him look especially deserving of the part, both on and off screen. She was confident in her abilities as an artist and professional—as were countless colleagues and peers who'd come to respect her talents. She would succeed in her task. The rest was up to Don.

As her brush moved across Don's face in the last stages of preparation, she listened to him as he spoke with his executive assistant.

"I'll be hiring the same guy Stallone used last month. Fever or whatever his name is. He's flying down here from L.A. tonight."

"*Gideon* Fevere?"

"Yeah that's the one. He's supposed to be good, an ex-secret agent-turned-bodyguard or something."

"Actually he was CIA, injured on the job and forced to leave the field. He runs his own security agency now. I've read so much about him in the papers recently. He must have made quite an impression with his last few jobs. Should be interesting having him about."

"I don't really care so long as he looks scary enough to keep these protestors at bay. Hopefully, after he gets here and does his thing, I won't get any more threats from these bozos."

"I thought it was just one person issuing the threats." Johnson the Assistant, as Catherine always privately called him, looked alarmed. "Have there been others since we left the States?"

Don shifted and Catherine stilled him with a hand beneath his chin as she continued working. "The guy's a part of some religious group, I'm sure of it. Just look at all the picketers outside the lot today; they're coming out of the woodwork. They're all probably in on the letters."

"I still think you should go to the cops."

"You think it might be good for publicity? I don't know how much weight Sydney cops will pull with the media. I've never filmed in Australia before. But it might work." Don sounded interested in the idea.

"Who cares about *that*? It's your safety I'm worried about."

And no doubt his paychecks, Catherine thought. But Don had received threats from stalkers before. He would, considering all the controversial roles he chose to play, so Catherine wasn't too worried about them yet.

"Keeping me safe will be up to Gideon. But your idea of notifying the police might be a good idea. I'll check with my publicist and see what he thinks. It could be a good way to make some tongues wag."

Johnson the Assistant laughed fondly, but Catherine guessed it was just as fake as everything else around her. "You're shameless," he twittered.

"You better believe it." Don somehow managed to chuckle without moving beneath Catherine's ministrations. "I'm as shameless and daring as they come."

Gag me with a mascara wand, she thought exasperatedly as the two men continued their discussion. Men were the most arrogant, self-important creatures in the world.

Chapter Two

GIDEON FEVERE DOWNED HIS second shot of bourbon. The bar was full of people, the noise just barely above tolerable. This wasn't his usual hangout, but then he was new to this town and hadn't found a favorite watering hole yet. His thigh ached fiercely, the twisted muscles and tendons—unwelcome trophies of a run-in with a shrapnel bomb—reminding him of why he seemed to frequent watering holes more and more often of late.

Tired and aching, he felt so much older than his thirty-five years should inspire.

Four years ago he'd been a good field agent. CIA all the way, tried and true since he'd turned twenty-one. But all that had changed so quickly. He'd only just heard the deadly click of a detonator, and Gideon had known his number was finally up. He'd been lucky. Only his leg had been mangled in the blast of the so-called dirty bomb. But two of his best men had lost their lives.

He'd been given a healthy pension, one he could live off of comfortably for a while. Or he could have taken a desk job in the agency. But neither of those lives would have suited him. So he'd started his own security agency, to protect the rich where before he'd protected the innocent.

It was a living. It could even be fun at times. And though Gideon missed the thrill of his old life, he was learning to revel in the sudden freedom of his new one. No more did he obey orders that were not his own. No more did he worry about emotional entanglements that might interfere with his work. Being a bodyguard was easy work after his battle days, affording him lots of free time where before he'd had none.

Unfortunately, he was just as much a loner now as he ever was. But then, he was set in his ways. And old ways died hard.

Sultry female laughter reached his ears and he glanced up from his empty shot glass. The woman presently drawing his attention was an attractive petite blonde. Though beautiful, he wasn't in the market for a woman tonight and she probably wouldn't have held his attention for long had it not been for the large group of men hanging around her.

He counted five in all. And each of them was eagerly panting to have her, vying for her attention with humiliating insistence, competing with one another like animals. More than their own behavior making them appear like a pack of wild dogs after a bitch in heat was the woman's own demeanor towards her audience.

Ruthless was the word that sprang to mind. Heartless and cold-blooded soon followed. The woman managed to encourage, yet discourage each man in turn. With a look and a touch she managed to flirt with them and lead them on, while from her mouth spilled caustic remarks that should have unmanned them completely.

Ordering a beer, he moved closer to an empty table and listened in on the group's activity.

"I was an MP in the U.S. Army reserves until 2001," one man boasted.

"Oh yeah? Right before war broke out, you mean," the woman countered in a goading tone. Her smooth, Australian accent sounded odd to his ears—for reasons he couldn't have said—but it stirred his senses nonetheless.

"Yeah, I guess."

"There's no guessing. War started after September eleventh, in one fashion or another. But that's okay— you're still cute—why don't you show me the size of your dick so I can decide if your cowardice isn't a bad enough mark against you to disinterest me."

The man laughed, albeit uncomfortably.

"Come on. Show me your package. Aren't you the one who said you have twelve inches stuffed down those tight jeans you're wearing?"

Another man eagerly spoke up. "No, that was me!"

The woman eyed him critically, and at the angle Gideon was sitting, he could tell she was doing it more for her own amusement than out of any real interest in the man. "Well I'm almost tipsy enough to look past the disappointment of your face. But only just. Why don't you show me this massive organ of yours then?"

The man actually got up and started unzipping his

pants. Gideon was stunned, but then he'd seen drunken guys do crazier stuff to impress a girl. It was just that this girl was so cutting. And the men didn't seem to notice or care.

Gideon studied her more closely. Her bright blonde hair was long, cut in several different layers and given to curl at the ends. It was darker at the roots and bright as platinum at the tips. Her neck was long, swanlike and lovely. Her skin was pale as cream and delicate. Her mouth was deep red, full and pouting, a cupid's bow. She was stylishly dressed in a spaghetti strand top and skintight suede pants. Her breasts were full and high—probably implants—and braless as she was, her nipples noticeably stabbed through the thin material of her top. She exuded feminine heat and raw sex appeal.

Yes, she was beautiful. Gideon's cock noticed that and saluted her accordingly. But it was her venomous personality that should have withered any interest he might otherwise have had in her. It should have done the same for the men around her. But, despite the sly digs and cuts that underscored her every word, her charisma was undeniable.

There was just something about her that captured his attention, and actually managed to hold it transfixed.

It had been so long since he'd noticed a woman—really noticed one. His work and lifestyle had, of course, kept him single over the years—beyond the occasional fling. And immediately after he'd left the agency he'd been so focused on building a reputation among the Hollywood beau monde, that he hadn't even thought about dating. Time had passed and still he hadn't started any new relationships. No woman had piqued his interest. But now this woman, venomous and deadly, was giving him a hard-on that threatened to burst his zipper.

He must be more deprived than he'd thought.

Now the young buck before her had his cock out in his hand—falling at least a couple of inches short of his claim to twelve—and was brandishing it proudly.

"Good grief, boy, put it away," the woman scoffed. "My smallest dildo would put you to shame. You're wasting your time here. Go find a virgin schoolgirl who'll actually be impressed by that little thing."

The man blushed but laughed her insult away, as if what she'd said hadn't been all that demeaning. "It's all in how you use it you know," he defended with a wink.

"Whoever said that had a pencil dick for certain."

God, the more this woman offended, the more Gideon wanted her. Not in tenderness or passion, but in lust—pure and simple. He had the overwhelming urge to dominate her, to gag her poisonous mouth and master her completely.

She was a challenge to the male ego. That had to be it, Gideon decided. Her very attitude goaded and dared those men around her to test their manhood in the most absurd ways. She was a femme fatale who inspired sexual aggression in the bold, while emasculating the unworthy.

Gideon was as bold as they came.

He would have her. Focusing his eyes on his prey he rose from his seat and stalked over to her table. Sparing not the slightest glance for her companions he spoke to them in his most commanding and dangerous tone.

"Beat it, guys. This one's mine."

The men disappeared from the woman's table in record time.

"WELL THAT WAS STUPID of you. *Yours* indeed. As if I'd swoon over such a declaration—you must be deluded," the woman sneered disdainfully.

"Just stating the facts as I see them," he responded easily, enjoying her fire. "What's your name?"

She snorted in disbelief. "You've got balls. But I'm bored so I'll go ahead and give you a thrill. The name's Kitty. As in Kitty-Kat. *Meow*."

"Do you ever purr or just hiss, I wonder?"

"I'll scratch your eyes out if you don't watch it, mister big balls."

"The name is Gideon Fevere. But in the bedroom you can call me Master."

Kitty's eyes widened and darted over his face and Gideon wondered briefly if his words excited or merely alarmed her. It was a bit bold, even for him, to be so crass. But she was clearly the type of woman who needed that in a lover. He sensed it as instinctively as he sensed there was more beneath her wicked personality than she would have ever comfortably admitted.

"I'm not interested, Mr. Fevere." Her voice was suddenly clipped and dismissive, far too proper after her earlier behavior, and her unusual accent fell flat. "I believe it's time for me to call it a night." She glanced at her watch for effect and Gideon felt his lips twitch in a smile at her abrupt switch in behavior. "I hate to say it wasn't nice meeting you, but then I'm sure you're used to hearing that from women."

"I'll drive you home."

"I'll take a cab."

"You're skittish without an audience. Or is it my presence in particular that has you jumping up to leave?" How he enjoyed sparring with this woman! He was a little surprised by her retreat, but determined all the more to have her in spite of it.

"I can't believe how arrogant you are. As if you could make me leave if I didn't want to. Trust me, I only do what *I* want to do." Kitty grabbed her purse and rose to leave, but not before Gideon heard the hitch in her breathing and saw the nervous dart of her tongue over the crimson pout of her lower lip.

Whether she consciously knew it or not, she wanted him to dominate her. On an elemental level, he recognized this and responded to it. Her nipples were stabbing points beneath their flimsy covering. Her breasts shuddered with every erratic breath she took. The pupils of her eyes were dilated so that they almost swallowed the deep brown of her irises. Her cheeks and neck were ever so lightly tinged with a blush and her mouth was engorging with blood in anticipation of his kiss.

There was no escaping years of elite training in observation. Gideon could clearly see her growing excitement. There were countless signs to tell him what he wished to know about her state of arousal. She wanted him almost as badly as he wanted her.

When she would have walked past him he grabbed her wrist, hard. "You're a liar. You *want* to go with me. I can see it in your eyes. So why the sudden retreat? Or are you just scared?" he taunted.

Kitty rounded on him, eyes wide. She clearly wasn't used to men pressing so insistently after a flat-out rejection. "I'm *not* scared," she scoffed.

"Then come back to my hotel room. I'll give you the thrill you've been seeking here tonight."

"Egotistical," she murmured. But Gideon knew she was interested in his proposal. Her pulse had fluttered beneath his fingertips in response to his boast.

"I've every reason to be," he promised, unable to keep the husky note of desire out of his voice. And if her erratic pulse was any indication—and he knew it was—she was not unaffected by that telltale lapse.

Oh yes, he definitely wanted her. More than she could even guess. His cock burned with it, eager to be buried in the hot, wet core of her. She was wet now. He could smell her arousal like a perfumed scent, but he would need her far more aroused before he could easily enter her.

Unlike the young buck who'd boasted of his cock size, Gideon had every right to claim such proportions. No woman in his past had ever complained, and he swore this woman wouldn't even have the breath to fabricate a complaint once he was done with her.

"Is that so?" Her lazy drawling words brought him back into their game of wits. He schooled himself. If he wasn't careful, he could lose himself in her, and that would surely spell his doom with this sort of woman.

"Let me prove it, so there'll be no doubt in your mind."

The woman seemed to war with herself. It was a fierce battle if her sudden tension was any indication, but her desires won out with whatever reasoning her higher brain provided. Gideon felt a surge of satisfaction when she replied in her sultry voice.

"All right. Let's go to your hotel. We'll see if you're man enough for me."

"Darling, I'm man enough for two of you."

Chapter Three

GIDEON WASTED NO TIME. Seeing the conflict in Kitty and knowing she could change her mind at any time, he quickly drove her to his hotel, breaking several laws in his rented car as he hurried. Her perfume enveloped him in the confines of the vehicle, making his head swim. Normally he wouldn't like such a heady, seductive scent on a woman. But on Kitty, it seemed right. By the time they reached his hotel room, he was drowning in her scent.

He practically shoved her into the room, careless with his greater strength. And he was a careful man, especially around women. For years he'd been trained and molded into a fierce killing machine, and as such he was ever conscious of how much weaker others could be. It was a mantra in his mind, more often than not, to gentle his actions around others so as not to frighten or intimidate unnecessarily.

Kitty, however, brought out the savage in him. He

would have to be very careful that she understood and agreed to the rules before he let himself go completely—or as completely as he would allow. The woman might be a predator, but then he was something else entirely and it wouldn't do to take more from her than she was willing to give.

He may be a savage, but he was no monster.

Kitty regarded him from under long, black lashes—a stark contrast to the bright blonde-tipped hair atop her head. She no doubt used a heavy hand with her mascara. Her skin, however, was porcelain fine. Clear and translucent under her loose powder, it was fragile, lovely and undeniably sexy. Undeniably feminine.

He wanted to bite that skin while he fucked her.

"Take off your clothes," he commanded, his voice thick despite an effort for calm.

Kitty's eyes widened. "What, no verbal foreplay? No lame-ass offers of a drink and conversation before the fuck-fest?"

Her crass words inflamed him sexually—even as her Aussie accent slipped a little into a wholly American one— as nothing else had in far too long a time. And he was damned if he could figure out why. She was beautiful, it was true, but she was definitely not pleasant company. He wanted to know why he felt this sudden obsession with such a vicious woman after months of abstinence.

Her limpid brown eyes were the first key to helping him discover the reasons why. In her eyes, he saw the first hints, the first clues. Deep within their velvet depths he saw an open, festering wound and a pain so profound that it shook him. This woman had been wounded, mortally so. Her eyes were dead but for that pocket of suffering buried in the depths of her soul and reflected clearly to anyone willing to see it.

He was no stranger to pain, to suffering. Perhaps it was this common thread between them that pulled at him so. And perhaps it was only the tip of the iceberg that awaited discovery within her. He vowed to discover all he could, if only to be able to completely purge his mind of the woman once the morning came. This was one woman he didn't want to think about after their liaison was finished. The lady was bad news all around, and he'd be a fool not to see it.

He'd been called many things, but never a fool.

Realizing he'd been quiet for too long, studying her too closely, he smiled and answered her question. "If you'd like a drink, that's fine. But you seemed eager enough at the bar to get down to business."

"Well, since you put it that way, forget the drink."

She surprised him by immediately pulling her top over her head and tossing it to the floor. Her breasts, full and gorgeous globes—a beautiful testimony to the skill of her cosmetic surgeon—swung gently with her motions. Her nipples, large and rosy, peaked tightly before his gaze.

Her slender, long-fingered hands came up and stroked over them. "Do you like what you see?" she asked, knowing damn well that he did indeed.

He swallowed, watching her fingers pluck at the long pebbles of her nipples. She lifted a breast and licked the crest with her glistening, wet tongue. He shuddered. She smiled wickedly.

Her hands fell, moving to the fastening of her pants with slow, seductive movements. As if by magic, her pants and shoes disappeared, leaving her standing before him in naught but a wicked crimson thong and an entirely too-knowing smile. Gideon's control snapped and he was on her before she could manage to blink.

"Don't tease me," he growled into her neck.

"Why not? You were obviously enjoying the show."

He didn't want to give her any more feminine power—she already had far too much—but he had to warn her. Had to give her some idea of what to expect. "It's been too long, and I'm very close to losing control with you, Kitty."

Her eyes filled with shadows and she shifted beneath him uncomfortably.

"You're a passionate woman and a beautiful one," he began.

"Look, don't get any ideas about any lasting ties between us, all right? This is nothing; it means nothing. Don't get all bent out of shape over it," she drawled. Yes. Her accent was now definitely more American than Aussie.

Her face was an expressionless mask. She was an enigma, even to someone like him, who had lived and almost died by easily reading the emotions of others.

Then he realized what she had said, and what she had taken his awkward warning to mean. He gritted his teeth. As if he'd ever allow himself an emotional attachment to such a harridan.

He tried again. "You don't understand—"

"No, *you* don't understand," she interjected once more. He clamped his hand over her mouth. She struggled immediately, but he easily held her captive despite her obvious anger at being manhandled. "Shut up."

Her eyes blazed at his command but she stilled beneath him. Gideon was sure it was more out of curiosity than any fear she might have of him.

"I'm not close to coming in my pants because I have any affection for you. I've been abstinent for a while and I'm just a little overeager."

He ignored the derisive glint in her eye as he admitted it. No doubt she worried that his prowess might not be up to her standards with such an admission. She needn't have feared. He had more than enough stamina for her, of that he had no doubt.

"Now. What I was going to say before you interrupted was that you're obviously a passionate woman, but you might not be prepared for someone like me. I'm bigger than you. I'm a lot stronger than you. I'm a very demanding lover, even when I'm not so desperately edgy, and I want to make sure you are prepared for it before we take this further."

He pulled his hand away to allow her a response.

She snorted. "Your ego is as big as a house! I think the real question should be whether or not you can handle *me*." She wriggled beneath him, undulating her pelvis against the more than obvious evidence of his sexual hunger. "Or will you go all soft before the party really gets started?"

He smiled darkly. "Don't worry about me. I'll give you the fucking you so obviously need from me. If you're up to it." He ground his pelvis into her. "As you can tell, I'm up to it. But I'm giving you a chance now, Kitty, to back out of this with no hard feelings."

"Oh, just bone me and get it over with. You'd think we were planning to marry with all this talk. I don't think I've ever said so many words to a lover in my life."

That dead pool in her eyes rippled with her words and then quieted. He wondered at it, but she chose that moment to rub her plump breasts against his chest, drawing his attention to a much more urgent matter.

"I warned you," he breathed before pouncing.

The dark swarm of his passion rose and was met by hers, as he let loose a small measure of his control.

He flipped her over and fell upon the tender slope of her back with all the demanding lust that raged in him. He scraped his teeth against her spine, dug his fingers into the soft cushion of her hips, and let his hair tickle her shoulders and back. The gasp of surprise that escaped her lips was signal enough for him to continue.

As he kissed and licked and bit—oh to bite into her tender skin at last—as he stroked her from her nape to the backs of her knees with his calloused hands, he listened to the music of her rising arousal. Every sigh, every quiet moan, was a triumph to him. His victory in the battle of their lusts.

Her body taught his what she liked most. And as in every other aspect in his life, he learned quickly from her. Her preferences were important to him, her pleasure his foremost objective. She liked having the globes of her buttocks squeezed and nibbled upon; he could easily tell by the way her legs tightened and her back arched. Every movement she made was carefully observed and catalogued by his higher brain, in order to please her better.

And once she was replete, when she was too sated to speak her vile words with her poisonous mouth, he would have all the time he needed for his own pleasures.

From behind her, he reached around and found her clit beneath the flimsy silk of her panties. She whimpered and moved against his hand with unabashed sensuality. Her skin was sheened with perspiration. The heat of her rose and brought with it her scent, smelling overwhelmingly like crushed and bruised flower petals. The wet nectar of her sex pooled on his fingers.

She keened quietly as she came.

He flipped her over once again, this time a little more roughly, though he was ever careful not to hurt her. Her face was flushed, her lips full and dewy. Her breath came in gentle gasps and her brown eyes had gone black and glassy.

He felt no small amount of satisfaction upon seeing the evidence of his own prowess written on her face.

Carelessly he ripped his clothes away, tearing fabric and popping buttons in his haste. He paused before removing his jeans, knowing that she would have to be blind not to notice his injured leg, and wondering what she would have to say about the unsightly scars. But his indecision passed as quickly as it came, as he realized the weakness of vanity inside him. Let her see his scars. He wouldn't care what she thought so long as she didn't turn away from him because of them.

Within seconds he was nude. To take the edge off his lust he palmed himself and stroked the hot, tight flesh of his cock. His eyes roved to the object of his greatest desire, and widened to find her juices already soaked through the barrier of her thong. She appeared too content to even notice the scars.

"Wait here a second, babe." He rose from the bed unashamed in his nudity, even knowing that Kitty followed his every movement with her lazy, feline eyes. He strode to the bathroom, where his overnight bag waited, still unpacked. Within it he found a box of condoms—unopened but always with him on long trips just in case—a handkerchief, and a pair of silver handcuffs.

A quick search of the bathroom and the living room provided him with the rest of the necessary items. He smiled, satisfied. Whether she knew it or not, Kitty-Kat's night was only just beginning.

Chapter Four

"KINKY ARE YOU, DARLING?" Her tone was an incredible mixture of boredom, sarcasm and—hidden deeper, no doubt deliberately—arousal.

He focused on her arousal. It was either that or be unforgivably insulted, especially after the intense orgasm he'd just given her. She was a derisively sly fox, this Kitty. But he knew she was merely putting on a show now, knew that beneath her bitchy exterior lay something far more interesting. He was learning more and more about her, whether she wanted him to or not.

Kitty was obviously apprehensive now. Scared. Not of the handcuffs in his hands or the lust in his eyes, but of herself. He could see it in her face and in her gaze. There was fear in her. And pain. Along with a wash of other emotions, deep emotions, unsuitable for the role of a hard-shelled virago she seemed almost desperate to portray. There was the predictable lust, but also a softer, more feminine desire kept deeply hidden. There was intelligence, cool and calculating. But the most telling, the most revealing was her tenderness.

It was in the way she moved when he touched her. In the way she sighed and moaned softly in her release. Though it seemed evident that Kitty hated men and merely used them for her own ends, it was becoming more and more clear to Gideon that she was perhaps not all that she seemed. No woman who truly hated could respond so honestly to a man this way.

This woman, whoever she truly was, had a deeper self. One that she was determined to protect and keep hidden away. Gideon wanted to know why.

"Just relax," he said softly, coaxing her with his voice.

A hard glint in her eyes did nothing to disguise the sweet acquiescence of the hands that he secured over her head. She wanted this to play out between them, perhaps as much as he did. The metal handcuffs bound her wrists, while he used one of his silk ties to knot the chain of the cuffs to the headboard. He leaned down and kissed her slightly parted lips, a small token for her show of cooperation.

Next he used another of his ties and employed it as a blindfold. There was a moment of resistance from her, a tiny flash of fear, but he dispelled it with a stern look. If there had been more fear, fear of him, he might have let it go. But he could almost hear the pounding thud of her heart and smell the sweat of excited lust on her skin, and knew she merely needed a firm hand to guide her further into their game.

Once her eyes were covered, he realized for the first time just how small and vulnerable she was. There was something about her eyes that made her seem stronger, more self-reliant, and now that they were hidden she seemed to dwindle and gentle beneath him. Incredibly she seemed an entirely different person, and even more a stranger to him.

A thought occurred to him and he spoke before he could caution himself against it. "You wear colored contacts."

Kitty went stiff as a board beneath him. "Okay, fun's over."

He was incredulous. He hadn't expected that response from her. "Why?"

"Let me up or I'll scream." Her voice was flat.

He gritted his teeth. "Some people might call you a cock-tease for this display."

"And you only just noticed that about me? What kind of a cop were you?"

Now it was Gideon's turn to stiffen. "How did you know I was a . . . a cop?" Well, he'd actually been a government agent, but her calling him a cop was close enough not to quibble over it.

She stilled, as if she hadn't meant to reveal her suspicions about his profession. "I didn't. It's just that you've been analyzing me all night. You just happen to have a pair of standard issue cuffs in your luggage, and you put them on like a pro. And you've got this air of command thing down to a science. I thought about it and it fit, but with that game leg of yours I figured you were retired."

So she *had* noticed the scars on his leg. "So? I was a cop, but now I'm not. What does it matter?"

"It doesn't, I guess."

So maybe she was just wary around cops—most people were. But there was something about her demeanor that suggested she was more than a little uncomfortable about it. Maybe she had something to hide. "I'm not a cop anymore."

"Look, this was a mistake. I knew it was a mistake from the minute I saw you. Let me up."

"No."

She hadn't expected that response; it was clear in the shocked tones of her voice. "You can't keep me here, it's illegal."

"So? I'm not in law enforcement anymore. Who cares what's legal?"

"You do! You have to."

Knowing there was only one real way to diffuse the situation, which had gotten too far out of hand in his opinion, he removed her thong.

"What the fuck—" she exclaimed.

"Exactly." And he meant to fuck her. His cock was so hard he could have beaten a criminal over the head with it, but he'd much rather beat her with it. So to speak.

Despite her attempts to close them, he easily opened her legs and spread them wide. Just to make things even easier he retrieved two more ties—he was rapidly running out—and secured her ankles to the footboard posts. The slick, pink flesh of her cunt was shining in the light and totally exposed to his gaze.

"You look like a fucking rose down here, Kitty-Kat." He stroked the lips of her sex with the tips of two fingers.

She was so wet. If she'd been any less aroused he might have felt guilty as she continued to struggle against her bonds.

"Let me go!"

"No. There's no reason to."

"I'm going to scream for the police."

"No you won't. You want this as much as I do." He stroked her juicy cunt once again, just to emphasize his words as truth.

She whimpered.

"Shh," he coaxed gently, stroking her more steadily now, watching his fingers slide in and out of the pink seam of her. "It's okay. I won't try to 'analyze you' any more tonight. I promise."

His fingers found her clit and she sighed, relaxing almost instantly. He smiled. Obviously he'd found the right button to push to make her more agreeable.

"You're soaking my fingers. Can I taste you? I want to taste you and lap up all those sticky, sweet juices until you come for me again."

Her breath caught. He deliberately let her feel the warmth of his breath on her sex, but continued to stroke her lazily with the tips of his right index and middle fingers. Her hips bucked off the bed. He lightly kissed the crown of her sex, which was shaved completely bald but for a tiny, heart shaped tuft of hair just above her slit.

She was a natural blonde, but not so light as the platinum locks on her head might otherwise suggest.

He inhaled deeply. "God, you smell so fucking sweet." He pressed her engorged bud.

She squeaked and bucked up against him again.

Still only using the tips of his fingers, he spread her lips wide and blew down into the valley of her sex.

Kitty shuddered.

"Do you like that?" He did it again.

"Yes. Oh yes," she breathed shakily.

He delicately pinched the folds of her wet flesh and pulled on them until she began to undulate rhythmically against his every motion. He rimmed the very core of her, tracing the thin circle of flesh around her pussy hole, but never penetrating her. He watched, fascinated, as that hole began to pulsate with the onset of an orgasm.

He pulled back abruptly and administered a gentle slap to her sex, effectively halting her release.

She cried out in surprise but spread her legs wider, eager for more.

"Did you like that?"

"Yes," she moaned, sounding plaintive.

"Good. Me too." He kissed the sting away and stroked her cunt. Again he rimmed the sensitive opening of her sheath, watching her closely for any sign of oncoming re-lease. When it came, when the flesh of her entrance at-tempted to suck his fingers into their heat with their fluttering pulsations, he pulled back once again and slapped her sex gently with the same hand he'd used to gentle her.

"God," she cried out.

"Call me Master," he commanded softly.

"What!"

He slapped her sex, harder this time. "Call me Master."

She seemed to think about it, if her hesitation was any clue. "No," she finally answered.

Gideon smiled, enjoying their game of wills. Taking her completely by surprise he fell on her. He used the tip of his tongue to prod and stroke the seam of her cunt, but only just the tip.

Kitty spread her legs as wide as they would go against the ties that held her ankles. She rose up against him, her pussy lips unfurling for the exploration of his tongue. But Gideon was careful not to let her mash her sex against his face, though he wanted it as much as she. He wanted to drive her wild with her own need before he gave her what she wanted.

"Please, please," she begged.

But he wanted more. "Call me Master," he murmured against her pussy before tonguing her again.

"No."

He breathed over her clit and watched it swell with arousal. "Do it." He tugged gently on the lips of her sex and marveled as a river of glistening moisture ran down her pussy and onto the bedclothes.

"Okay, okay, I'll call you Master. I will." She surrendered.

"Say it."

"Master. Oh, Master, *please*." Her legs shuddered and quaked with the force of her desire.

"Tell your Master what you want," he commanded, letting his lips play over her flesh with every word.

She moaned. "Lick me. Bite me. Spank me. *Fuck me*."

He pulled back and waited a full minute, giving her enough time to mourn his loss before he spoke again. "Beg your Master. Beg for it, if you want it."

She performed for him beautifully. "Please Master, I beg you. Please lick and bite and spank and fuck me. Oh, Master, please, *please fuck me!*"

"So impatient," he murmured with a satisfied smile.

He buried his face into the burning hot juices of her. She keened high and long and bucked up against his face, riding his lips and tongue as they rooted deeply into her. He slurped the full lips of her pussy into his mouth, tracing the delicate hole of her, and savored the swollen bud of her throbbing clit.

She was beautiful. And she tasted even better.

He felt the pulsations of her climax against his tongue, and buried it deeply into her. The feel of her muscles squeezing him, sucking at his tongue like a tiny mouth, made his cock burn. He breathed her in, burying his nose deep into the musky perfume of the woman. He loved it.

He speared her as deeply as his tongue could reach until her tight nether mouth suddenly released him, spent as the climax abated. Without pause he continued to bathe her with his mouth. God, but she was the tastiest pussy he'd ever had. He couldn't get enough of her.

With his rooting mouth he sucked on her clit the way he wanted her to suck on his cock. He raised her up and laved the dusky seam of her ass in the way he would have liked her to lick his. He ever so gently bit the flesh of her pussy lips in the same way he would have liked her to bite the skin of his testicles.

Kitty enjoyed every second of it. Her moans and cries and undulations were like small treasures to him, every single one. Gideon loved the way she shuddered when he came too close to her asshole. Adored the kittenish, mewling noises she made whenever he suckled her clit and lips. And when he dug his fingers into the cushion of her bottom—too roughly he feared—she let out a tiny scream and came against his mouth once more.

She was perfect in her passion.

Gideon pulled away and rapidly slid a condom over the thick, engorged flesh of his cock. Kitty moaned and protested the loss of him. He gently slapped her pussy. "Don't be so impatient, kitten. We've got all night."

"Please, Master," she bucked her hips, blatantly showing off the dripping flesh of her cunt for him, knowing instinctively that he would be watching.

His eyes never left her, and the sound of the word "Master" on her lips inflamed him as much as her seductive motions. He positioned the wide head of his cock against her. Pressing only deep enough to warn her of the reality of his size, he held still.

Kitty's head thrashed against the pillows and she moaned.

Gideon lowered his head and sucked one of her coral nipples into his mouth. Here was territory he hadn't paid nearly enough homage to. Rolling the puckered flesh between his lips and teeth, he squeezed and plumped both globes in his hands. Definitely implants. And while he wasn't a man who appreciated the perfection of such artifices, preferring a woman's natural state, he found hers to be incredibly pleasing.

He suckled and bit her nipple until it was rosy red, then moved on to the next. This time he took as much of her into his mouth as he could, and fed deeply on her. He sucked hard, burying his face in the pillowed flesh, taking her nipple to the back of his throat. And every move he made was reciprocated. Kitty's body undulated beneath his, as much as her bonds would allow, and she moaned and thrashed until the sounds of her pleasure echoed in his ears.

Finally, able to stand no more of the sweet torture of resting at the very liquid heart of her, he thrust himself home. Burying himself deep, feeling the tight fist of her clamp down on his length, hearing her broken cry of surprise and pleasure-pain, he felt like he'd finally reached heaven.

Chapter Five

GIDEON LAY ON HIS side, his cock buried deep into Kitty's ass. Hours had passed. His box of condoms was almost empty. He'd pumped himself into her so many times . . . but not nearly enough.

He'd taken her that first time, missionary style, and it hadn't required more than a few strokes to make her come around him. Needing to take the edge of his rapidly growing lust, he'd straddled her face and let her suck him off to completion.

The woman had a wickedly gifted mouth.

Since then he'd fucked her pussy three more times, until the pink flesh had begun to look perhaps a little too well ridden, and then he'd fucked her breasts, her ass and her mouth again. Each time he came, he made sure she came with him, wanting—no, *needing*—her to find release with him for a true completion.

Now he was deep inside of her again, riding the tight

portal of her lubricant-filled ass with an abandon that should have alarmed him. He'd never felt like this. Never been so free with his strength and desire. But Kitty seemed more than woman enough for him. Whenever he pulled away from her, whether to catch his breath or change his condom, she moaned and pleaded prettily for more.

"Master" was now a mantra on her lips, and oh how he loved the sound of it.

Three of his fingers were thrusting gently inside of her pussy—he too could enjoy their ministrations, feeling them with his cock in her behind—making wet, slurping noises to match those of his thrusts in her ass. They were both covered in a sheen of sweat and Kitty's juices. Kitty's legs had long ago been freed, but Gideon loved seeing her held captive and so the handcuffs had stayed.

He felt the clench of her pussy around his fingers a second before her ass clamped down on his cock. She came with a hoarse shout, but the sound was no louder than a whisper. Kitty was tired. Gideon gripped her hips tightly and with a final, deep thrust, he emptied himself one last time.

Their shuddering breaths echoed in the sudden silence of the room. Night had passed them by and the dawn was already rising. Gideon pulled himself gently out of her, kissed her shoulder and peeled off his sodden latex sheath. He retrieved the keys to his handcuffs and freed her.

Kitty smiled, her makeup long since worn off to reveal a delicate peaches-and-cream complexion that was even more beautiful than the powder she'd been wearing earlier. Her mouth was swollen from his kisses and from his gently thrusting cock. Her breasts had his fingerprints stamped all over them and her nipples were longer than any others he'd ever seen from the continued tugging and pinching of his fingers.

The marks of his gentle love bites dotted her from neck to knees. Her stomach and thighs were pink from his whisker burns. Her pussy was red and swollen and her ass was glistening from the generous amounts of scented oil he'd prepared her with.

She was beautiful.

Gideon kissed her, long and thoroughly, stabbing his tongue deep. Reveling in her sweet flavor. When he pulled back she was heavy lidded and dozing off from exhaustion. Feeling the relentless need for sleep himself, he tucked his prize gently into his arms and faded into the land of dreams. Where Kitty's crimson mouth waited and smiled.

THE ANNOYINGLY SHRILL RING of the bedside phone awoke Gideon an hour later. He'd forgotten all about his six o'clock wake-up call. Had forgotten all about his new job that would start in a mere half-hour. But he smiled when he realized the reason for his uncharacteristic loss of memory.

He turned in the bed and was surprised to discover Kitty had gone. Not only was the bed empty, but her clothes and purse were gone along with her, so presumably she hadn't merely risen for an early shower. He cursed a violent blue streak.

Damn the woman anyway. He'd meant to look in her purse for some I.D., to find out where she lived and what her real name was. He was certain it wasn't Kitty. But now it was too late, and she was gone. He'd probably never see her again.

He tried and failed not to be too disappointed about it.

With a black mood brewing he rose and showered. Don Garrison's arrival on the set wasn't scheduled until 11 a.m., but Gideon would be there to whip his crew into shape a lot earlier than that. He had been hired to do a job, and he would do it well. Don Garrison's staff would hate him before it was all over, but Gideon was determined to protect his client from any and all threats.

It was too bad he hadn't protected *himself* from the only threat that had ever come close to actually outgunning him. Kitty had been a dangerous liaison. The woman was too deep for him to figure, and he was a man accustomed to figuring out the most complicated puzzles with ease. A woman like that could get under his skin and he should thank his lucky stars that she was gone.

But he didn't; he damned himself for a fool, but he knew in his heart that he didn't.

Chapter Six

CATHERINE GATHERED WITH THE rest of Don's personal staff to greet Mr. Gideon Fevere. He wasn't exactly as she might have imagined him, but then she'd never met a CIA agent, ex or otherwise. He was all business as he greeted her and the others, asking them each a few curt questions about what they knew of Don's situation.

Don was open with everyone in his entourage, and they all knew exactly what they were up against. They'd each had their run-in with the vociferous protestors outside the Hollywood and Sydney studios since filming had begun on this picture, and they'd seen the e-mails and letters Don had received over the past several days.

Today Don had received the most alarming hate mail to date. A letter, threatening his very safety and the safety of those around him, had been left for him in his trailer before dawn. There had been no witnesses to the strange early morning visitor, and everyone had been questioned just to be certain, but to no avail. It had clearly not been difficult at all for this intruder to slip undetected onto the set.

Gideon was not a man to be trifled with. It was plain for all to see. Within an hour of arriving he had secured the entire area. No one came or went without his knowledge or say-so. It had taken Catherine ten minutes longer to get past security this morning than was usual, all because Mr. Fevere had said no one could pass—either arriving or departing—without his express permission. Catherine could have done without such domineering impertinence, but then she supposed since it was to benefit Don, it could be borne.

For a little while.

She tried to pass for invisible before him. It was usually quite easy for her. No one noticed a pale-faced woman with carelessly styled, chin-length dishwater blonde hair, murky blue eyes beneath a scant fringe of light brown lashes, dressed in stylish but deliberately unflattering clothes. Catherine had perfected the "unnoticeable" look and it had taken years of hard work to do it. She had fun being invisible, after all. But now she wondered if anything escaped the watchful eyes of Mr. Gideon Fevere.

In fact, that's what she was most afraid of.

Handsome in a dangerous, rugged fashion, Gideon was built like a football player with all those huge muscles on his shoulders and thighs. His glossy chestnut hair was a bit long for the look though. Pulled back in a ponytail now, it would fall to his shoulders when freed.

His face was stunning. The very definition of masculine sensuality, he looked like a rogue pirate. His mouth was to die for. Sculpted into a sultry line, his upper lip was much fuller than his bottom one. His nose looked like it had been broken once before, but the crooked line of it saved him from being entirely too lovely. His skin was smooth and unblemished, but the shadow of his beard darkened the clean, strong line of his square jaw. A deep cleft marred the perfection of his chin, and added a dangerously sexy look to a body part Catherine had otherwise previously taken for granted on a man.

His eyes were his best feature. Almond-shaped and violet-blue in color, his eyes should have appeared feminine beneath their long fringe of lashes, but they were all male on the strong planes of his face.

Holy hell, but the guy was scrumptious.

Gideon came before her and shook her hand in greeting. There was an instant when her heart nearly froze in her chest when he seemed to be studying her a little more intently than he had any of the others. But after a moment's pause he seemed to shake himself and moved on. She sighed her relief and left to ready her station for Don's arrival.

The usual protesters came and went outside the studio compound. But nothing was said or heard about the threatening letter Don had received that morning after Gideon had collected it from the shaken actor. Now even Don seemed subdued, remaining uncharacteristically close-lipped about his worries while she and the special effects makeup crew worked their magic on him.

Catherine was more than a little disturbed by that telling fact. Don was usually more concerned with his public image than with his personal safety, but this new development seemed to have shaken him. He was pensive and quiet, and even Johnson the Assistant couldn't draw him out of his shell with the news of the rising positive hype surrounding the film.

It was a long and unsettling day, but it was as easy as ever for Catherine to lose herself in her work. Gideon was everywhere and nowhere, passing before her sight every few hours, but never coming any closer than within nodding distance to her. When Don's shooting schedule was finally over, eighteen hours had passed in strained sluggishness and Catherine was never so happy to go to her hotel as she was then. Even if she did have to go with a security guard as per Gideon's orders that no one leave for the hotel without an escort.

She had braved the long hours, and many more stressful ones would come if Don's stalker had anything to say about it. It should have worried her, if only for Don's sake, but more than anything else, it wasn't the potential threat that concerned her. It was Gideon Fevere who was increasingly on her mind.

She thanked her lucky stars that he didn't know the truth about her.

KITTY GLANCED AT HER watch. As bored as she was, time was creeping by at a snail's pace. Another night off, another night wasted at a singles bar, and she wasn't any better off than when she'd arrived. As usual when she arrived, shooting off her scathing words and laughing too often to be unforgivably insulting, the men crowded around her like bees to the hive.

But tonight it wasn't enough.

There was no satisfaction to be gained in baiting these boys. And *boys* they were. Whenever Catherine looked at one she found herself comparing him to Gideon . . . and finding him sorely lacking. Gideon was a man. The only real man she'd had in her bed in, well, *forever*.

Gideon, Gideon, Gideon. He was all she could think about. It had only been a week since she'd been with him, but already it felt like months. An agonizingly long time. Her body yearned for his masterful touch. Her mouth ached for his tender, yet passionate kisses. She'd been a hopeless wreck since she'd left him the morning after their glorious night of hot, wild sex.

The morning after. It was a time zone all its own to Kitty, after years of playing the singles scene. One-night stands were her specialty, and she liked it that way. No emotional attachments. No hassles. No risks.

No love.

Definitely no love. But then she didn't want love. Couldn't stand the idea of it, because that's all it was, really. An idea. Love was not real. It never had been for her. She'd learned young to avoid it, and in a most unforgettable way. But she wouldn't think about that now.

And she wouldn't think about Gideon Fevere.

But god! He'd been the most amazing lover she'd ever known. Tender and rough in all the right places, and ever conscious of her pleasure before his own. Their night together had been the best ever for Kitty. And now she was beginning to fear that he had ruined her for all other men.

It was a terrifying and depressing thought, that. More and more she was beginning to suspect that she'd made a mistake in her morning after by leaving him without a word the way she had. While forever with Gideon was an option that didn't even enter her mind—not *really*—it would have been nice to have shared a few more evenings with him.

If only to get him out of her system all the more swiftly.

But no matter. Such was life. Ships passing in the night and all those old chestnuts. Kitty was as her feline name implied—at least she hoped so—and she had no doubt she would land on her feet when she reached the bottom of her unexpected fall from grace.

Damn Gideon anyway. No man ever truly mastered Kitty-Kat. Not for long, anyway.

Chapter Seven

TWO WEEKS PASSED. TWO new threatening letters arrived. Don was visibly strained by the worry, as was the rest of his staff. But Gideon Fevere was as calm and cool as always, ever the bastion of strength and purpose in a sea of disquiet. He seemed to have the situation well in hand, had even intercepted the last letter from its paid courier, who was now going to court after being charged with criminal trespass on the lot.

But the true culprit had yet to be found.

Catherine had dealt with the rising tension the best way she could, burying herself in her work, and keeping a close eye on Don when she could. She hadn't had a solid evening off for the past week, putting in far too many hours on the set. But it didn't really matter. She couldn't have enjoyed the time if she'd had it. She felt helpless. Everyone did. And as the filming progressed, the crew seemed to grow more and more vigilant whenever the protesters were nearby . . . and then even when they weren't. The studio compound, and the nearby hotel, had become tiny prisons of a sort for the uneasy crew.

Watching Don rehearse one of his upcoming scenes, Catherine found her mind wandering over the many duties she had yet to perform before the day's work was done. She sighed wearily.

"May I have a word with you, Catherine?" Gideon's voice broke into her reverie.

She started and turned what she hoped weren't entirely guilty eyes to his. "Sure."

"Walk with me."

They turned away from the set and meandered back towards the lot, where stagehands hustled to their chores in the bright afternoon sun.

"Have you heard anything from Don or the others about our stalker?" he asked.

"No," she admitted truthfully.

His hand fell on her back as he guided her easily and gallantly through a small, oncoming crowd of workers. It was warm and strong, that hand. And Catherine had a hell of a time ignoring it, especially when it lingered long after the need for its guiding presence had passed.

"I realize you're in a position to hear a lot of what goes on here. Things even I may not be privy to. Are you sure you haven't heard anything recently that might suggest that Don has received any more threats? Think hard."

Catherine did, but knew she hadn't heard anything of value and told him as much.

Gideon nodded, accepting her response. "Things have

been relatively quiet. Too quiet. I was beginning to wonder if perhaps Don had received more threats without telling me. He doesn't seem as worried about this as he probably needs to be." He cleared his throat. "So. Catherine. You do go by your full name, don't you? Not Cathy or Kate or Katie?"

She swallowed nervously. "No, it's just plain, boring old Catherine."

Gideon's hand moved up and down the line of her spine teasingly. "Not boring. Never that." He smiled down at her with such a look of promise and knowing that she shivered.

Catherine had no idea how to respond. As usual, she was at a loss for words in the face of such blatant invitation. Her quiet, cautious nature asserted itself and she promptly averted her eyes. What Gideon might see in them, she didn't want to chance.

Longing. Need. And a secret knowledge that could damn her if he but looked hard enough to find it.

They arrived at the entrance to her trailer. Catherine stepped forward, unlocking the door with unsteady hands. Knowing it was foolhardy to spend more than the bare minimum of time in his presence, she couldn't fight her growing desire. "Would you like to come in for a cool drink or something?" she asked, part of her hoping he wouldn't hear the need in her voice.

While another part of her hoped he would.

He was close, too close, behind her. The warmth of his breath stirred the fine hairs on her neck and his hand came to rest at her hip. Squeezing.

"I'd love to come in for a cool drink . . . or *something*," he answered in a whisper, his mouth moving against the shell of her ear.

No sooner had they stepped into the trailer, no sooner had the door closed, than they were in each other's arms.

Catherine clutched him to her, the rage of her pent-up passion making her far more eager than she otherwise would have been had her mind been ruling her actions instead of her libido. Gideon seemed as overly eager as she, his hands cupping her bottom into the hard cradle of his thighs, his mouth feeding on hers hungrily.

Their lips, teeth, and tongues clashed. The sound of their ragged breaths filled the silence of the room. Hands too desperate in their need ripped the clothes from their bodies until both were practically nude. Gideon's fingers slipped into the liquid warmth of her pussy and she moaned. Catherine reached between them and cupped his heavy cock in her hand, squeezing until he moaned with her.

"God, I've needed you so much, Catherine," he said against her mouth. "You're so fucking gorgeous in your primness."

Hooking one leg over his hip, riding his hand as it thrust over and over between her thighs, she could barely pay attention to anything he was saying. But it sounded good, his voice sounded good. That was all that mattered, wild as she was to have him, this man whom she barely knew.

But she knew him enough. If only he knew just how much she did know . . . Best not to think about that.

"Take me," she begged. "Please take me, Gideon."

Everything was happening so fast. But it didn't seem to matter. Reason had no place here, in this storm of need and passion. Gideon lifted her up. Catherine wrapped her legs around his waist eagerly. Her back rested against the wall. His mouth burned against hers, against her throat, against her breasts as they rose and fell before him.

Hard and fast he entered her, thrusting to the hilt as if he knew how well they'd fit without testing her first. And they did fit. Perfectly.

His hips moved, thrusting in and out of the wet well of her eager body. Short, gasping screams tore from her throat, over and over. Gideon caught them with his mouth, his tongue stabbing deep and hot. His masterful fingers came between their bodies, unerringly finding the swollen bud of her clit. Pressing, rubbing, squeezing her there, he thrust ever harder, ever faster.

Her head butted against the wall behind her. But the pain was short-lived, and barely noticeable at all. Her body shuddered, trembled, and then came completely undone. She sobbed her release into his mouth, scraping his back with her nails, clutching him tighter to her.

"Oh fuck. *Yes*, kitten, just like that." He moaned as her body squeezed his, her pussy milking his cock hungrily. "Just like that. Take all of me."

With one last mighty thrust, he came with a scalding hot splash into her womb.

Catherine tried hard not to dwell on just how difficult this new development would make their working relationship, then nearly laughed at the absurdity of such a thought. In so delicious a situation as this, what could it matter? She'd been the serious working girl for far too long. It was time for a little adventure.

For the first time in six years she would have fun with a lover as Catherine. Not as the daring Kitty.

TWO DAYS OF SECRET pleasures followed. Gideon visited her every chance he got, in her trailer, in her hotel room—wherever they could find time for a private interlude of passionate lovemaking. Catherine fought the urge to seek him out as well, unwilling to appear too needy in Gideon's eyes, but desiring him so much—all the time in fact—that she couldn't help but entertain the notion in her weaker moments.

It wouldn't do at all to become addicted to the man, she cautioned herself.

Caution be damned, she was already addicted.

For now, Catherine was alone in her own tiny trailer, cleaning her numerous brushes and bottles. She was clearing up to leave when there came a knocking on her door.

"Come in," she called, expecting it to be the arrival of the next day's shooting schedule.

What she didn't expect was the arrival of Gideon Fevere.

"Is something wrong?" she asked, deliberately keeping her back to him while studying her motions as she cleaned her station. She didn't want him to see how very much she wanted him. Her body ached with need already.

"Yes," came his curt reply.

She started and turned to face him. "What?" she asked,

when he wasn't forthcoming with any other conversation, tensions rising.

"The very idea that you seem to think you could have fooled me for this long. That's what's wrong."

Catherine shot up from her seat and put the chair between them. Gideon towered over her, even with the space that separated them as he stood before the door. Her heart pounded a fierce staccato in her breast, and fear—fear unlike any she'd ever known—assailed her with pounding force. Did he think she was behind the letters and threats? Surely that was it, for he couldn't have guessed at the other . . . surely. "W-what are you talking about?"

His eyes burned as they studied her, and Catherine shuddered in apprehension and elemental awareness. For the first time all day she allowed herself to look at him— really look at him—and felt herself melt a little at what she saw, despite his obvious displeasure.

He was every inch the predator, wild and mysterious in the soft light of the room, and no doubt he knew it. His smoldering violet gaze met hers a long moment before he deliberately turned and locked the door behind him with a deafening click. Catherine repressed the urge to flee in the wake of such a telling gesture.

He turned back, but still said nothing. Her unease grew with every passing breath. She studied his face for any sign of his intentions but was sidetracked by his unmistakable male beauty. Sculpted into a sultry line, his upper lip was much fuller than his bottom one, but it had a devastating affect on her libido. She wanted that mouth on her skin. On every inch of her skin.

His heated gaze roved over every inch of her, studying her, drinking her in, before settling once more upon her face. Catherine shifted beneath the intensity of that strong gaze, but refused to avert her own, preferring to challenge him head-on. She knew nothing could be taken for granted about this elegant beast. He was clearly one not to be underestimated, and she was wise enough—and female enough—to see that immediately.

Several minutes passed and neither of them moved or spoke.

"How do you manage to change your appearance so dramatically without changing much at all, Kitty?"

Catherine started. She'd expected him to accuse her of being Don's stalker, but now she realized she should have expected this all along. He was ex-CIA for chrissakes; he was trained to notice even the most minute of details.

She didn't bother to play dumb; it would have done her no good and insulted them both. "I wear extensions in my hair, brown contact lenses, and a lot of makeup. It also helps to hold my face in a stern mask most of the time. Plus the men seem to love it."

"And you dress like a sultry tease," he added, eyeing her plain, concealing tunic and pantsuit derisively.

"Yeah, that too," she allowed.

His hands fisted and his lips twisted as he seemed to be fighting some intense emotion. Catherine only hoped he didn't fly off the handle and strike her. She knew firsthand just how strong he could be even under the most gentle of circumstances. Her pussy actually grew wet with the memory.

"How could you not be honest with me? Tell me who you were? Did you think I wouldn't notice?"

She straightened her posture proudly, something she rarely did when she wasn't dressed as Kitty. "I knew there was the chance that you would. I'm not an idiot and neither are you. But most people wouldn't notice. I almost expected you not to. I take care to keep the resemblances few between myself and Kitty."

"You *are* Kitty."

"I know. But I almost think of her as a separate person. As Catherine I don't act anything like her, really."

"Liar. You treat men abominably no matter what face you're wearing."

She gasped. "I do not!"

"You do. You're friends with no one on the set. No one really knows anything about you, except that you're good at your job. And the men are all afraid of you. Iron Ass is what they call you behind your back."

Catherine almost smiled at the nickname. She'd heard it before, of course. "They just call me that because I've turned at least two of them down when they asked me out."

"And because of how curt you are. And your eyes are hard as nails when you do speak a few words to any of them."

"I'm quiet, *okay*? I don't talk to anybody that much, male or female. I'm not a man-hater, so quit making it sound like I am."

"I heard and saw how you treated those men in the bar that night, Kitty. I'm not blind. You loved making them squirm. You liked beating at their pride."

She snorted. "And so what? Did you hear them protesting? It's all a game to them, to every one of them. Survival of the fittest, the best man wins the girl. The man who can take the most punishment and still keep his dignity is the one who gets to fuck me. It's the same in every city, in every country. The single dating scene is a sea of sharks and guppies."

"Or cats and mice."

Catherine chuckled, unashamed of his comparisons to her nickname. "Or cats and mice. Whatever floats their boat."

"It's all lies. Everything about you is a lie. Even these past few days have been a lie, haven't they?"

She gasped. "I never lied to you."

"Your appearance was a lie. Your fake Aussie accent was a lie. Your hair was fake, your eyes were fake—hell, even your tits are fake. I don't know if you're this quiet, unflappable Catherine—tender in bed and all business outside of it—or the raucous, derisive Kitty who thinks of men as nothing but playthings. Is anything real about you? Is anything you do sincere?"

Heart hurting at his words, she clutched her breasts in her hands. Yes, they were implants, and she'd gotten them at a time when she had been very insecure about the small size of her chest. She'd never heard a man complain so vehemently about them as Gideon had, though. "My tits are none of your business," she exclaimed, refusing to address the other, more hurtful things he'd said.

Gideon advanced on her threateningly, his eyes dark and stormy as she'd never seen them before. "You didn't say that when my dick was cushioned between them only this morning," he bit out.

She gasped again, and immediately choked on her air. "Don't you dare speak to me that way—"

"Lady, you haven't got any idea of what I can dare to do. Not yet. Not by a long chalk."

"If you're threatening me, Gideon, I swear I'll get your ass fired."

"Go ahead. I hate working for that pompous brat you call a boss anyway. Just seeing you rub your tits against him while you work makes me sick. And you will call me Master, Kitty-Kat." He spat out her name like it was a distasteful epithet. "I thought you'd learned that lesson by now."

Catherine was at a loss for words. As Kitty she was a pro at handling male egos and umbrage. But she had no idea how to handle an angry Gideon, as Kitty, Catherine or otherwise. His words hurt her, cutting her to the quick. But she'd be damned if she'd let him see that. Her pride simply wouldn't allow it.

"You're an asshole, Gideon. I am never anything less than impeccably professional in my work. Neither Don nor I would allow for less. You can impugn my personality and my appearance, but never my work. Just as I would never impugn yours." She kept her words clipped and staccato, wanting more than anything for the conversation to end.

"I feel like I don't know you," he said, surprising her.

"Of course you don't know me. You know nothing about me. We've only fucked, you and I. Whether I was Catherine or Kitty, that's all it was. It wasn't important for us to know anything tangible about each other." She folded her arms across her chest, avoiding his gaze. But she was so shocked by his next words that her gaze immediately shot back to his.

He eyed her intently, making her edgy and nervous beneath his unwavering gaze. "Your name is Catherine Meagle Stowe," he said, "age twenty-seven, very close to twenty-eight. You were born in West Palm Beach, Florida, though you later moved to Atlanta, Georgia, at the age of eleven."

Catherine started in surprise.

"You're practically estranged from your parents, who have been divorced and remarried twice. You live alone and have ever since your third year in college, which you never finished because of a row you had with your boyfriend."

"Fiancé," she whispered brokenly, but he didn't seem inclined to hear her and merely talked more rapidly over her small voice, listing the contents of her life as though he were reading the ingredients of a cereal box.

"You've worked hard to be one of the best in your field, making yourself indispensable to your rising star of a boss. At the age of twenty-four you began to use your free evenings to perfect the image of Kitty, picking up men in bars like a kid in a candy store. I could list the exact number of flings you've had over the years, but I'm sure you don't want to hear it so bluntly. None of your relationships have lasted more than a week since college, yet you seem to revel in that fact, not lament it. Between work and the endless dating, you have few friends. Your favorite food is—"

"Stop, stop. *Just stop it right now!*" Catherine's breath sobbed as she fought against the unexpected urge to weep.

"I don't care how you know all this, or why, but you can just shut up about it. I know who I am. I don't need to hear you criticize the way I live just because your male pride is all bruised and sore."

"I know everything about you, Kitty. Things even you have forgotten about yourself."

"So?" It took every ounce of willpower she possessed not to burst into tears at the look in his eyes. The burn of anger was being replaced by dull disgust and she couldn't bear to see it directed at her so unflinchingly.

"So don't say I know nothing about you, because you're wrong," he replied. "I know plenty. And if you'd only care to ask, I'd tell you everything you could ever want to know about myself."

They stared at each other in silence for a long while. Finally, he swept his fingers through his hair, releasing it from the tie at his nape. It was as beautiful unbound as it was tied back to reveal his strong, masculine face. But it made her heart bleed to see it so close and know that she'd never get to run her fingers through it again.

His gaze cut her open and laid her bare. His hoarse questions surprised her. "Didn't you feel anything these past few days we've spent together? Anything at all besides basic lust?"

Catherine failed to keep the tears at bay after all, and her vision swam with them as her eyes flooded with the sea of her pain. She searched for an answer that they could both accept. "I can't answer that," she said finally.

Gideon was upon her before she could blink the tears from her lashes. His fingers bit cruelly into her shoulders, lifting her effortlessly onto the very tips of her toes. He looked down into her face, gritting his teeth against the force of his pent-up emotions. "You can't or you *won't* answer that?"

She lashed out in an effort to defend her breaking heart, a heart she'd felt certain was impervious to any attack before now. "Just what do you want from me, Gideon? An apology for pulling the wool over your eyes, however brief a time it was? Will that assuage your wounded pride?"

"All I want is for you to tell me that the time we've shared has held some meaning for you. That you regret leaving me that morning and lying to me, even through omission, these past weeks. And especially during these past few days. I want you to admit you want me still, even knowing your secrets as I do."

But she couldn't give him what he wanted. Her pride was the only thing that kept her going, the only friend she'd ever really had. To let it go, especially for him, was to lie down and die at his feet. Her feelings for him were the greatest weapon he would ever have against her, and she'd once sworn never to arm an opponent with such a deadly arsenal again. So she said what she could to ensure her freedom. She spoke the words she knew Gideon would find most unforgivable.

It was the hardest thing she had ever done.

"But I don't want you. I had you once as Kitty, and several times as Catherine. That's enough for both of my selves. Now leave me alone, or I *will* get you fired for sexual harassment."

Chapter Eight

CATHERINE INWARDLY FLINCHED AWAY from the cut and betrayed look in Gideon's eyes. Now that she'd said such callous words, she regretted them wholeheartedly. She wished to call them back, more than anything, but it was too late. The pain on Gideon's face was enough to let her know that she had won. He would leave her alone now. The threat to her heart was averted at last.

Why then, did that traitorous organ hurt as if struck by a mortal wound?

Softly, oh so very softly he spoke his final piece. "You're incredibly lovely, Kitty. But you're so very full of spite. And why? Because you were hurt once—*once*. Some women would kill for the chances you've had in life. You'll never be happy, carrying around as much emotional baggage as you do. But I guess you will be *safe*. And that's what's most important to you, isn't it?"

A long look from his deep, violet eyes and he was gone.

Without another word or glance in her direction, he turned and left the trailer. The door banged softly shut, even as Catherine swayed unsteadily on her feet.

"Oh God, I'm sorry," she whispered, giving in to the tears at last. "I'm sorry, *sorry, sorry*." She sank to her knees and wept, knowing she was no better than anybody who'd hurt her in her own past. And that was when she realized she no longer had any pride left to sustain her. Any claim to self-righteousness was lost to her when she'd opened her mouth and cut into Gideon with her lies.

And she had lied. From the beginning. To herself and to Gideon.

A long while later, eyes swollen and cheeks stained from her tears, Catherine exited her trailer. For the first time since Gideon had arrived on the set, she ignored one of his principal rules: Only leave the lot in the escort of a security guard. She left the studio grounds and made to walk the short blocks to her hotel alone.

And that was why she never saw her abductor, until it was far too late to scream.

SEVERAL MINUTES AFTER HIS confrontation with Catherine, Gideon felt a bit more in control of himself again. Enough to seek her out and talk to her once more. He was determined to get her to admit to her feelings for him. He wasn't blind. He knew she cared. It was just hard for her to admit to any *tendre* between them, to herself as much as him, he knew.

But when he arrived at her trailer, he was surprised to find her already gone.

For the past two weeks, ever since that first day on the set when he'd realized almost at once who she was—or who she was to him—he'd been studying her every move. She'd never once left her trailer, or hotel room without his knowledge and watchful eye. He'd tried to assure himself that what he was doing wasn't exactly spying; she was, after all, in his care as one of Don's entourage. And then, as his tentative lover. Therefore, it wasn't entirely unethical for him to follow her so doggedly.

Right?

The things he'd witnessed while following were the best reasons he was so certain she *did* care for him. After all, when she'd gone to a bar barely a week after their first encounter, she'd been edgy and unapproachable all evening. No man had gotten within ten feet of her without being blasted by her withering scorn.

He felt no shame at the self-satisfied pride he'd experienced when he realized that she'd been comparing each and every man to him. He could see it there, plain as day, in the lines of her face. She was pining for him, as much as he was for her. Though he knew she'd never in a million years admit to it.

She hadn't gone out as Kitty since.

Finding her gone from the studio lot, he went to check in with his many security guards for any reports of her departure. It would have been catalogued by time and date and whoever had escorted her off the compound.

But to his surprise there was no record of her ever leaving.

Following instinct more than reason, he left on foot in

the direction of her hotel. All of Don's people were staying in the same lodgings and he knew the route well. After the first block, his instincts kicked into overdrive and he began to run.

It was a fortunate thing too. He was just in time to see Catherine being stuffed like a sack of flour into the trunk of an old and rusted sedan. Despite the terror in his heart, his mind was a sea of well-trained calm as he noted every detail of the car and hailed a passing cab.

Chapter Nine

"WAKEY, WAKEY, LITTLE FISH."

Catherine's mouth felt cottony and dry. A sweetly soured taste coated her tongue like milk and her head throbbed and pounded painfully. It was dark, her vision black, but it took her only a few short seconds to realize it wasn't blindness she was suffering. A thick hood covered her head in suffocating blackness. Her hands were tied behind her back, and she was lying on a cold, concrete floor. Other than that she had no idea what was going on.

"You awake, girlie?"

She moaned softly as she tried and failed to rise from her prone position. Her head swam violently and it was a long while before she could hear the man as he continued to speak.

"Now don't try and get up; there's no need to stand on manners here. You just stay down there and keep quiet."

It took her three tries to be able to speak audibly.

"What do you want with me?" She hated how powerless she sounded, and no doubt appeared, but there was no helping it. That's what powerlessness really was, she supposed.

A sharp and brutal pain exploded in her face as her captor struck her cheek in swift reply. Had he used his fist or foot or something else? It felt like the last, though she'd never been struck with any of them so she couldn't be sure.

"I told you to keep quiet! Don't make me hit you again, you sinning whore. The chloroform hasn't worn off yet, and I don't want to lose you too soon."

It was the sinning comment that made her realize just how dangerous her situation was. This was no idle crime, but a well-planned abduction with a horrible purpose. Catherine had no doubt she was in the presence of Don's stalker, the religious fanatic who was none too happy over the film that dared to show some of the apostles *in flagrante delicto*.

His next words proved her hypothesis true.

"You Hollywood types are all a bunch of corrupt sinners, full of greed and loose morals. It's about time someone taught your kind a lesson, and I'm just the God-fearing man to do it, amen."

Catherine was afraid to say anything, afraid he would strike her again. She wasn't sure she could handle it. Sure, in the movies, the hero and heroine always seemed able to get up and win the battle after being dealt such a blow. But in the real world, Catherine felt like she'd already lost what fight might have been left in her after such a brutal punishment. Her face felt like half of it was missing, like the bones were crushed and mangled, though she knew it couldn't possibly be that bad.

Though the warm trickle of salty blood against her lips did make her wonder just how much damage was real and how much was imagined.

"Ain't you got nothing to say now, girlie?"

She barely managed the murmur, "But you told me not to make a sound."

A sharp pain stung her shin. It was definitely his boot that had struck her this time; she'd felt the leather and laces as he lashed out. In the sea of pain that was drowning her, she found there was enough sarcasm still left within her to lament that her captor hadn't worn softer tennis shoes instead.

"Don't sass me! Don't you dare sass me."

Catherine wisely kept quiet.

"You know why I'm here, don't you? You little whore. You and all your people have been watching for me, haven't they? Well, God and all his avenging angels are on my side, and your hoity-toity bodyguards will never even get close to catching me no matter how hard they look."

He laughed, and to Catherine it sounded maniacal and wholly twisted. She began to shake in fear and, she supposed, a bit of shock as well. Her body was going cold and she was still drowsy from the chloroform he had used to drug her into submission. She began to wonder if she'd ever see Gideon again.

She would give anything to take back her angry words to him. If she died here, if this man killed her, she didn't want Gideon to remember her hateful lies in her trailer. She wanted him to remember their recent time together, when she'd been more herself than at any other time over the past six years. When she had begun to love him.

She did love him. But had she shown *him* how she felt? She hadn't said anything. Before now had she even dared to acknowledge it to herself, this depth of feeling she'd never hoped to feel again? But Gideon was a man who seemed to see everything. Had he seen the thawing of her icy heart? Had he known he'd finally mastered and commanded her love, both when she'd been Kitty *and* Catherine? She supposed she'd never know now.

"Now that you're awake, let me tell you how things are going to be. You make one sound and I'll kill you. No screaming, no moaning, and definitely no escape attempts. You understand?"

Catherine nodded, and hoped the man could see the motion beneath the enveloping hood.

"Good. Now I'm gonna step out and get some more rope and make a more comfortable place for you to rest. You may be a sinner and a whore, but God is merciful and so will I be."

Catherine dared to ask the one question she needed answered most desperately. "What will you do with me?"

He seemed inclined to answer her this time. "Well, let's see. I'm gonna fight and win against the powers of evil. If your boss won't drop out of this film, and if this studio won't quit making this abomination altogether, I'll send them pieces of you. One at a time, until they have to quit, to save your life."

Warming up to his topic with the true fervor of a zealot, he continued. "I'll start with your fingers, and then move on to your toes, and if that don't work—I think it will—I'll send them your cute little ears. They'll have to stop production sooner or later, else I'll run out of parts and start sending 'em your organs."

Catherine shied away as the man patted her shoulder in what was probably meant to be a soothing manner. Terror filled her throat with the sour sting of bile.

He laughed again. "Don't you worry none about the pain, though. I got enough painkillers and chloroform here to take the edge off for you. And I won't let you bleed to death. You won't suffer too much, girlie."

Catherine heard him stomp away, each step sounding like a death knell in her ears. A door slammed, presumably leaving Catherine alone to dwell on all that the man had said. Dear, sweet heaven, she was dealing with a total madman. How, she wondered amidst her nearly overwhelming terror, was she going to get out of this alive?

A long time passed in silence and darkness. It was stuffy beneath the hood, and before too long Catherine almost began to hope that she'd suffocate before her captor could get a chance to mutilate her. It felt like hours had passed, though she had no way of knowing for sure how much time had really elapsed. Each minute was an eternity of dread in her mind.

She struggled to sit up, though it was a difficult, slow, and very painful process. Her face was definitely swollen, though the bleeding seemed to have stopped. Her shin hurt, but it was a trifle compared to her face. Finally, she managed to push behind her with her bound hands, and with the strength of her stomach muscles she sat up into a sitting position.

Not sure what bound her wrists, whether it was rope or

duct tape or something else, she struggled to loosen the restraints. But to no avail. Her captor had secured her well. Catherine had no idea what to do next, but she knew she had to do something if there was to be any hope for her survival.

Unexpectedly the door opened and slammed once again. Catherine whimpered, seeing her chance at escape flee in the face of her captor's return.

It was therefore quite a shock to hear Gideon's voice in the dark of her frightened world.

"Catherine, baby doll, are you hurt?"

She sobbed out her relief. "Gideon! No, I'm okay. Please get me loose before he comes back."

Gideon was already working on her bound hands and soon they were free. He pulled the hood from her face before she even had a chance to, and he took her face in his hands. The pain in her cheek was insignificant as he rained kisses all over her face.

"I've never been so scared in my life, woman. Don't ever pull a stunt like this again," he commanded imperiously.

Catherine gasped and felt her tears dry instantly. "Don't blame me for this, you arrogant son of a—"

The twinkle in his eyes let her know he'd goaded her for just such a reaction. "Feel better at all?"

She smiled. "Yeah." Looking down, she noticed the handgun he held. "You saved me," she said softly.

"I'll always save you, kitten."

"I'm sorry I said all those horrible things to you." Her voice cracked.

Gideon pulled her close into the protective circle of his

arms and held her. "Shh. I'm sorry too. We can make it up to each other later, but for now, let's get out of here."

Catherine looked around at her prison. It looked like a small garage, full of tools and dusty equipment. It smelled like gasoline and the floor was covered in oil stains. A small, dirty cot was nestled against a bare wall. Catherine wondered if her captor slept there.

Gideon gave her one last squeeze and made to rise. Before they could gain their feet, the door to the garage opened and banged shut. Her captor had returned.

"Well, well, well. I can't leave you alone for a minute, can I?" Taking Gideon by surprise, the man raised an iron bar and swiftly knocked the gun from his hand. Gideon quickly pushed Catherine behind his back but not before she got a good look at their aggressor.

The man was small, not much taller than she. He was thin and gaunt, but well groomed. His hair was a graying blond and slicked back over his high forehead, his nose a beak over thin, pursed lips.

Catherine noticed his union-issue jumpsuit and immediately recognized him. "You're one of the Gang Grips on the set. That's how you came and went, dropping your notes off in the early hours without anyone noticing."

"Doing my eight 'n skate just like always," he said, referring to his eight-hour shifts that started at six a.m. most mornings. "No one notices us peons with men like your boss running around."

"Are you working alone or have you some accomplices waiting in the wings to bail you out?" Gideon asked him softly.

The man seemed unhappy to have to speak to Gideon, and

sneered. "Me and those hundred others protesting this film are never alone. God is on our side and He will prevail, amen."

"Then you are alone. Why don't you come quietly and this will all be over without anyone getting hurt?"

The man smiled, then chuckled. He pointed at Catherine who peeked out from behind Gideon's back. "Your whore's already been hurt for opening her fool mouth," he goaded stupidly. "She learned real quick not to mess with divine justice, hallelujah."

Gideon glanced back at her, and Catherine realized that in his hurry to get her free and clear of danger he hadn't even noticed her bruised cheek. But he most certainly did now. His eyes hardened and darkened as a storm of anger stained them almost black. Surprising both her and her captor, Gideon turned and rushed the man in a blindingly quick move.

The man had no chance to raise his weapon, Gideon was that fast. As he landed a solid punch to the man's nose, there came the deafening crunch of broken cartilage and bone, and Gideon quickly followed with another punch to his jaw. The man fell back, unconscious and unmoving. That quickly, that easily, the threat was over. Gideon hadn't needed a gun or an iron pipe at all. His fists had done the job as well as any weapon could have.

"Fucker. I should beat him to death," Gideon grumbled even as he stepped away from the fallen man.

"No. Let's just get out of here and let the cops deal with this." Catherine shuddered.

"You're right. Well, at least your boss will get some publicity out of this. He should like that."

Catherine laughed, then winced as her cheek throbbed. "Yeah, there is that."

Gideon pulled her close and lightly touched her cheek. "It's not broken, but it'll bruise really badly before all's said and done."

"Great. At least I have something to look forward to," she grumbled.

"What are you complaining about? I know firsthand how well you can ply your cosmetics to fix a little bruise," he teased. "Come on. Let's get you back to the hotel and cleaned up. We'll get my guys over here to make sure this creep doesn't leave. Other than that, I don't want to see the bastard again. You're right, the cops can clean this mess up."

Catherine had never been so happy to lean on another person in her life, as Gideon led her from the building.

Chapter Ten

IT WAS SEVERAL HOURS before Catherine could lie down to rest after her trying ordeal. Gideon was right, her cheek did swell and blacken, but the bone was thankfully unbroken, and her shin was tender but otherwise fine. After speaking to several police officers and detectives, her face felt like it was throbbing with fire, but there were so many questions to answer that she couldn't simply crawl into a corner and sleep, as she so desperately wanted to.

To her surprise the garage where she'd been held was actually a storage and repair room on the studio lot. Gideon had followed her abductor through back alley after back alley before the man—a Mr. Thomas Sean—had doubled back to the studio. All of Mr. Sean's tail-losing maneuvers had been no match for the seasoned cab driver Gideon had procured, however. Promising the cabbie a rich fare had ensured that their prey stayed well in sight until the end of the odd chase. And strangely enough, despite Sean's paranoid behavior, he hadn't even seen his pursuers.

Thomas Sean had worked alone, to some people's surprise. After all the picketing and protesting of the film, many expected there to be a whole conspiracy of stalkers involved. It was hard to believe that Don's crew had lived in fear of just one man. But Sean was a true zealot, a loner with crazy ideals that went far beyond the boundaries of reason. His sort worked best on their own.

After the police had gone, and after her kidnapper had been taken away, Catherine felt as if an immense weight had been lifted off her shoulders. Gideon was there with her the entire time, keeping a close watch on her, seeing to her every comfort and need. Though she protested his decree that she remain out of work for at least a few days, she was touched that he seemed to care so completely for her in the hours she needed him most.

In Gideon's hotel room, where he'd taken her immediately to get her a bath while they waited on the authorities, she finally fell asleep on the long sofa. Dawn was already rising beyond the windows; a new day had come at last.

She didn't hear when Gideon rose from his seat beside her and quietly left the room.

"WAKE UP, SLEEPYHEAD."

For a moment Catherine thought she was still in that storage room, and that the voice belonged to her kidnapper. But her vision cleared and she saw Gideon's handsome face staring down into hers.

"Here, drink this." Gideon handed her a glass of water and some aspirin. "How badly does it hurt now?"

Catherine reached up and felt her face. The swelling had gone down considerably and though it was sore when she touched it, it was no longer throbbing. "Much better."

"Well it looks a helluva lot worse." He eyed her critically.

"Gee thanks," she quipped and downed the aspirin.

He rose and moved to the kitchenette counter where several paper bags waited. "I bought you some soft foods. You shouldn't chew on that side of your mouth for a few days. It'll heal faster if you don't."

"Did you get me a steak to hold against it for the swelling?"

"No. I've found it doesn't work all that well and makes your skin smell horrible."

Catherine laughed. "I thought all macho men put steaks on their black eyes."

"Only if they want to attract any dogs in the area." He looked back with a grin.

Catherine watched as he put away the supplies. One paper bag remained when he turned and came to perch before her on the coffee table, and he was suddenly serious.

"You could've been killed last night. Very easily. I could've gone looking for you a minute too late and you'd still be stuck in that storage building right now going through who knows what kinds of tortures."

Catherine felt a surge of terror at the thought. "But you weren't a minute too late. You saved me." She started realizing all that he'd said. "You mean you actually came looking for me? After our fight?"

Gideon sighed. "We need to talk about that, you and I. We need to talk about a lot of things. But first"—he reached over and took her hands between his, holding them in a fierce grip—"you're going to swear to me that you'll never break one of my rules again. Whether on the set or anywhere else."

"Wait, I'm not going to promise that."

"You will promise it, Kitty. I mean it."

"My name is Catherine, Gideon. You've used it before."

He ignored her. "Promise me."

"O-okay. I promise. I didn't really mean to break the rules, I just wasn't thinking clearly at the time," she defended.

"I don't care. Your obedience should be automatic."

Catherine straightened her spine at his imperious tone. "I'll obey myself and no one else unless it suits me."

Gideon winked. "Then I guess I'll have to make it worth your while to obey me all the time." He rose and pulled her up from the couch. "Come on."

She dug in her feet for a moment but he only dragged her behind him, heedless of her stubbornness. "What do you think you're doing?" she demanded.

Gideon pulled her into the bedroom before he answered. "I'm going to show you how fun it is to obey your Master."

Catherine shuddered, but for the first time in twenty-four hours it was with something other than fear. It was with desire.

Chapter Eleven

I'VE BEEN PREPARING THIS room for the time when I'd get you back here. It's why I've kept you away the past couple of days we've been together. I didn't know if you'd noticed that, by the way," he said.

She had. But she'd assumed he hadn't wanted to make love to her in the same bed he'd so recently had Kitty—a woman he should have thought was an entirely different person altogether—so she hadn't given it much thought. And she'd certainly never guessed he'd been keeping them out of his room for any other purpose. Especially this.

Catherine looked about the room with wide eyes. Gideon had turned the bedroom into a collage of forbidden sexual devices. A pleasure swing graced one corner, a collapsible rack in another, and the bed had been rigged to accommodate all sorts of rope bondage possibilities. Her pussy was soaking wet and her mouth was dry by the time her eyes met his once again.

"You can't be serious," she managed. Oh, how she hoped he was.

Gideon merely smiled in response.

"I'm not doing this," she lied.

"If you won't do it willingly, I'll have to force you."

Oh please do, she thought. "Try it and see what happens."

He was on her in the space of a breath. Using his full strength, and arousing her to a feverish pitch, he tore her clothes from her body with ease. The tatters of cloth dotted the room by the time he was finished and she was standing, naked and panting before him.

"What will it be first? The rack or the swing? I've been dreaming of using them both for too long, so choose quickly."

"Neither," she defied, standing proudly in her nudity before him.

"Then I choose the rack. You're in sore need of a spanking, slave."

Catherine squealed as he easily caught her and carried her to the rack. The design was such that it was merely a sturdy metal frame from which a person could be suspended or merely secured. Gideon cuffed her arms and legs to the rig so that she stood high on her tiptoes, legs braced far apart, her wrists held wide over her head. Surprising her, Gideon turned and left the room, but was back within seconds with the last paper bag he'd had in the kitchenette.

From the bag he pulled a small cat-o'-nine-tails whip and brandished it before her with a smile. But instead of the usual soft leather tails such a whip sported, this one sported long, thick braids of silk. He also showed her the other contents of the bag. A slender, petite butt plug made of clear glass, golden-chained nipple clamps, pussy weights and scented oils. By the time he was through showing her his treasure trove of toys, Catherine was panting loud enough for them both to hear her rising excitement.

Gideon had been a busy boy.

"Are you ready, kitten?"

She moaned and licked her too-dry lips.

He chuckled and laid the items, side by side on the floor in front of her where she could easily see them. Slowly, with a secretive smile, he brought the oil and glass anal plug to her. He let her smell the oil, a delicious strawberry scent, and bid her kiss the plug. She did so, to his obvious pleasure, and he watched her lips press against the cool clear glass with the hungry eyes of a predator.

He stood behind her and kissed her shoulder. Having him stand just beyond her line of sight was unsettling, but incredibly arousing. It reminded her of how erotic it had been to be blindfolded that night, not knowing when or where he would touch her, his every move a surprise.

She felt his mouth move down her shoulder to her spine. He traced the long line of her back with his lips and tongue, laving her with the liquid heat of his kiss. When he knelt behind her and spread her bottom cheeks wide, she stiffened, but in surprise not protest.

The bonds that held her hands were a blessing that kept her from collapsing on suddenly weak knees when she felt Gideon lick the seam of her anus. He laved her thoroughly and she moaned, the pleasure so intense it made her dizzy.

She felt him prod a well-oiled finger, knuckle deep, into her anus. And all the while he continued licking and kissing her tender flesh, easing the way for a deeper penetration.

With her legs spread wide, ankles secure, she could only dangle there as he gave her the wicked loving. Her pussy was wet and throbbing. Every lick and suck he gave her made her pulse with pleasure. She was shaking with need when finally she felt the cool prod of the glass plug.

Gideon's mouth eased her flesh as it protested the intrusion. His tongue laved away any small discomfort and heightened the helpless pleasure as the plug slid home. Soon it was seated fully inside of her, filling and stretching her, heavy and hard in the depths of her bottom.

She felt him pull away and saw him pass in front of her to retrieve the whip.

"I'll wet the silk to make it sting. You've been a very naughty girl, kitten."

He poured a generous amount of oil onto the braided silk strips of the whip, soaking the material.

"G-Gideon," she started nervously.

"Shh," he said and kissed her mouth gently. "Trust me. You'll love it."

It was hard but she held back her nervousness as he once again moved behind her. Several seconds later it was a surprise and pleasure to feel the sting of the whip on the flesh between her spread legs. The whip stung her pussy again, and again, until it was burning with desire and soaking her thighs with the juice of her arousal.

Gideon used the whip on her buttocks, still filled so pleasurably with the glass plug, and on her thighs, until she was trembling and moaning with tortured lust. She was on fire with need. Her body burned from head to toe, her nipples were hard and aching points, and she'd never had so much fun in her life.

She was so dazed with pleasure that she hardly noticed when he came before her again. But she definitely noticed when he bent his head and took her breast deep into his mouth. Moaning around his mouthful of flesh, he vibrated her nipple until it elongated and throbbed.

With a loud pop, he released her and moved on to the next, leaving the first to be played by his masterful hands. His fingers pinched and pulled one nipple, while he bit and licked and sucked upon the next. Catherine moaned and thrashed against her bonds, seeking to arch up into his hungry hands and mouth. Gideon merely pinched her nipple cruelly in erotic punishment for her struggles.

Catherine was almost sobbing with need when he finally eased his torment. He secured the nipple clamps over the wet, erect flesh of her nipples, the golden chain dangling heavily between them so that she was aware of the sweet torture at all times.

Soon he was as naked as she, though she'd missed his disrobing, a sight she would have dearly loved to see. He squatted beneath her spread legs and brought his mouth to the red, aching lips of her sex. It was just the balm she needed. Within seconds she was coming, raining her juices unchecked down into Gideon's waiting lips and mouth. He sucked her dry and when she was spent, he released her from her bonds and carried her, limp, to the waiting pleasure swing.

Positioning her with ease, he sat her in the cradle of the sling seat and secured her ankles so that they were widespread and high in the air. He stepped between them and entered her with one long, smooth thrust.

"Oooh, I'd forgotten how big—" she moaned and was stunned as another small orgasm shook her.

"You'll never forget again after I'm through with you, kitten," he promised.

Still embedded within her he fastened the small pussy weights to the lips of her sex so that they unfurled, wide and open to his thrusts. He moved, in and out of her wet heat, over and over until she was keening like a wild, tortured animal.

She was almost upside down as she lay back in the swing, her ankles up about Gideon's shoulders as he moved within her. Her body was so wet it made sucking noises every time he withdrew. The plug in her ass stabbed deep and heavy with every slight motion they made.

Through the aid of the swing he controlled the force and angle of his thrusts with ease. "Oh Master, yes, yes," she murmured over and over, mindless to anything other than him and his complete dominance over her every pleasure.

Soon she was coming on every down stroke, tiny orgasms that lasted only seconds but gripped her body in a mercilessly erotic grip. Gideon's fingers dug into her hips with each and every pulse her body made around his cock. He held back as long as he could but soon he was pounding into her body with the force of a battering ram, speeding towards his own release with helpless abandon.

Catherine shouted and felt her pussy clamp down on his pistoning cock, milking him. The most intense orgasm she'd ever experienced wracked her body until she was thrashing about in the swing. As the release took her deeper and deeper into ecstasy, she heard him shout along with her and felt him pump his hot seed deep into the well of her body.

His essence spilled out onto the hot flesh of her rear, stinging her with its delicious heat. Gideon groaned hoarsely as his cock pulsed one last time in the milking fist of her cunt. His head fell back, sweat pouring from his face and shoulders, making him shine like a god.

Minutes later, after they'd calmed, he freed her from the swing and carried her to the bed. He surprised her by tying her wrists securely from the rig suspended above it.

"So you can't leave me before I wake." He winked at her.

He gathered her in his arms, gently removed the glass plug and positioned his cock at her rear. Gently, slowly, he slid into her. Feeling stretched and dominated she cried out and felt him reach around to soothe her with circular strokes against the tight swell of her clit. He thrust deeper, seating himself fully and they both moaned with the pleasure of his mastery.

Burying his lips in the crook of her neck, Gideon sighed, and fell asleep, buried balls deep in her anus. Exhausted, Catherine soon followed even as pleasure sang through her blood. Sleep had never been so good.

Chapter Twelve

CATHERINE SLOWLY AWOKE TO the feel of full thrusts of Gideon's cock, deep within her soaking pussy. Her ankles were bound, her legs spread wide. Her nipples and pussy were still held in their clamped weights, which swayed deliciously with his every motion. She moaned and thrust back as best she could against the restraints that held her.

"I love you, Catherine," he said and kissed her fully awake.

The bed creaked with their motions. His loving was gentler this time and somehow deeper. He rocked softly atop her, thrusting deep and strong, his arms holding her close. It was one of the most beautiful and frightening experiences Catherine had ever known.

For a long time, Gideon slid in and out of her welcoming heat. Catherine gasped and moaned, soft and tender in the moment. Lost in the beauty of Gideon's generous heart.

"Free my hands," she begged in a breathless whisper.

He did so, never breaking his gentle rhythm. Catherine put her hands around his sweat-soaked back and held him tight. Her chained breasts rubbed deliciously against the fur of his muscled chest. Their mouths met in kiss after scorching deep kiss. Their moans filled each other's mouths, making a sweet music in the air around them.

The pace of their thrusts increased. Gideon groaned and shook above her. Catherine bit her lip and felt her womb open and tremor. With one last, deep drive home, they both came in perfect unison, crying out softly even as they kissed and found release together.

Gideon collapsed onto her, his heavy weight pressing her down into the mattress. His sweat-dampened hair fell over her face like a dark curtain as they both fought for breath. The drumbeat of his heart was an echo of her own as they slowly calmed.

Pulling back, his violet gaze burned down into hers. "I do love you, you know."

She didn't know how to respond.

He sat back, pulling her into a sitting position in front of him. "You love me too, Catherine. It's all right to admit it. I would never hurt you like he did."

Unable to meet his gaze she turned her head away. "I'm not scared that you would," she lied.

"Good. Because you're old enough and wise enough by now to know that not all men are dumbasses like Mike was."

Her gaze shot back to his in surprise. "How did you find out—?"

"I've got my ways. It wasn't hard." He turned and reached under the bed and lifted a thick, manila folder onto the bed. "Mike's entire life is in these pages, from birth to now. If it's any consolation, he's just as much a loser now as he ever was." He held it out for her to take.

She snorted, both surprised and confused that he'd bothered to find out so much about her past. "I'm sure he is."

"Do you still love him?"

Laughing, she pushed the folder aside. "I was never in love with him, only with the idea of being settled down, I think."

"That's good. Because if you did, I'd have to make his life a living hell. It would be no sweat off my back to, at the very least, destroy his credit and criminal record with a couple of phone calls."

She started. "Can you really do that?"

"Say the word and I'll do it now," he promised, in all seriousness.

"No way. He's *so* not worth the effort," she laughed. "I promise you, I'm over him."

"But you're not over the pain he and Norah caused you."

He'd managed to surprise her again. She began to realize just how resourceful he was, and how determined he'd been to uncover her past. "No, I'm over it." And she really was, she finally realized. "I've just been stuck in this role of being a bachelorette, loving men and leaving them, with no emotional entanglements to muck up the place."

In a surprisingly swift move he pounced on her, spilling

Mike's folder and its contents onto the floor. He laid her back and thrust into her, stunning her with the strength and force of it after such a gentle loving.

"I promise you that you'll love me, but never leave me, not again. There will always be plenty of emotion between us. And you can get used to the idea of settling down all over again—in some form or another—with me. I'm not letting you crawl back into your invisible shell ever again."

"You're so bossy," she teased and wriggled her feet. "Are you gonna untie my ankles now so I can wrap them around your waist?"

Her words clearly inflamed him, and his cock grew even harder deep inside of her body. He reached down and easily freed her ankles without ever leaving her. "A Master is supposed to be bossy," he groaned as she wrapped her legs around him, thereby deepening his angle of penetration.

"Maybe so, but I can be just as bossy." She panted as he began to thrust in and out of her body with strong, quick movements.

"We'll see," he gritted out, and then there was no more room for conversation. They both needed all their strength to ride out the storm of their passion.

Epilogue

Three days later

GIDEON MOANED AS HE was awakened from a deep, exhausted slumber. He felt the wet heat of Catherine's cunt as it swallowed up his cock when she sank down on top of him. He tried to move his arms and widened his eyes to find himself completely tied down and unable to move. Trying his ankles, he found they were bound the same with the rigging ties on the bedposts.

Catherine laughed up above him. She was wearing her Kitty perfume, its thick floral scent drowning him with lust. "I've been thinking," she said as she rose and sank down upon him, over and over.

"Oh yeah," he gritted out against the mind numbing pleasure of her body on his.

"People are going to start to wonder what happened to

us. We haven't left these rooms for four days. Shouldn't you be guarding Don or something?"

"I've got security teams covering it." He threw his head back as her inner walls clamped down on him. He groaned. "But I don't think Don needs their protection much anymore," he finished.

"Well that's good. I wouldn't want anyone to think you're not doing your job." Catherine leaned back, reached behind her, then brandished her prize. She unfurled the braided whip in her hands with a devilish smile.

"What are you going to do with that?" He tried and failed to keep his hips from thrusting up into her tight, wet sheath.

"I'm going to show you how pleasurable it is to obey me," she teased and lightly caressed his chest with the whip.

"I'd like to see you try." And he would. Oh how he would.

She stopped moving and waited for him to look at her. "I love you," she surprised him by saying in her soft, husky voice.

He shuddered. "Oh kitten, I love you too. I'll always love you," he vowed. She thrust down upon him and he gritted his teeth against a nearly overwhelming urge to come. "Not that this conversation isn't the most stirring and satisfying I've ever had but . . . could you please move faster? I *need* you," he groaned.

She leaned down and kissed him, the motion sending him that much deeper inside of her. "What do you need? Tell me what you need, Gideon," she said into his mouth.

"I need you to fuck me, kitten. I need you to fuck me hard."

With a wicked smile she pulled back and immediately stilled her motion. Caressing the silken whip against her face she commanded him with a devilish twinkle in her eyes, "That's Mistress Kitten to you, slave. *Meow*."

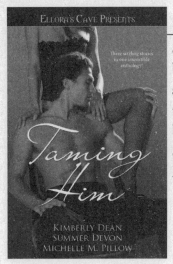
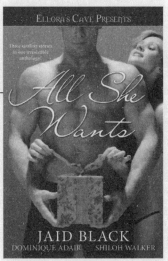